DEADLY CURRENTS

DEADLY CURRENTS

DEADLY HIDDEN CURRENTS OF TERRORISM

WILLIAM W. BENNETT

Auctorem House
276 5th Ave, Ste 704-2591
New York, NY 10001
www.auctoremhouse.com
Phone: 1 888-332-7718

Published by Auctorem House: 09/26/2025

ISBN: 978-1-968059-08-8(sc)
ISBN: 978-1-968059-09-5(e)

Library of Congress Control Number: 2025920932

To my sons, Jeremy and Jeff

Special thanks to my beloved wife, Cathy.

But He gives a greater grace. Therefore it says, "GOD IS OPPOSED TO THE PROUD, BUT GIVES GRACE TO THE HUMBLE." Submit therefore to God. Resist the devil and he will flee from you. Draw near to God and He will draw near to you. Cleanse your hands, you sinners; and purify your hearts, you double-minded. Be miserable and mourn and weep; let your laughter be turned into mourning and your joy to gloom. Humble yourselves in the presence of the Lord, and He will exalt you.

–James 4:6-10 *NASB*

CHAPTER 1

Jim rose early, something even marriage hadn't changed, slipping quietly out of bed without waking Cecilia. For a moment, he stood and looked down at her. Her auburn hair was spread in disarray, her eyes moving beneath the lids in REM, indicating that she slept soundly. Her mouth was open, one hand close to her lips, the fingers curled gently inward. She was beautiful, and Jim breathed a prayer of thanksgiving to God for this wondrous gift.

As silent as a moving shadow, he left the room, padding to the private bathroom he now shared with his wife. There were things on the counter and in the medicine cabinet that he never thought he would see in one of his bathrooms. Smiling at the thought, he shed his shorts and stepped beneath the shower, testing it first with his hand to be sure it was warm enough. Even in the shower, Cecilia made her presence known in his life, and he looked with amusement at the soaps, shampoos, and conditioners he would never have placed there.

Two minutes later, he was finished and stepped out to dry himself. He looked at his physique critically in the mirror, his opaline green eyes taking in every detail, and decided that he was still riding that wave of physical prowess necessary to survive for a soldier. Well, no one was guaranteed survival, but top physical fitness gave one an edge and tipped the scales in favor of survival. Experience taught him that truth.

With that sobering thought, he dressed quickly in his work uniform. His crew wore tan pants, shirts, and baseball caps with the company logo on the front. The shirts were typical Navy uniform style, and his shoulder epaulets showed four double strands of gold rope on a dark blue background, forming four stripes or bars indicating he was the vessel's captain. Over his uniform, he put on the waterproof jumpsuit and boots everyone on the crew wore outside during the colder weather.

On the Mediterranean, fall was an uncertain season. Storms came quickly, unexpectedly, and sometimes brutally and destructively, sending unwary sailors into the unfriendly waters. Leaving his quarters quietly, he made his way to the kitchen, where Abe handed him an insulated mug of fresh iced tea. One of the men always had his iced tea ready and waiting. Nodding his thanks, he walked to the ship's bow, the first to arrive. In the east, the hint of dawn made a thin, almost gray line between the ocean and the sky.

Leaning against the tool locker, he heard the hatch open and heard the voices of his brother John and their best friend Wade talking together as they came up. Andrea followed on their heels. Andrea was a bluff seaman in his early sixties, his face weathered and wrinkled by the sea air, his blue eyes twinkling with pleasure as he breathed in the morning air.

His brother and Wade were the same age, only ten months younger than Jim, and they grew up together in Boston. Wade stood six feet five and a half inches, and John was an inch taller than Jim's six feet two inches. Despite being out of the military for three years now, all three of them still sported the traditional jarhead haircut.

As one, they raised their cups, three steaming coffees, and one iced tea and then turned to look around them. It was a tradition for them to greet each morning this way, and they rarely missed the chance to join together to welcome the day. Fog settled over them, growing thicker, and though they could tell it was getting lighter, there was no sign of the sun through the heavy fog.

"It will be an unusual day," Andrea said with a shiver, resting his cup on the tool locker and thrusting his weathered hands deep in his pockets. "We will be needed today, I think, my young nephews, if my senses are correct. There is a feeling in the air, a feeling of menace and danger. Do you not feel it?"

He always called them his young nephews, although Wade was technically unrelated to them. Wade didn't seem to mind being included in that statement. Jim nodded solemnly. He felt it, too. John raised one eyebrow, his gray eyes ironic as he looked into the stormy green eyes of his brother. He trusted his uncle and his brother when it came to these premonitions, especially on the sea.

"I guess the vacation is over!" he said with a shrug. "Probably the honeymoon, too!" he grinned at his brother, who smiled back.

For the past three months, they had traveled at their leisure from port to port, visiting places they'd never been to before, literally on a world cruise. It had been a honeymoon for Jim and Cecilia, and though they had company the entire time, the crew was respectful and gave them plenty of privacy when they wanted it. Jim felt the crew had earned that rest and recreation time and did not mind spending the money. Success in their work provided the funds necessary for such a prolonged time. That did not mean that they neglected physical fitness during those months.

Of course, they were all still soldiers, so rest did not mean that training and practice did not continue. They all knew the reason they kept their skills honed to near perfection. Their lives depended on it. None of the men showed any sign of resenting the rigorous schedule and hard work. Routine ruled each day, and the men appreciated the results.

A month past they put into port in Plymouth and picked up their newest crewmember, Marvin Winston Finn. Stolen from the British Navy, Finn came highly recommended as an administrative assistant. His reports from superiors were quite impressive but did not tell the whole story. With their recruit, they were heading now for Naples, to be on hand in the Mediterranean theater, ready to battle against the new terrorism threats developing in that part of the world.

The sound of a twin-engine seaplane could be heard in the fog above them, very close to the surface, as though it might be landing nearby. All four looked at each other with wary eyes and a sense of impending conflict. Military men develop that unique sense when danger lurks near; at that moment, all four men sensed danger.

The call for help came even as Jim and Andrea expressed their sense of impending need. Sean Oxton was on the radio when it came. Calls for help came in different ways, from collected factual statements to terror-filled cries. This one made the very hairs on Sean's neck stand up as a hoarse whisper filled with terror sounded suddenly in the quiet room. Zeke, at the command intelligence center, punched the record button automatically. Sean responded as only someone familiar with the situation could.

"This is *Bring It Up Coral*, a deep sea search and rescue tug near your location. Just tell me what's going on; we're coming to help. Over," he said quietly, just above a whisper.

"Oh God!" the voice whispered, shock and horror coming upon each word. The captain and mates are killing all the passengers and crewmembers. I hear someone coming!" the last was whispered in a whimper.

"Copy. Keep hidden and quiet!" Sean replied. "Over."

Just as the man keyed the microphone to reply, Sean heard the distinctive sound of a silenced pistol spitting twice. The sound went dead. Sean looked at Zeke with sadness even as his hand pressed the alarm. A loud klaxon sounded throughout the ship, bringing every crewmember out of bed or away from his duties and heading straight for the ready room.

After an early morning squall, fog shrouded everything in a soft liquid blanket of impenetrable gloom. At the wheel, Dorf stood with his chin thrust forward, his eyes scanning back and forth between the sea and his instruments, his knuckles white from the strain. Sean stepped onto the steering bridge, and without looking away, Dorf questioned him quietly. "I've got a steady signal less than a mile out. Is it bad?"

"Worse," Sean said tersely. "Bloody murderin' pirates."

Andrea appeared on the bridge and put a hand on Dorf's shoulder. Dorf released the wheel into Andrea's hands and nodded to Sean. Neither needed to speak. They headed to the weapons room together to prepare for a rescue. As the men hurriedly got into their gear, Jim spoke.

"Zeke is going to play back the recording. This is bad. It's pirates, I think. We have to go in fast, and we're going blind," he nodded to Zeke, who paused in his dressing long enough to hit the play button. The men listened to the recording. Each one had a unique way of listening as he worked.

"Why do pirates need a silencer?" Frank Miller asked quietly at the end of the recording. Because of the first letters of his name, Frank was nicknamed FM by his friends. Jim sometimes wondered if the man had some kind of antennae that detected trouble. He'd gone right to the heart of the issue with unerring accuracy.

"Maybe because sound carries in the fog, and we're near enough to land for other boats to be in the area," Jim mused, checking his magazine in his H&K Mark 23 .45 caliber pistol. He replaced it and slid the weapon into its holster. "That tells us these are bad people, so be ready for anything. First men on deck, get the Rigid Raider ready to go," he added, heading out the door with about six men at his heels.

"Andrea, bring her to a full stop about three hundred yards away so they can't see us through the fog. We're going in on the Raider," Jim said into his microphone.

"Already slowing to all stop. We'll be there in two, Captain," Andrea replied. Rarely did he call Jim "Captain," but this was one of those times when he followed protocol. The ship was indeed slowing, the bow settling though on the rear deck that wasn't immediately obvious. Jim didn't bother answering but took his place in the Rigid Raider with fifteen other soldiers. Master Chief Warner was already at the controls, lowering the boat into the water.

Cecilia appeared on the bridge, gently touching Andrea's arm and turning to look out the rear windows as the Rigid Raider accelerated away from the stern, rounded the boat, and sped past. This Rigid

Raider had been made especially for the team, powered by a matched pair of two hundred and fifty horsepower outboard motors made by Volvo. It could carry twenty-four fully armed men, twice the number of the traditional Rigid Raider. Watching the boat speed by, Cecilia breathed a prayer for their protection.

At the moment, the raider carried sixteen men. Jim Shepherd was their Captain and leader, commonly called Shep by the men when they weren't in port or around strangers. Though Jim never thought of himself this way, his men considered him a legend, a former SEAL team Captain, and the best Naval Intelligence operative.

John Shepherd, his brother, was his second in command, holding the rank of Commander, known affectionately by his friends as JR. Jim and John began in the Marines, but Jim soon moved to the Navy. Their best friend, Wade Adams, was always with them. Wade had the unlikely moniker of Beer Bottle. In the Marines, he and John served together in Force Recon, distinguishing themselves and looked upon with the same respect as Jim. Wade served the crew as Lieutenant Commander.

Jim had two men who held the rank of Lieutenant. Sean Oxton referred to as Ox by his friends, was a field physician and soldier Jim stole from Australia's SAS. The other Lieutenant was Waldorf Bernard, or Dorf, as the men called him. Dorf served with Jim as a SEAL and was the tallest of the soldiers at six feet nine inches.

Three men held the rank of Ensign. The Kline twins, Zeke and Bill, known as Uncle Zeke and Sparks, were identical twins, both having served with Jim in his SEAL unit. John Smith, inevitably nicknamed "Smitty," was the third. He was also a former SEAL.

Jack Boswell, a former SEAL, was a Petty Officer First Class, and Frank Miller, another SEAL, was a Petty Officer Second Class. Jack could drive anything, and he was nicknamed Driver. Because of his initials, Frank was referred to as FM. Like Jim, Frank began his service in the Marines and was plucked out of a Force Recon group to train as a SEAL.

Lee Roy Brown, known affectionately as "Lunch Box," Chance Edwards, and Phillip Eustus were the other three from the Australian

SAS who came with Ox. Phil was called "PU," pronounced *Pew*, and everyone called Chance by his first name.

Clancy Franklin and Vincent Hall were two Marines from John's Force Recon unit who completed the team. Clancy's middle name was Garrett, so the men called him C.G. Vince was simply known by his first name. All five of the latter were Seamen on the boat.

The military unit of sixteen brave and true men was called *Omega Force*, and they were considered the last word on Terrorism. Formed as a black-on-black unit, they answered to six men. President Jack Royce, Sir Edward Marsh, Director of Operations (D.O.) MI6, Ira Lehman, D.O. Mossad, Petros Kladas, D.O. Greek Intelligence, and General James March, Commander of Australia's SAS. Through a brilliant plan, the mission was launched without bureaucratic oversight. Jim and his team did not exist on paper anywhere. To the world, they operated a Deep-Sea Search and Rescue operation.

At this moment, they were Omega Force, risking their lives to save as many people as possible in a very bad situation.

CHAPTER 2

Whatever the pirates expected, it wasn't a skilled military unit. The two men on the stern of the yacht with machine guns went down before they could fire their weapons. As their guns barked in the fog, the sound of a seaplane engine revving caught Jim's ears. As he leaped to the deck, he spoke into his microphone. As he spoke, his eyes swept the decks, noting how his men moved to maintain cover fire.

"Four of you stay on the raider and see if you can stop that plane! If not, get a tracer on it!" He ordered. John was at the wheel, and he simply waved, pushing the throttles forward so that the nearly empty boat leaped out of the water and plunged toward the seaplane. Jim knew it would be a close race. The Raider was fast, and if John managed it, they could stop the plane from taking off or at least put a tracer on it. He could only hope.

Jim moved with purpose, leading his team down the starboard side of the yacht, while Sean led his team down the port side. Dorf was leading his team down into the bowels of the yacht. They encountered no opposition, and Jim turned to watch the seaplane take off. Even as it did, the Rigid Raider appeared next to the pontoons for just a moment, long enough for C.G. Franklin to lean over and slap a homing device on the underside where it couldn't be seen. Nodding in satisfaction, he listened as Dorf's voice came over the radio set.

"Jesus, Mary, and Joseph!" That was a bad sign, Dorf's Catholic heritage coming out in stress. "There's a huge explosive unit right next to the fuel tank in the engine room set to blow in thirty seconds! This is a professional job, Jim. I can't stop it without setting it off!" From the sound of his voice, Dorf was already running for the deck, his crew before him.

"Everybody meet the Raider at the stern now. Move it!" Jim snapped, even as he followed his team.

It was a mad race, desperate, the men sprinting at full speed. Leaping from the stern railing into the Raider, landing awkwardly, being helped to their seats, and turning to help others, they moved with purpose. Once Jim was on board, John jammed the throttles forward again, and the boat hurled away from the waiting explosion. Ten seconds was not enough.

"Down!" Jim yelled, just as the explosion lit the area with a bright white light and a tremendous concussion. Shrapnel from the ship whizzed past them. Something heavy slammed into Jim's shoulder with the force of a pile-driver, nearly unseating him. Only his bulletproof vest and body armor protected him from broken bones, but he knew he was hurt. Screams from some of the men told him there were worse injuries. C.G. Franklin took a melting piece of fiberglass through his left thigh, pinning him to the seat for a moment before he ripped it free and threw it overboard, burning his hands in the process.

John was holding his left hand against his chest, and Jim could see a piece of glass sticking out of it, blood dripping from the end of the glass. It had pinned his hand to his vest, and he wisely left it there. Smitty took some glass in his face, and Lee Roy Brown had another piece of fiberglass sticking out of his side. Usually, the body armor protected them from projectiles, but the bomb was much more powerful than a bullet.

"Sound off!" Jim said into his microphone. The men had an order for this, and they all got quiet quickly. Jim listened as each one answered in the affirmative that they were accounted for. Only five admitted to being wounded. Jim could see the count would go higher, though they had escaped truly serious life-threatening injury. He sighed as he gave his report and said that he'd been hit with something on the shoulder that had done some major muscle and tendon damage. His eyes swept over the men most injured, but they were holding up.

Bring It Up Coral appeared out of the fog, moving slowly toward the explosion, and halted as the boat came into view. The landing was a little awkward since John couldn't use both hands. Once the boat was secured, lifted out of the water, and settled on its cradle, the men stood and stepped onto the deck. Vince was helping C.G. walk. Chance and Phillip were helping Lee Roy off the boat. No one else needed a hand walking, Jim was glad to see. Sean immediately took charge.

"You're bleeding or hurt; you come with me to the medical wing," he said, touching the men he wanted to get moving as he stepped through them. Jim was already following C.G., still being helped by Vince. He stepped around Chance and Phillip, helping Lee Roy, and took C.G.'s other arm, lifting it over his shoulder.

"Hey, didn't I hear you say you were hurt?" C.G. said, looking at Jim's pinched face.

"High on the back," Jim grimaced. "Hauling your heavy carcass hurts like the blazes, so let's cut the chatter and get down below," he added, grinning at C.G. "How are you doing back there, Lee Roy?" Jim asked, looking over his shoulder. Watching the man slowly raise his head, he studied his eyes carefully. His men expected him to take a personal interest, and he was careful to respond appropriately.

Lee Roy was hunched over in pain, the piece of fiberglass still sticking out of his side. He lifted his ebony face and grinned at Jim, a feral grin that said volumes about his pain.

"I'll make it, Shep," he said through gritted teeth. His Australian accent was strong. "Could ha' come without these two pelicans, though," he added. "They could be helping their mates haul that oversized raider out of the water and clean it up a bit. I tried to convince them I could walk down on my own, but they weren't listening!"

"I'll look into it, Lee Roy. Dereliction of duty is frowned upon on this ship!" Jim said with a grin at Chance and Phillip. They both smiled slightly, knowing the captain was just being facetious.

"Hey, if we're going on report, how about this blighter?" Chance said. "I bet he doesn't even put his own gear away!"

"And all three of you are in barney if you don't shut up and get to the medical wing," Sean retorted, coming alongside and checking Lee Roy's face. Jim saw him wink at all three as he stepped ahead of them all and opened the door to the infirmary. Chief Medical Officer Charles Wozniac met them, and his wife, Chief Nurse Millie Wozniac, was behind him with Cecilia. Despite his pain, Jim smiled at the sight of his wife, but it was a fleeting smile. Letting go of his friend truly hurt, and he felt light-headed and dizzy for a moment before recovering.

Cecilia helped C.G. and Lee Roy get settled and helped with the surgery required to remove the piece from Seaman Brown. Jim watched the twenty-minute surgery and stitching, then watched the three wash up and go to work on C.G.'s leg. His hands were also treated, though the burns weren't too severe. John's hand and chest were next, and after that, the cuts from flying glass on faces and arms. Last, the three came to Jim.

Cecilia helped Jim remove his equipment and looked at the black and blue bruise spreading over most of his left shoulder. Doc stepped in, examining him, moving his left arm, and feeling around the muscle. She could tell it hurt, but Jim bore it stoically as she knew he would. Only a slight tightening of his eyes told her that specific movements caused pain.

"Well, this is going to hurt for a few days, but it should heal up just fine," Doc said, putting a cooling salve on the bruise. "You're officially on the injured list until I release you," he added, smiling at Jim. "No lifting anything heavier than a nightie with that arm," this last he added with a wink at his wife and Cecilia, both of whom were trying hard not to laugh. Jim knew it was because the last comment had flushed his face crimson.

"Think you could find a nightie for me to lift, Doc?" C.G. asked with a straight face. His leg was badly bruised and needed eight staples to close the wound. The burn would make it worse once the local wore off, but his face was relaxed at the moment, even mischievous.

"I'll ask Dr. Gregg if he could spare Mary Ann or Barbara," Doctor Wozniac replied without missing a beat.

"Hey! Have a heart! They're both nice enough, but I was thinking of someone a little younger," C.G. laughed despite the pain in his leg. Imagining either of those worthy ladies getting their hands on him when injured would have put him at a definite disadvantage. "You know how those spinsters are, Doc," C.G. added in a whining tone. "Never really give a guy a chance to rest!" Everyone laughed with him.

Wade and Zeke burst into the room at that point, and Wade was carrying what looked like a model flying saucer. Jim raised an eyebrow as the two stopped in front of him.

"I've been working on this for a while," Wade said. "It's a drone, and I had surveillance in mind when I built it. Zeke just programmed it to follow that plane."

"The plane has a half-hour lead on us!" Jim said, pointing out the obvious.

"Not on this baby!" Wade said with pride. Zeke was nodding his head. "We've been testing it. That seaplane will have a top speed of two hundred and thirty knots. This baby can do nearly seven hundred knots!" Looking closely at it, Jim saw it was modeled after a stealth 117A fighter design. That it could travel that fast was something of a surprise, and he smiled at Wade and Zeke, impressed. He should have realized that if Wade had designed it, it would have been fast.

"Will they be able to detect it?" Jim asked, now interested, as he looked the model jet over.

"No. It's too small, and all it will do is track them. Zeke put a chip on the pontoon, which we can see from the satellite if necessary. This can home in on that chip and send back detailed digital data," Wade replied.

"What are you waiting for?" Jim asked.

"Sharky's going to give us fits because we don't have the proper permits to fly this," Zeke said quietly. He looked around to ensure Jim's new administrative assistant was not standing by the door. "You know how he is," the disgust on Zeke's face was tangible, and Jim nodded without smiling, knowing precisely what Zeke meant.

Jim sighed. Marvin Winston Finn was a first-class administrative assistant. Stolen recently from the Royal Navy, he served the *Bring It Up* officers. Already, his exacting ethic and nature were rubbing some of the officers the wrong way. He wanted things done correctly the first time, tended to nag, and was extremely narrow-minded about rules and regulations. Finn was much more interested in the "letter of the law" than the intent.

"Send a message to Sir Edward and get us the permits. Get that thing in the air now, and if Finn fusses, I'll deal with it," Jim said. He looked at Cecilia, who was trying not to smile, and grinned. "This is all your fault!" he complained. She giggled at him, unable to hide it anymore, knowing he blamed her for suggesting a secretary.

"My big, strong Captain is having difficulty handling a dry little man like Mr. Finn?" Cecilia asked, her eyes wide and innocent.

Jim headed to his newly remodeled office, which had a door leading to Finn's tiny cubicle and another door on the opposite wall leading to Cecilia's somewhat more spacious office. On the way, they passed Finn, who came to attention and saluted Jim smartly. He saw the jet in Wade's hands.

"You shouldn't fly that without the proper permits, sir!" he said carefully.

"You have my orders, Lieutenant Commander, Ensign!" Jim nodded to Wade and Zeke, his face devoid of any emotion. "Get that drone in the air in the next ten minutes! Dismissed."

Hiding grins, they hustled to obey after saluting Jim officially. Marvin was now wrestling with a conflict. In the Navy, one obeyed the captain, and one obeyed at sea. Captain Shepherd had given a specific order and used the men's ranks rather than their names, giving it more weight. Finn kept his mouth shut and followed Jim and Cecilia back to the office. He still didn't know his Captain well enough to understand how his reservations might be received.

"Sir, you are aware that proper permits are required to fly the drone, correct?" Finn finally asked. Jim sighed inwardly.

"Sir Edward Marsh is personally seeing to the permits, Marvin. Rest easy. Although we don't have them in hand at the moment, they are already approved." Jim felt immediately uncomfortable with the deception, but Marvin would nag him about it relentlessly unless he thought the proper procedures were being followed.

"Sir Edward Marsh?" Finn asked, impressed. "Oh yes. Everything goes through him, doesn't it?" Jim grinned, knowing Finn had a long way to go to understand the nature of his team. He paused at the door, his eyes filled with concern. "Are you alright after the explosion, sir? I heard you were among the wounded."

"Took a hit to the shoulder. I'll be fine in a few days. Thanks for asking, Marvin." Jim was always polite to his men, even those he didn't particularly like. Finn was a good man and a first-rate assistant. Jim's dislike of the man was not about his work. It was the man's pettiness.

"Right then!" Marvin said, nodding emphatically. "Mrs. Shepherd will make sure you follow the doctor's orders."

He didn't mean it to sound condescending. It was just that he couldn't help himself. Jim sighed inwardly and went to his desk, alarmed at the stack of papers filling his "in" box. Marvin saw the look.

"All those require is your signature, sir. It's routine. If you have any questions, I'm here," Finn called from his office.

"Thanks, LT," Jim replied with a sigh.

Marvin was a little over average height, thin, in good shape, and a conscientious worker. Jim's work had become much more organized and a good deal simpler since hiring Finn. Jim supposed that his name was what prodded the men to nickname him Sharky. When Finn was practicing a rescue exercise with the crew, Dorf said it first. "There's a Finn in the water!" It stuck, and Marvin didn't seem to mind being called Sharky, although he obviously preferred his name and, more particularly, his rank. His rank, for some reason, was very important to him.

An hour later, Jim managed to sign the last report. His shoulder bothered him, and he sat awkwardly in his chair. He hated weakness of any kind, especially in himself. The injury was making him miserable and reminding him that his body was not at full capacity. Cecilia came into the office, looked at him, and suggested they go up to the computer room to research the vessel that now lay at the bottom of the Mediterranean. Knowing it would be best to get her husband away from Finn and this type of work, she was happy to suggest it. He agreed, shoved the stack of papers at Finn, and left.

Cecilia already had the salvage rights and put them on Finn's desk as they walked out of the office. Finn grunted his usual response to more paperwork and kept working. Cecilia smiled. Although the man was exacting and somewhat of a prude, she liked his efficiency and was willing to put up with as much as necessary to ease her husband's workload. Since Finn joined the crew, her husband has indeed found his workload to have lessened considerably.

CHAPTER 3

Zeke was already busy watching the drone track the seaplane in the computer room. Two blips appeared on his radar screen, one slowly catching the other. Jim saw the markers and paused.

"If you can track those by radar, why can't they track your drone?" he asked.

There was a pause of some seconds before Zeke answered. "I can track the drone because I'm not actually using radar signal transmission, Shep. I'm tracking the homing device on both aircraft," Zeke said without turning away from the console. "Each device gives off a unique signal," he explained.

"So, how did you get them both to track on the radar screen?" Jim asked, intrigued.

Again, there was the usual pause before Zeke answered Jim's question. "Well, every plane today is equipped with a little black box, and that box emits a sound at a certain frequency unique to that aircraft. A radar unit receives that transmission. All I did was program the unit to receive the signals from the homing devices by entering their frequencies into the program," Zeke answered.

"Neat!" Jim said, clapping Zeke on the shoulder.

"Uncle Zeke is watching you!" Zeke replied quietly. Everyone was so used to hearing that phrase that no one laughed, but it somehow endeared this interesting mix of personalities they knew as Zeke Kline. In the truest sense of the word, he was a computer nerd and a former Navy SEAL.

Zeke was perhaps the fastest thinker among them, one of the reasons he was constantly making people laugh. He thought in binary code as often as he thought logically. Perhaps that helped him to stay extremely focused. Quickly deciding, even though he liked to examine all the possibilities and alternatives, his mind never ceased to amaze his colleagues. Jim valued Zeke and relied heavily on his genius. His skill with computer programs was a legend among the crew, and in two years, he'd proved his worth.

Cecilia traced the yacht's ownership to Paul Klaus of Athens, Greece, at another computer console in the command intelligence center. The report said Mr. Klaus was a developer who built casinos and hotels on the Mediterranean. That told them that the man could afford the yacht and that it was probably insured. Ten minutes later, a Lloyds standard contract was faxed to the ship for the salvage of the insured yacht.

Zeke and Wade were busy watching the drone follow the seaplane. It landed in Venice harbor, and they drew Jim's attention to the monitor. The drone took pictures of the departure of four men herding a woman in her forties, a teen girl, and a younger boy. The latter were obviously prisoners and showed all the signs of shock and terror. Studying the images, Jim noticed that the woman's panties were around her ankles, forcing her to walk oddly, and the man pushing kept stepping on them, tripping her, and catching her before she fell. Her daughter, seeing all of this, seemed to be screaming at the man pushing her mother while the boy kept trying to leap at him, his captor holding him and laughing. With those pictures logged in the computer, the men turned the drone around and punched in the commands to return to the ship.

It took forty minutes for the drone to return, and Jim watched it splash into the water in spectacular form, like a flying fish diving beneath the surface. A few seconds later, it surfaced, and the Rigid

Raider launched to pick it up. The film was processed quickly, though the digital images were already saved in Zeke's computer.

Enhancing the photos of the four men in the seaplane took some work, but Zeke was quick on the computer and, in a short period, had four pictures that could be identified. He sent them through the proper channels and waited patiently for a reply. Sir Edward did not disappoint them, and when the answer came, Jim began to understand the picture forming around these men. One was a former friend and disciple of Gerhard Richter of the Red Army Faction (RAF), sometimes called the Baader-Meinhof gang, high on the most wanted list of INTERPOL. The other three were equally noteworthy as wanted criminals.

"We better get down to the yacht and see what we can find!" Jim said quietly. He knew they would have to wait at least three days for everybody to heal enough to carry out the work of bringing the yacht to the surface. Jim hated waiting. Just then, his shoulder reminded him that waiting was something he had to do. Wincing, he shifted a little to ease the pain.

For a moment, his eyes met Zeke's, and he saw in them what must be in his own. These terrorists were killers and kidnappers, and for injuring Jim's team, they would pay dearly. Both men nodded at the same time and Cecilia saw in her husband's eyes the deadly resolve that thrilled and frightened her at the same time.

No one knew better than she the terror that evil men could bring into the lives of innocent people. Her entire family was dead at the hands of terrorists. Jim rescued her and allowed her to watch when justice was finally served on the man who led the terrorists that attacked her. The fact that Jim loved her still surprised and thrilled her. His love brought her back from the brink of self-destruction.

That was something liberals never thought about. Victims of violent criminals who specialized in terror often ended by destroying themselves, primarily through suicide. Those who were sexually abused despaired of ever being seen by others as anything but tainted goods, usually blaming themselves. She was still going through therapy to help her overcome the false guilt every victim felt so profoundly. Jim's devotion and ability to see her for who she really was changed everything for her. That and her faith had seen her through to near recovery. But for victims, the battle was never over. The memories haunt for a lifetime.

Jim was aware that this marriage blessed him. Cecilia did not want to change him from what he was, to keep him out of harm's way. She understood the need for soldiers and the dangers they faced. Jim felt safe in his relationship with Cecilia. He could tell her anything and had the freedom in their relationship to be who and what he was. They smiled at one another and even knew what the other was thinking. Jim leaned down and kissed Cecilia gently, once again lost in the wonder of those soft lips pressed against his.

"Hope you brought enough for everybody!" FM quipped, stepping lightly through the command intelligence center door.

"Sorry, those perks are for the captain," Cecilia said, smiling and touching his cheek lightly as he bent down as though to receive a kiss.

FM put his hand on his cheek and opened his eyes wide. "Wow! She touched me! Wait till I tell the other guys!" he exclaimed. Everyone laughed. "Just came to ask if you wanted us to set up the crane and rig for bringing up the two pieces of that yacht," he said to Jim when the laughter died.

"I assume by this conversation that you and TRT are already at work doing just that?" Jim raised an eyebrow at FM. FM shrugged.

"Could be, Shep. Not that we would ever usurp your command or nothin'," he added with a wink at Cecilia. "But we know how busy you are these days with all your new responsibilities."

Jim grinned. "Get back to work!" he said gruffly, the smile still in his eyes.

FM snapped off a perfect salute at attention, spun on his heels, and returned to work. As he exited the door, Sharky arrived with half a ream of fax paper in a neat file folder. He came to attention as soon as the door closed.

"These are the regulations on flying that drone, sir," he said, holding out the thick file. "I didn't know who should have them first, so I brought them to you."

"I'd better look them over before I give them to Lieutenant Commander Adams," Jim said formally, leafing through the papers slowly as though skimming them. "Thanks, LT. You can get back to your regular work," Jim was careful not to make eye contact because Finn always acted uncomfortable under direct eye contact. Finn saluted smartly and left, a pleased expression on his face. Jim knew letting Finn know this was outside his normal duties would please the man. He shook his head and waited a few seconds before handing the file to Cecilia.

"Whatever you do, don't let Sharky see you have these already. File them somewhere, will you?" he asked, leaning down to kiss her again.

She smiled and rose gracefully. I've got the Lloyds contract in here. I'll take them down with that, file them away, and give the contract to little Lord Flaunt my Rank, High Commander," she said with a mischievous grin.

"Little Lord, Flaunt my Rank, High Commander!" Zeke said lightly. "Officious little prude is more like it," he muttered in an undertone.

"One of the many worker bees the Navy seems to create," Jim commented, moving toward the door. "Unless we corrupt him, he'll never rise much further in rank, even on this boat!" Jim added with a grin.

"He's incorruptible!" Zeke said after a pause. "Even Bright Eyes can't charm that one!" Bright Eyes was the nickname the guys had given Cecilia shortly after she came on board as a crew member.

Jim knew that Zeke didn't like Marvin because Marvin tended to invade their lives with his officiousness, and Jim knew that Zeke's nature included a hatred of invasiveness. People were complex sometimes. Jim grinned at Zeke and waved a salute. Zeke was already rapidly clicking a keyboard's keys, his eyes glued on a computer monitor.

CHAPTER 4

After three days, Doc and Ox decided the crew was healthy enough to get back to work, and Jim ordered the submersible to be sent down to examine the wreckage.

Jack Boswell, commonly called "Driver" by the crew piloted the craft. Frank Miller went down as chief engineer, and Sparks tagged along in case any electrical problems arose. Sparks was Bill Kline, one of the Kline twins, who was the head electrician on the ship. He served with Jim as part of Jim's Navy SEAL team, as did seven of the team, before they formed their new unit, so they had a long history together. Because he knew the men intimately, he could hear the excitement in their voices as work finally got underway. His men were unused to downtime, and the injuries had hampered operations for three long days while the men chafed to return to their usual routine.

A host of crew members checked seals, fittings, and connections around the submersible. Jim watched the work go on with a pleased expression. Cecilia came up beside him, snuggled against him in a most satisfying manner, and put her hand in his.

"Hey, Shep!" FM shouted from the hatch of the submersible.

"Go, FM," Jim replied, not bothering to move away from Cecilia.

"If you're not too busy, could you get me a couple of new filters?" FM grinned wickedly as he spoke. He was looking at Jim's good hand, the expression on his face comical as he noted Jim's calloused hand engulfing Cecilia's tiny hand.

"I don't know," Jim replied with a straight face. "I only have one good hand, and it's busy right now. Is it urgent?"

Cecilia laughed delightedly as she and Jim moved off to the hold to fetch the filters. They walked down into the semidarkness, Jim descending the steep steps first, holding her hand over his shoulder. A year ago, he would never have thought he would enjoy contact like this with a woman. Still euphoric over the novelty, he continued into the hold. He would never have guessed how much Cecilia was secretly pleased by his attention.

They fetched three new filters and brought them to FM, who was no longer at the hatch. Smiling, Jim disengaged his hand from Cecilia, climbed the ladder, reached down and received the filters from Cecilia, and shouted down the hatch.

"Hey, FM! If you're going to interrupt me from my important duties to fetch some filters, the least you could do is hang around until I bring them back!" he shouted. "What makes you think I have time to hang around this hatch waiting for you to remember you asked for these filters?"

"You catch me hanging around waiting, and I'm liable to get a dressing down from the Captain, Shep!" Frank said with a grin as he climbed up to receive the filters. Jim grinned back.

"Yeah! I heard he's really tough since he got married!" Jim replied. "We better stay busy."

"Best if we do," FM replied with an easy smile. He looked at the filters. "Bloody design makes these things iffy at best," he groused.

"What's the problem?" Jim asked, interested.

"It's the design of the slot. No matter how carefully we slide these things in, they can be ripped, and then they don't work," Frank answered.

"Design problem or necessity?" Jim asked. He was immediately interested in the problem.

"A little of both. I've been working with Inchworm, but so far, we can't figure out how to change the design to make it work better," FM answered. He nodded at Inchworm as the mechanic sauntered past.

After a moment of thought, Jim said, "Here's what I want the two of you to do." He called Inchworm over. "Inchworm, come here a minute. You need to hear this, too." Inchworm was a newer crewmember, Walter Rule, serving as Petty Officer, Second Class. His name made the nickname inevitable. There was certainly nothing slow about PO2 Rule when it came to work.

"I've been talking to FM about the filter problem. I want the two of you to make drawings and send them to Calvin Beardsley. Ask him to work with the company on making a change and get drawings, detailed plans, and necessary parts back as soon as possible."

"Got it, Shep!" FM nodded easily, heading back down into the bowels of the submersible. Inchworm noted the easy reply and gave one of his own.

"FM and I will get on it as soon as possible, Shep," he said easily. Moving quickly, he still managed to make it look like he was ambling his six-foot-three-inch frame off on the errand he'd been taking care of before Jim interrupted him. Jim grinned. The man was definitely unbending.

"Well, I see you're too busy at the moment, honey," Cecilia said with a grin. She loved teasing Jim.

"I'm not too busy!" Lee Roy Brown said, coming to stand beside her. He was still on light duty because of his wound, but Jim noted that he was standing easier.

"You get back to work, or I'll tell the captain!" Jim said, climbing down off the submersible.

"Spoilsport!" Lee Roy said, grinning.

"How's the side?" Jim asked, joining them.

"Better, thanks. I can breathe easier, and I could do some exercises this morning. About three more days, and I'll be ninety percent or better. I'll give you Yanks a run for your money in two weeks." Jim loved listening to the Australian talk.

"Those of us from Boston are proud of our Yankee heritage!" Dorf said, coming to stand beside them, dressed in his wetsuit and holding his mask, snorkel, and fins. Dorf could mimic the snootiest Boston accent when he wanted to. Towering over them, he grinned down at the three of them. Dorf was six feet nine inches tall and powerfully built, though his build was deceptive. He was quick and sure.

His best friend and almost constant companion, Mark Drumheiser, arrived at that moment, also wearing a wetsuit. Mark was a diminutive five feet four but sported the body of a gymnast. He was perhaps the deadliest fighter on the crew, master of eleven martial arts. No one made Mutt and Jeff jokes about the pair. Mark nodded to them and tapped Dorf's arm, and the two moved off.

Soon, the submersible was deemed seaworthy and lifted by the crane into the water. Dorf and Mark were there to attach all the hoses, check the cable, and give a final okay. Working in tandem with Driver, Master Chief Warner lowered the submersible cables connecting the vessel to the mother ship. The submersible could operate independently under battery power for nearly seventy-two hours. Connected to the ship, it could stay down indefinitely.

Driver took the controls of the Kockums Salvage Bathyscaph, developed by Swedish submarine designers Kockums and christened The Steel Crab. Four electric motors propel and steer this ugly submersible, and a fifth electric motor manipulates the arms and other attached tools. It is capable of diving 36,000 feet and is equipped to stay beneath the surface at that depth for three days before needing to surface to recharge batteries and life support systems.

Slowly, as they sank into the depths, Sparks read off the depth gauge in fathoms, instantly converting the readings into feet in his head. The blue-green waters of the Mediterranean made the descent pleasant to the eye. Slowly, perceptibly, the light faded, and when Sparks called out one hundred fathoms, six hundred feet, the light was almost completely gone.

Driver switched on the dive lights. These powerful beams penetrated the dark waters for nearly thirty yards, surrounding them in a fixed globe of visibility. At one hundred and thirteen fathoms, six hundred and seventy-eight feet, they came in sight of the bottom, which in this locale was marked at nine hundred and seventy-five feet. Both sections of the sunken yacht were immediately visible in the dim light. To the men on the submersible it was always an eerie sight to come upon a sunken ship.

When they were within two fathoms of the bottom, Driver expertly brought the submersible to a stop, hovering where the blades wouldn't disturb the silt. A severed arm of one of the murdered victims lay on the bottom, several feet from the wreckage, the denizens of the deep already gathered around for the grizzly feast.

"*Steel Crab* to Uncle Zeke," FM said into his microphone.

"Uncle Zeke is watching you. Go ahead," Zeke replied. It was his favorite saying, and the men on the submersible smiled when they heard it again.

"Ask the Captain what he wants to do about the remains of the victims," FM replied.

"Try not to tear them up too much, but leave them at the bottom. They died at sea; let them be buried there," Jim's voice replied immediately.

"Oh, you're there!" FM said too innocently.

"What did you mean by that?" Jim asked, his face turning red.

"We thought you might be off TDY somewhere, busy with someone, I mean something else!" FM replied. Everyone laughed, including Cecilia.

Jim understood the need for the moment of levity. He could see the image of the arm on the bottom, too. All the men knew that death at sea was a very real danger, every day you were on it, and they had great respect for those who lost their lives at sea, especially those who just perished in the piracy raid.

Using the manipulator arms and great care, FM was able to drag the two visible bodies out of the wreckage and deposit them respectfully near the arm. In a few days, only the skeletons would lay there. He hoped the men loved the sea the way he did. Thinking about resting in her depths wasn't something he did often, but it did give him some comfort to know his body would serve some purpose, even in death. His soul, he knew, would be gone, so what happened to the body didn't really matter.

Part of the bow was smashed outward, as if something heavy shifted and almost escaped in the sinking. Curious, Driver positioned the sub above the hole, and they looked in at a huge safe, hidden where a safe should not be. No wonder the pirates didn't find it!

"Hey, Shep, you seein' this?" FM spoke into his microphone.

"That's a Worthington 1000 safe!" Zeke said.

"Bring it up!" Jim commanded. "Let's see what these pirates wanted so badly."

It took three hours to cut away enough of the bow to bring the safe out, and when they did, FM grunted in surprise as the submersible shifted. "This thing is heavy!" he said. He put it expertly into the sandbox Master Chief Warner lowered earlier in case they needed to pump silt out of the pieces to lift them clear. Often, it was FM's job to set up the sandbox. Today, it had been lowered from the ship. Typically, the sandbox would not be loaded with something quite as heavy as the safe. It was rated for that weight, barely.

"Hoist the sandbox!" FM ordered.

Slowly, the crane took up the slack in the cable, and the sandbox began the long trip to the surface. Designed to hold the weight, it rose steadily, if slowly. In his usual expertise, FM placed the safe so it rested in the best possible location, and the sandbox rose level to the top. Dorf and Mark were there to receive it and guide it to the rear of the ship, where it would be unloaded.

On the observation deck, Jim stood with a powerful pair of Zhumell signature waterproof binoculars, slowly rotating to ensure no one was watching them. There were no ships or boats near them. He radioed that information to the dive team, who prepared the safe to be lifted to the deck. Scanning the sky, he saw no surveillance aircraft, but that didn't mean they weren't there.

This was completed quickly and with a minimum of fuss. As soon as the safe was on the deck, Inchworm appeared with the hose to wash away the salt water. When he finished, John and Wade moved in with two cans of WD-40 and two rags to spray and wipe the safe down. Once completed, the safe was tipped onto a specially designed forklift that could lower things from the deck to the hold and lift things from the hold to the deck.

Chance drove the forklift, expertly operating the complicated machine. In less than ten minutes, the safe was secured in the hold. All the while, Jim remained on the observation deck with his binoculars, making sure that no one saw the safe dropped into the hold. He was relatively sure that no one was within range of even a powerful telescope.

"Did you really expect anyone to be watching?" Cecilia asked, stepping up beside him and laying a hand gently on his forearm as he lowered the binoculars.

"No, I think they believe that the yacht was destroyed in the blast. From the plane, they could see it explode and sink almost instantly. And I don't think they believe the safe they're looking for is on the yacht, or they wouldn't have blown it. I'm guessing that's the reason for the hostages; whoever owns this safe will want it badly. But I always try to be careful, especially now that I have a beautiful young woman on board." He complimented her, smiling down at Cecilia.

"Oh! And when did you bring her on board?" Cecilia asked facetiously, looking around. She smiled up at him, and he bent down and kissed her lightly. "Thank you for the compliment, Captain," she said demurely. Breathing in the fragrance of her hair and skin, he smiled into her eyes, and for a moment, everything else faded.

CHAPTER 5

Laughing together, they made their way down into the hold. Mark and Dorf were still in their wetsuits, but tanks, fins, masks, and snorkels were parked on the diving platform. Every SEAL team member learns the basics of breaking into safes. Surprisingly, Dorf had a unique talent in that field, and he kept some equipment in the war room that, if found, could land him in prison in any of a dozen countries.

It took him seven minutes to crack the safe, and when it opened, the hiss of air told them all that the seals held. Everything in the safe was dry. As always, they stared into the cavernous safe for a few minutes. Mr. Klaus was very wealthy, and the contents of his safe were no surprise to the men.

There were three bundles of currency, about eighteen inches square, tightly shrink-wrapped to keep the bills dry. One was U.S. currency, one was Euro currency, and the other was British. All the notes were new, sequential, and wrapped with strips most common in the Grand Cayman Islands. Nearly five million dollars in currency sat there, neatly stashed.

There were checkbooks, bank records, and another wrapped rosewood armoire filled with fine jewelry. Two black jewelry cases were filled with diamonds and other precious stones. Their worth might top the currency! It was, however, none of those things that finally caught the crew's attention. There was a notebook, a plain blue covered spiral binder one could purchase in any office supply store in America or Europe, filled with coded entries.

"This is what the pirates were looking for," Jim said. He was wearing surgical gloves as he held the book carefully, touching only the brass spiral binding. He studied page after page as he flipped them, like a flip chart, and read them sideways. "We're upgrading them to terrorists because of this. Let's see what Uncle Zeke can do with it," he said, putting it in a plastic zip-lock bag and handing it to Cecilia.

Cecilia took the book up to Zeke while the men ensured everything was returned exactly as they found it. Mark, who had an eye for such things, adjusted things a little until satisfied. They closed but did not lock the safe.

"Will anyone be able to tell we've opened this?" Jim asked. The safe certainly looked untouched.

"I was able to use my new toy to watch the tumblers, so I opened it with the proper combination. I doubt anyone can tell it was opened once we lock it again and wipe it down," Dorf replied confidently. "As long as everything is still in there, no one will suspect it was opened, or if they do, not be sure."

It took two days to lift the two parts of the yacht and secure them safely to the inflatable pads that would keep them afloat as they were towed into Athens. The open ends faced the rear, and it looked odd to tow both halves that way. Men worked around the two pieces for nearly half a day, securing everything before they could set off. Jim decided to go slow to minimize any hazards along the way.

Zeke did not disappoint him either. He broke the code on the third day. When his computer whistled to let him know the code had been broken, he watched the sheets print out, taking each one and scanning them quickly. As he read, his eyebrows climbed up his forehead. After the third page, he depressed the talk button on his communication headset.

"Shep! CIC! I need you now!" he said tersely.

"Sir! How dare he!" Marvin Finn said, stepping into Jim's office as Jim rose to leave.

"Excuse me, LT?" Jim said, momentarily perplexed. His mind was on what Zeke might have found, and Finn's reaction surprised him.

"He gave you an order, sir! I'll write him up and deal with this immediately!" Finn said, outrage in his voice.

"Whoa, Finn!" Jim commanded, holding up both hands as if to fend him off. "You will do nothing of the kind! You assumed something that wasn't there. Zeke's been with me for years and wouldn't tell me he needed me unless it was urgent. Lighten up, LT. You'll give yourself an ulcer!" Jim said, heading out of the office, shaking his head. He didn't see Finn's expression, but Cecilia did. She knew the man would mope for days for being called out like that. Some men, especially men like Finn, were like that, as touchy and crotchety as an old maid sometimes. Mrs. Shepherd sighed.

"He really didn't order the captain anywhere, you know," Cecilia said lightly. "He did say he needed the captain immediately. His words were, if I remember correctly, 'Shep! Computer room! I need you now!' That was a plea for immediate attention," she finished. Watching him carefully, she saw he wasn't following her.

"Well, it sounded more like an order to me! And he's only an Ensign!" Finn replied petulantly. He looked like an angry child, his lips set in a thin line, his eyes expressing disapproval.

Cecilia sighed. "You'll find that rank means very little on this vessel regarding teamwork, Marvin. Each man is respected for his expertise and trusted, sometimes with the very lives of every other team member. When you trust someone like that, it doesn't pay to think about rank. Jim looks at every man on this vessel as an equal, a co-owner of the company. You'll get used to it eventually," she added when she saw his mulish look. At least, she hoped he would get used to it eventually. Right at this moment, that wasn't happening. She decided to add one last warning. "I wouldn't suggest talking to Zeke about this either, Marvin. He's a SEAL, and you might find yourself in a lot of trouble," she finished.

Finn didn't believe her. She could tell. And she knew he would talk to Zeke. Hoping Zeke would merely ignore the man, which was probably what he would do, she realized that Finn could be frustrating, and Zeke might decide to teach him a lesson in humility. Cecilia sighed. Marvin would be a handful for the crew until he learned the ropes.

In the computer room, Jim sat down next to Zeke. John and Wade answered the summons as well, taking the remaining seats. Zeke handed the printout to Jim, who began reading, handing a finished page to John, and so on until the pages returned to Zeke. In silence, the men read for nearly half an hour before Jim handed the last page to John. He sighed deeply, his head bowed, his green eyes staring at nothing.

"An agent in place!" John was the first to speak. "How many more poor suckers did the communist regime leave hanging out there, suddenly cut off, without direction?"

"This guy is good," Wade said quietly, handing the last sheet to Zeke. He's kept in the dark all these years and used his training and connections to build a multi-million dollar business. I wonder what his communist bosses would have said about that?" He grinned at the other three men in the room.

"Okay!" Jim said suddenly, straightening in his seat and looking at the other men around him. "We have an agent in place that no one knows about except his former KGB connections. He, of all people, is approached by Kalil to launder money for this "committee of five" that Klaus refers to. Klaus doesn't know who they are yet, but he has tied Kalil to Chechen rebels (and we know they were influenced and financed by Al-Qaeda). Kalil also has some former members of the Red Army Faction working for him. Klaus guesses that the Russians used Kalil to supply and possibly train terrorists during the eighties," Jim looked at the men to make sure they were following him. He saw in their eyes not only understanding but also quick assessment, looking at the situation to determine the dangers that might be lurking just beneath the surface.

"Somehow, Kalil guesses or discovers that Klaus is gathering information on him, and he decides to kidnap the wife and kiddies to make him cough up the code book. Kalil probably has someone in the household employed to spy on Klaus. Anyway, Klaus either hides the safe on the yacht or uses it as a secure hiding place, having it built into the forward ballast compartment on purpose. Kalil doesn't know where the safe is, but he searches the yacht anyway, or his pirates do before they blow it up," he continued.

"Which means Klaus is frantic because he probably knows by now that Kalil has his wife and kids, but he also knows the safe was on the yacht, which means he has no way to get them back," Wade said after a pause.

"Kalil will kill them if Klaus doesn't come up with the book," John said quietly. "Hopefully, Klaus is smart enough to tell Kalil where he hid the safe, and Kalil will wait."

"Well, let's radio in and let Klaus know, through the insurance company, that not only have we raised his yacht, but we also have his safe," Jim suggested.

"He'll take it off our hands, give the book to Kalil, and then what?" Zeke asked. As usual, his hands were busy with the computer console before him.

"Either Kalil will think himself safe and leave Klaus alone because of his value as a money launderer, or he will kill everyone," Jim stated flatly.

"Kalil is careful. He's remained hidden all these years. I think he'll kill everyone," John said quietly. Wade nodded in agreement.

"We'll just have to prevent that," Jim said. "Zeke, can you carefully mark this book and everything else in the safe to avoid detection?"

"The book and money will be easy," Zeke said confidently. I can mark the jewelry boxes, but probably not the jewelry itself. Let me see everything, and I'll let you know," he added. Those new tracking chips are top-of-the-line. We'll know within a few yards of where the book or money goes. That will give us an edge."

"I think the money and the book are the keys here. Leave everything else alone. And, Zeke, good work!" Jim said, putting a hand on his shoulder. "Unlocking this code has given us some really solid information!"

"Thanks, Shep," Zeke said with a grin.

"Oh! One more thing," Jim said, his face suddenly troubled. "Finn thinks you gave me an order, and knowing him, he will make an issue of it. Deal with it as you see fit."

"He does outrank me, Captain," Zeke pointed out.

"Yeah, well, when did rank mean anything to us?" Jim replied with a wicked grin. "Just don't publicly put him in a hurt locker," Jim added.

"Why not? The little prude will do his thing publicly!" John snapped.

"Okay!" Jim said, suddenly laughing and holding his hands up as if to avoid a blow from his brother. "Jeeze, you Marines are a tough bunch!" he added.

"Yeah!" Wade interjected. We ate higher-ranking officers for breakfast on a regular basis. I don't know about you guys, but it always gave me the runs!" Everyone laughed at that comment, and Jim bowed to the wisdom of his crew. Either Finn would learn or leave.

"I seem to remember a Gunnery Sergeant who had you for breakfast once," John said with a laugh, slapping Wade on the back. The two shared a look and a laugh, and then Wade blushed, remembering the incident.

"I had that coming," he admitted. "And I never disciplined him, either," he added. "I did hope it would give him the runs, though!" John and Zeke burst out laughing, and Jim grinned.

"I trust you to handle it," Jim said, slapping Zeke on the back.

"Ow!" Zeke said, rubbing his shoulder. "Us computer geeks ain't tough like you Marines!" he whined.

"It's a good thing we're all wearing boots here!" Jim said, laughing at Zeke's mockery. Zeke was as tough as anyone Jim ever met in the military, and that was saying something. "Because this geek is slinging it mighty thick in here!" he added. Everyone laughed.

"Hey Geek! Oops! I mean, Zeke," John said, enjoying the fun. "Is there any way we can keep track of Klaus's business, home, and mobile phones once he receives notice of his recovered safe? He's bound to call Kalil or contact him," John added.

Zeke turned his chair back to his command intelligence center and began to type on a keyboard, then moved to another and yet another. He went back to the first and added more commands. Two minutes of silence passed, and then the computer screens began to change. He nodded as if pleased and continued typing on the three keyboards. After five minutes, he looked up at his three friends.

"Got 'em all!" he announced with pride. "Whatever calls Klaus makes on his known phones will now be recorded."

"Will he know?" Jim asked.

"Uncle Zeke is watching! He won't know anything!" Zeke said as if stung.

"Sorry, Uncle Zeke!" John said with a laugh. "After all the things you've done with that command intelligence center of yours, we should stop doubting. And you don't have to say it! We know! Uncle Zeke is watching!" They all laughed.

"Huh!" Zeke grunted. He was already working at his center. Wade, John, and Jim looked at each other, grinned, and left the center to Zeke. His genius created the center and devised a system where the ship's motion hid the signal from his feeds. Jim didn't know all the technical aspects of it, but the unfolding dish on the communications mast was almost always open these days. Zeke claimed that no one could trace his infiltrations, and Jim believed him as they had yet to be even questioned.

CHAPTER 6

That night at dinner, Jim watched Finn make his way to Zeke's table. Everyone else also saw it happen, and the dining hall grew quiet. Marvin looked around and noticed that everyone was watching. That suited him. He wanted everyone to realize that things would go according to the book from now on.

"Yes, Sharky?" Zeke replied when addressed.

"I prefer you using my rank as opposed to my name or any nickname you may have attached to me," Finn said haughtily. Jim groaned inwardly. The man just didn't understand! His tone was condescending and autocratic, both guaranteed to fail with Zeke. Even his body language and how he addressed Zeke told Jim that Finn was sure of himself, which was a big mistake.

"My apologies!" Zeke said, sitting back with a grin on his face. "Yes, Lieutenant Junior Grade Sharky, er, Finn?" He said, pretending to stammer. "I'm guessing that, by your presence and sour expression, you have your usual vituperation to express fluently."

"You are addressing a superior officer!" Finn snapped, angry now.

"No, merely a higher ranking one. What do you want, Sharky? I'm eating." Zeke replied easily.

"You give me no choice but to write you up, Ensign Kline," Marvin said, drawing himself ramrod straight. "You gave the captain an order this morning, and now you completely disregard standard operating procedure! I will take personal pleasure in designing your punishment." Finn added. Jim groaned inwardly.

There was a moment of silence as Zeke looked at Finn, his grin never slipping, his eyes full of mischievous delight. Then he moved, and Marvin Finn got his first lesson regarding the nature of this crew. Zeke seemed to strike like a cobra, and Finn found himself dragged across the table, through the food, dishes scattering everywhere and breaking on the floor. Then he was snapped upright. He glared at Zeke, prepared to speak when pain mushroomed in his shoulder, and he fell to his knees. Speech was impossible, sound was impossible, all he could do was grimace in pain and stare in disbelief. He tried vainly to pry those fingers away but was helpless against Ensign Kline. It was impossible to believe that a man that thin could have so strong a grip!

"Do I have your attention yet, Finn?" Zeke asked easily amidst the laughter of the men in the room. Marvin wanted to fold onto the floor, but Zeke's other hand still held his shirt collar. "I'll wait for an answer," Zeke added.

Finn couldn't stand the pain and whispered a "yes" through clenched teeth. Zeke jerked him to his feet again, and the pain was gone. His eyes widened as his feet left the floor, and he realized that Zeke was literally lifting him clear of the floor with one hand. It didn't seem possible!

Although trained in the British Navy and somewhat conversant with hand-to-hand combat, Finn hadn't practiced in years. He tried to break free and discovered, to his humiliation, that he was utterly helpless in the hands of this man. After a few attempts, he found his face pressed against the tablecloth, his arm cruelly twisted behind his back, and his fingers burning with pain that made him scream until Zeke eased up on the pressure. Zeke remembered Jim's words and knew Finn would hurt for days because of this.

"We don't do everything according to the standard operating procedure on this ship, mate! Zeke said, his face next to Finn's, the grin still in place, eyes still playful. But they suddenly grew hard, and

Marvin, looking into them, realized for the first time in his life that he was in the presence of a man who could easily kill him. Those eyes made him think of fresh earth falling on his coffin. Fear came then.

"We work together, and rank don't mean shit unless the man wearing it deserves it!" Zeke suddenly realized he'd used a foul word in the presence of Cecilia. He looked over at her. "Sorry about the bad language, Cecilia. I let my anger get control for a second there. Please forgive me." He said humbly.

Cecilia tried hard not to laugh. Not daring to speak, she merely nodded in the affirmative to Zeke, who turned his attention back to Marvin. "Now, Marvin, I'm going to give you some good advice, and I suggest you listen carefully. Are you listening?"

"Yes," Finn groaned, his shame and anger growing almost hand in hand.

"I respect your ability to shuffle papers and make Shep's life easier. I respect that you're a good sailor and know your stuff. But you focus on meaningless, petty stuff, just like hundreds of other officers I've known. If Shep wants to discipline me, that's one thing. He's earned the right. You haven't. Try it again, and I'll throw you off the rear of this ship. Understand?" Zeke looked right into Marvin's eyes, and the man blanched white under that gaze.

"This is outrageous behavior, Ensign!" Marvin sputtered.

"Wrong answer!" Zeke crowed with a huge smile. Effortlessly, he hoisted Marvin into a fireman's carry and headed for the door. Almost everyone got up to follow as Finn beat at Zeke with his free hand and kicked about with his free leg. It was all to no avail.

True to his word, Zeke carried Finn to the rear diving deck of the ship and tossed him into the water. At that moment, they were going at an easy five-knot speed, towing the two parts of the yacht behind. Finn came to the surface only to be brushed under by the floatation pontoons. He came up gasping for air.

"Man overboard!" Zeke said into his microphone. Wade, who had the wheel, immediately began to slow down. When towing, as they were, the process took time. Knowing what was about to happen, Sparks threw a life jacket at the same time Zeke threw Finn so he didn't have to swim far to reach it. Six other crewmembers were lowering the Rigid Raider to pick Finn out of the water. Zeke merely turned and headed back to the dining room.

"I think you may have made an enemy," Jim warmed, turning to walk beside him. "Next time, throw him off and make him swim back." He added with profound disgust.

CHAPTER 7

Finn handed Jim his resignation almost as soon as he dried off and changed uniforms. Taking the paper from his hand, Jim sat back and motioned with his head to say that Finn should take a seat. Marvin remained standing stiff as a board at attention.

"Sit down, Finn!" Jim commanded firmly, making eye contact, something Finn hated and tried to avoid at all costs. Jim wasn't about to coddle this man anymore. Marvin looked hurt at the tone in Jim's voice but sat as directed without further demure.

Jim leaned back in his chair and read the letter through, then tore it into pieces and tossed it in his wastebasket. Marvin's eyes opened wide, and he came out of his seat. He found himself face to face with the captain, whose eyes turned as hard and dark as the barrel of a gun. Slowly, Marvin sat back down without saying anything.

Walking around the desk, Jim took enough time to cool off and sat on the edge of it. He knew that part of Finn's makeup included being tenacious and a perfectionist, and he was usually very narrow-minded. On many occasions, those qualities were not a detriment. When it came to teamwork, they were a disaster, and Jim knew it was time to introduce Finn to the idea. Making sure he talked softly and slowly, he began to lay out the facts, including many details, to keep Marvin's attention.

"Marvin, this company started as a pilot program three years ago to see if it was effective. Military solutions to terrorism are often the best and the most effective. Still, because bureaucracies run the military, the military is hampered in carrying out such solutions to their natural conclusions. Our paramilitary unit is different. A bureaucracy or a committee does not run us, and our missions have no military oversight. We go in, assess the situation, and act accordingly. If a military solution is the only way to go, we exercise that."

"Does Sir Edward know you have this freedom?" Finn asked. He was hearing this part of the operation for the first time, and Jim could see he didn't like it. Finn would always need someone to be in command and give orders, and the concept of such a unit belied that ideal.

"He was one of the founders of the idea. In the past, military solutions were withheld from situations that resulted in terrible loss of lives and useless wars. Terrorists are not really soldiers, Marvin. They're cowards, every one of them. Oh, they're brave enough when they're carrying out their plans against women and children. And they're fanatical enough to die for what they believe, strapping bombs to themselves, but their targets are rarely military. Even if they go after a military target, it is always from a safe distance with a car bomb or something like that.

"Some terrorists operate on a shoestring budget, while others have an almost endless source of money to finance their schemes. The latter are the ones we go after. We find out where the money is coming from and take care of that, and we find the terrorists and take care of them. Sometimes, a military solution is the only one that is possible. Most of the time, we've been able to amass enough evidence against them to send them away for life."

Jim pulled two sheets of paper from his desk full of facts and read through them for Finn's benefit. Then he drew an email from Sir Edward sent that morning. He handed the email to Finn last.

"Sir Edward wanted to speak with you personally," he said, handing the email to Marvin.

"Lieutenant Junior Grade Finn, Marvin: It is of the utmost

importance that you trust Captain Shepherd and his Team. Their contributions to the war on terrorism have been invaluable to the Crown. Advise you stand down and learn to do things their way immediately. EM/DO/MI6." It took a few minutes for the meaning of the words to sink in, and Marvin put the paper on the desk with a surprise on his face.

"This is very hard for me," Finn stated after reading the missive twice. "All my life, I've only known one way to operate, and it's served me well."

"Which is exactly why we chose you, Marvin," Jim replied, rising and returning to his chair. He sat down and stared at the ceiling for a few minutes, his fingers steepled, the tips pressed gently together.

"You are very good at what you do. I don't want to change any of that. But you need to learn to work with the men. This is a team project, and every man is part of that team. Even the men on the kitchen crew understand they are valuable to our team. The soldiers treat them with respect because they do their jobs well and try hard to work with every one of us.

"You're new. You haven't been on the boat long enough to be acquainted with exactly how we do our jobs. I want you to study us, especially the sixteen-man fighting team. Watch every man carefully, see how he does what is expected of him and how he interacts with others on the crew. Listen especially to how they address me and the other officers on the ship. You'll see quickly that we don't do things as you want and never will.

"Watch the support crew interact with them. Don't draw any conclusions until you have studied us for at least three months. By then, you'll know exactly how to fit in and be a team member and player, causing no friction with other crew members. By then, they will know you well enough to respect what you do, and you'll find that incidents like what happened this evening won't come up.

"I want you to spend at least two hours a day watching us train. Pick different two-hour chunks of time to watch so you see the whole program of training from a first-hand point of view. When the three months are finished, I want a full written report of your personal assessment of the crew on my desk. Then, if you want to quit, I'll accept your resignation."

At that moment, a pleasant series of bells sounded. Jim sighed. Now, three hours out of Athens, he had to meet with the Team for a plan of action. He waved Finn to follow him. "Come with me, LT. This will be a good time to get two hours of study in," he said, leaving his office. Reluctantly, Finn followed.

Cecilia, sitting in her office, listened to the entire conversation. She knew her husband was a respected leader of men, and now she had one more reason to appreciate that. He knew exactly what words to use with Finn to calm him down, give him a reasonable goal, and keep him on the crew. She smiled as the two men left.

Marvin had never been in the conference room for a meeting. He was surprised to find all fifteen men waiting for them as they entered and even more surprised when no one raised an objection to his presence. Looking around, he saw two members of the kitchen crew seated at the table, watching and listening. He joined them, sitting one chair away, pulling a pen from his pocket, and opening his notebook. Out of respect for Jim, the team stood as he entered and sat again when he waved them down. Finn noted the respect the men showed for Jim and realized he was seeing something he'd noted before but not entirely understood. Jim's men highly respected him and showed it in ways that didn't include what he was used to, such as salutes or the use of rank and title.

"Okay, gentlemen, we've got three hours to prepare to follow that book and rescue those hostages. What do we have on intel?" he asked to begin the meeting.

"Klaus made a call from his office phone to a hotel in Agordo. That call was routed to two different locations before hooking up with a cell phone, of all things, in Venice. If the person speaking on the cell phone is Kalil, I now have a voiceprint and a cell phone GPS fix for his location. Unfortunately, he was in an outdoor café having coffee when he took the call. Also, this one is cagey. He tossed the phone after using it," Zeke announced quietly.

"Why the rerouting of the call?" Jim asked.

"It's a way to keep people from tracing it," Zeke answered easily. "Oldest trick in the book, and it works for just about every system but ours," he added with some pride.

"Dang, Zeke, you're good!" Phillip Eustus said, shaking his head. "Our experts have been trying to break that one for two years now, and we still don't have the technology!" Jim looked at Phil and grinned. His last name was pronounced with a long "u" sound, and the men nicknamed him PU, which is pronounced *pew*. Eustus was a powerhouse with two hundred pounds of packed muscle on a five-foot-eleven-inch frame. His head was usually shaved, and his light complexion was often red in the sun.

"Duly noted, PU!" Zeke acquiesced. "I'll send the schematics and programming to them first thing in the morning," he promised. Jim knew he would. Sir Edward already had the same technology, and Admiral Runion had it almost before Zeke finished building the prototype.

"We're going to have to set this up quickly, Shep," Wade said in the silence that followed. "If Kalil decides to kill everyone, he'll move immediately. His kind never waits."

"I agree!" Mark said quickly.

"Time will definitely be of the essence! The question is: Do we go in with lethals or non-lethals?" John queried no one in particular.

"If Kalil kills Klaus, we go in with lethal weapons. If he doesn't, that gives us a window of opportunity, and we go in with non-lethal weapons," Jim replied after a few moments of thought. The men nodded in approval of the plan.

Two hours later, a somewhat stunned Marvin Finn followed the other men out of the conference room. Jim had taken suggestions, listened to his men carefully, and discussed just about every possible scenario. Not only did Finn have a new respect for these soldiers, but he was also beginning to see that they were indeed a breed apart. Everyone was brilliant and skilled in his profession to a degree he wasn't sure existed elsewhere.

Of course, being British, he knew the Americans had superior forces but had never thought about that superiority in terms of skill before. For him, it had always been numbers. American forces were just larger than other armies. Yet he remembered now the 20 Marines who went down behind enemy lines in a region in which he was stationed. Before they were obliterated, they had accounted for three thousand dead enemy soldiers. Military personnel in that city were so angry over their losses that they allowed the bodies to be mutilated, which proved to be a serious mistake. American forces moved in the next day and finished the work of those twenty brave men.

"LT, how will this contract stack up for us financially?" Jim asked Finn as they walked together, interrupting his contemplations.

"Our profit margin is just under forty percent on this one, Captain," Finn replied immediately. Jim knew he would know the figures, and he was pleased. He listened as Finn outlined the details despite his hatred of details like that. What he wanted was the bottom line, and Finn gave that right at the beginning.

"Well done, LT. That's good news for us," Jim confirmed, suppressing a sigh.

They arrived in Athens an hour later, where the Lloyds representative met them. He inspected the wreckage and handed over the check with a smile. Finn took charge of the check with far less officiousness than he had exhibited before. He asked Jim's permission to put the check in the ship's safe and left. When he was gone, a tall, gray-haired man appeared at the gangplank, asking permission to come on board. Jim guessed correctly that this was Paul Klaus.

Klaus was perhaps two inches taller than Jim, still in excellent physical condition, and looked every inch the business tycoon he was. His suit must have cost over a thousand dollars, and his watch and jewelry were all gold with diamond decorations. Since he was operating in Italy, Jim suspected the suit might be an original Armani. Mr. Klaus clicked his heels and bowed correctly in Greek fashion. Since his name was Greek, perhaps he thought it added to his disguise. Over the years, he had probably done this over and over until it became a habit. Jim didn't know. But he bowed in return.

"I understand that you recovered my safe," Klaus said immediately. I will gladly pay whatever you charge for safely bringing it up." His eyes said that he would rather not have to pay any fee. Jim smiled inwardly.

"Under the Lloyds contract, we have already been paid, Mr. Klaus. The safe is your property. You may see it now and arrange for transport." Jim waved him toward the forward hold.

Paul Klaus followed them into the hold and looked at his slightly rusted safe strapped to the hold wall. He could see no marks around the combination lock that suggested it had been oiled or opened. He grunted in satisfaction.

"I have a group of moving men prepared to take it now. Is that possible?" he requested respectfully, looking at Jim. It was a measuring look, almost challenging, and Jim remained stoic as he stared back, showing nothing but utmost cooperation.

"Absolutely," Jim replied expansively. "I'll have my crew bring it to the deck, and your men can take it from there."

"Mr. Bernard. Can you get some crew to bring this to the deck?" Jim asked, turning to Dorf. Dorf snapped a salute and hurried up the stairs onto the deck. In moments, he had Mark and FM help him load the safe onto the specially designed forklift and lift it out of the hold. They set it carefully on the deck.

"Do you think it will still open, and are the contents still dry?" Klaus asked, his eyes twinkling as he looked at Jim.

"We could have opened it," Jim admitted easily, looking bored with the conversation but politely answering. "If the salvage rights made it ours, we would have. It's a Worthington 1000, which is a very good safe. If your seals held, whatever is inside should be dry. It was nearly a thousand feet down, so I don't know if the seals held or not. No water drained out of it, though, so I think you should be fine."

"You could have opened it?" Klaus questioned suspiciously, his eyebrows slightly raised.

"We are a salvage operation. Sometimes, we possess the salvage rights, and anything we find is ours. We've been very successful in two ventures of that kind, but one was so old there was no safe, and the other was from the Great War, so the safe was easy to open," Jim replied honestly. Your safe was your property, so we didn't have the right to open it," Jim added.

"You are honest men, then?" Klaus asked, the twinkle back in his eyes.

"Lloyds doesn't hire salvage crews that don't play by the rules, sir," Jim replied. His manner was cool, as appropriate in the situation.

"My apologies, Captain!" Klaus said. He watched his men manhandle the safe onto a thin forklift that could travel the gangplank and slowly followed it off the boat. Jim grinned as he thought about Klaus opening the safe and finding everything as it should be.

"A suspicious man," Dorf commented quietly, standing just behind the captain, watching Klaus climb into a beige Bentley. "And he didn't seem overwrought about his family either! He didn't appear anxious or in too much of a rush to get his property off this boat.

"That's how he survived so long," Jim mused quietly in return.

"Will Kalil kill him?" Dorf asked.

"Probably not, once he has the book. He will have the upper hand. Killing his money source is bad business, and Klaus must love his family. We're going to rescue them," Jim added.

"Chopper?" Dorf asked.

"I don't know yet," Jim answered honestly. "Let's see where the book goes, and we'll know then. Kalil seems to be a very cautious man as well. He may have them secreted away somewhere difficult to reach. Zeke will know soon."

CHAPTER 8

Less than an hour passed before the homing chip showed the book in transit. Zeke followed it, first by road, then by air, and back to roads, this time in Italy. It stopped in the Dolomite Mountains near Cortina. He enhanced the satellite feed and whistled. Zeke called Jim to the command intelligence center.

We'll have to make a night insertion from the air, Shep," he announced, studying the pictures. "They're being held near Cortina, in what looks like a mountain fortress. The man in charge used to run a terror cell for the Baeder-Meinhoff group. Dietrich Murchenheim. Very bad character! Shall I have Sir Edward fix up the air transport?"

"That's a Good idea. I'll give you an hour to gather as much Intel as possible. When you're ready, get the team to the conference room," Jim replied.

The mountain fortress proved to be an ancient fortress, long abandoned, then used by monks, and finally bought by Kalil. Tracing the ownership had been a puzzle, but Zeke came through, hacking into two secure sites to gain the information so craftly that neither official site would ever log the intrusion. Most of his system intrusions were done with this protection in place to hide his presence and what he discovered.

Satellite photos enhanced on Zeke's computer, then fed to the laptops in front of the men, gave them an accurate layout of the buildings, walls, well, trail up and down, and the road that stopped at least two thousand feet below the fortress. Kalil added some Polaris four-wheel drive ATVs to transport men and women up and down the steep trails.

There were photos of people. One man, Jim, thought it might be Kalil himself, arrived after the notebook was identified, and a reasonable amount of time passed to be sure no officials followed the trail. He was a dark, thin man who seemed almost aware that photos could be taken from satellites because he kept his head down and never looked up like a normal person. Everyone occasionally looks at the sky outdoors, especially in a beautiful setting. Kalil didn't.

But even the most careful people made mistakes. Kalil was driving a rented Mercedes, and they now had one alias and a trail to follow. MI6 had an asset in Cortina that could help. He or she was there on other official business but would fit this into his or her plans. Knowing Sir Edward, whoever this man or woman was in Cortina, they would get the photos and the information without being detected, even by someone as careful as Kalil appeared to be. That was a common mistake of undercover agents. Most believed they could remain unknown. In this day and age, that was impossible!

Jim led the teams through the plan and listened to all suggestions, making refinements occasionally until everyone knew what to do. His team was sure the enemy was not expecting any kind of rescue attempt. Once Kalil, or perhaps one of his lieutenants, left the compound, guards posted became lazy and careless, basically putting in their time by smoking, talking when they met at various points, and even sleeping. Murchenheim seemed confident no one knew where to find him.

After dark, the teams made their way separately to the government airfield where a C130, now used for UPS in Greece, waited with propellers spinning. Once everyone was on board, the pilots took off without comment. Sir Edward was clever. This particular plane flew over that fortress three nights a week, and this was one of the scheduled nights. The guards would think nothing of the normal run. Satellite photos showed they rarely even looked up when the plane went over.

This would be a low-level insertion, always dangerous, doubly so in the dark in unfamiliar territory. If any of the team was concerned about the danger, Jim couldn't tell. Like him, they were good soldiers and accepted the risks that came with the job. When the time came, and the green light flashed, each man moved out confidently. Most trusted God to protect them; if they prayed on the way down, so much better. Jim offered one of his own for the protection of his team as he led the way out.

Buffeted by the wash from the plane, the skydivers swung wildly for a moment or two before settling for a speedy descent. Barely discernable were the men's footsteps landing, the chutes' woosh as they were hauled in and quickly folded. Other than that, there was silence, and Jim looked around, counting, making sure every team member was close by. They were.

Skill, training, practice, confidence, and grace worked together to get the men down safely. Some landings were harder than expected, but there were no twisted ankles, broken bones, or torn tendons or muscles. Those were real dangers in a night drop, especially a low-level drop. John suffered a small bruise on his instep, but it was bearable. Jim was glad to see Sean checking it carefully before giving him the thumbs up.

Finding their equipment didn't take long. They all landed pretty much in a circle around the package. In minutes, they were ready to go. Team 1 was the first to circle around. Everyone else waited until they were above the fortress, ready to lay down cover fire. Dorf, Jack, Mark, and Bill were armed with Heckler & Koch SA80s and their MP5/10SD rifles. The smaller, lighter sniper rifle gave them superior night firing through NV sights specially designed for such maneuvers. Their job was intense because they had to watch to make sure none of the team were ambushed or shot if discovered.

In position, Dorf keyed his microphone twice to let Jim know it was time for the other three teams to move. Team 2, with Jim in the lead, had the south wall. Team 3, with John in the lead, had the east wall. Team 4, with Sean in the lead, had the west wall. Team 4 left first; they had the longest distance to travel. Team 2 followed in ten minutes, and then Team 3. Once they were in position, the danger really began because once they started, they had to go fast and hard.

Dorf and his team watched the other teams move to the walls. Shaking his head and pursing his lips in a silent whistle, Dorf watched the team move in and execute the plan flawlessly. Jim crept to the wall directly under one of the guards standing, his rifle dangling from his right hand, smoking a thin cigar. Slowly, Jim straightened, grabbed the man's ankles, and jerked his feet out from under him.

There was no time for a cry. Just a startled grunt and the clatter of a fallen weapon was all the sound, and it carried all the way up to Dorf. The other guard turned at the sound, giving Sean a clear shot with his rifle butt, striking the man just below the ear. Jim's karate chop to the neck of his man was hardly necessary, but he did it anyway. John climbed onto the wall behind his man and clubbed him unconscious with an extending baton, the guard never realizing he was there. Ten seconds later, all three teams were inside the fortress without raising an alarm.

Sean took his team to one of the buildings where most of the men slept, ate, and played. Looking in the windows, he saw four at a table playing cards and three others stretched out on their cots, two asleep and one reading. He put up his fingers to indicate the number of men and motioned for his men to position themselves. Then, bold as you please, he entered the door and pointed his weapon.

"Just sit still and make no sound," he commanded in perfect idiomatic German. The men froze as Sean's team moved in. Each man was forced to breathe via a mask attached to a can of gas that rendered them instantly unconscious, all of them slumping in their seats.

"We're getting good at this," Sean commented, looking at the unconscious bodies. "No blood, no mess."

Team 3 was in the armory, making sure that all the weapons there would never be used to harm anyone. Shortly after they left, the whole building would go up in smoke. Explosives were used liberally and expertly placed for maximum damage. Whoever this group was, and whatever their objective, they would have to resupply arms, which would cost them time and money. It would also tell Jim if there was money behind what they were doing.

Team 2 had the job of surprising the guards with the hostages. Jim led his team to the house where they knew the hostages were kept, watching the ground for tripwires and finally stopping at the door. Zeke, FM, and Smitty took windows, checking them for warning devices. Thirty seconds later, Jim received their reports.

"Dime store warning device on my window," Zeke said with disdain.

"Same here, Shep," Smitty added, looking at the one fastened on the inside of his window.

"Either the light is out on mine, boss, or the idiots forgot to check the battery. Mine does not appear to be armed. Now ain't that somethin'?" FM's voice was casual, even if near a whisper. Jim smiled.

"On my mark," Jim said quietly. "Go!"

As one, the four men burst through windows and doors. Murchenheim was seated at a table with the teenage daughter tightly tied to her chair, and he was fondling her hair. He looked up more in irritation than fear and fell back without a cry as Jim fired a beanbag shot into his face. One other guard was in the room, and FM took him down. Smitty came into the bedroom, where a guard stood by the door. Because he had a gun in his hand, Smitty threw his knife, taking the man in the throat and killing him instantly.

Mom and the boy lay in a rumpled bed, hogtied cruelly, gagged, and hysterical. Smitty looked up as Zeke came in. He was cutting the ropes that bound their feet to their hands and hadn't taken out the gags yet. Those came next, then the ropes that bound hands, feet, and elbows. There was blood under the ropes. Zeke looked down at the dead guard as he passed and nodded once to Smitty. He saw the gun and knew there was no other way.

Jim and FM came into the room, slinging their weapons after making sure the safety was engaged. Jim helped the mother sit up, speaking quietly to her in Greek.

"Are you Mrs. Klaus?" he asked. She nodded in the affirmative. "You're safe now. Do you speak English?" Again, she nodded in the affirmative. "Good. Some of my men don't speak Greek, but they all speak English." She seemed to understand. "Will you come and help me with your daughter?" Again, she nodded, her eyes suddenly going wide.

Jim didn't know how to be delicate about it. He gave her orders, keeping his voice soft and calm. "Ask her if he touched her sexually," he suggested. Listening as mother and daughter spoke, he sighed in relief. Murchenheim hadn't gotten to rape yet. Suddenly, he looked at the mother. "Did he touch you?" She was a pretty woman, and her eyes fell, and she began to sob quietly, holding her daughter.

Without really thinking about it, Jim turned and fired a beanbag shot into Murchenheim's groin, watching with satisfaction as the man came partway to consciousness at the new pain, his body slowly drawing into a fetal position. Mrs. Klaus saw it, too, but it didn't help what she had to face. Still, she and her daughter jumped at the report of the shotgun and gasped as the beanbag hit home. The daughter's eyes suddenly narrowed, and she lashed out a kick, landing it where the beanbag had already done some damage.

Sean came in at that point, introduced himself as a doctor, and went to work examining the prisoners. Mrs. Klaus hadn't stopped crying yet, but Sean got the story from her. Murchenheim broke her will on the first day of captivity with rape and brutality while her children were forced to watch. Jim knew the story and hated it. He was twirling his knife, looking at the terrorist who had remained hidden so long. Sean saw the interchange, recognized what was probably going through Jim's head, and conversationally spoke.

"It's not really worth it, you know," he said quietly. "Tempting, but best not, don't you think?" While he worked, he kept his eyes on his job but glanced Jim's way once or twice in concern.

Jim looked at him, his green eyes as cold as the grave, but to Sean's relief, the knife went back in its sheath. Jim removed himself from temptation and greeted Dorf as the giant walked to the door.

"We're ready out here, Shep," he said simply. Jim nodded and motioned to the team. Dorf walked over, picked up the unconscious, and handcuffed Murchenheim, and everyone left. FM paused long enough to spray the remaining living guard. Smitty and Zeke were carrying the dead one.

Wade met them, hoisted the dead body over his massive shoulders, and began the trek down the trail to the road. A covered truck waited there for them and would transport them to a waiting military plane. Near dawn, everyone arrived at a Greek military post, where the Klaus family was turned over to Greek authorities. The dead guard was also received.

Only a few eyes watched the unfamiliar team climb into the transport truck and leave the facility. Murchenheim was awake now, watching his captors carefully, his mind racing, his mouth grimly closed. At a crossroads near the port, the truck stopped. Without a word, Jim jerked Murchenheim to his feet and threw him out of the back of the truck. Four MI6 agents picked the terrorist up and stuffed him roughly into a car. There, he learned that he was in the hands of the hated British and on his way to prison. His head spun as he tried to understand it.

"So, you used a NATO team to capture me?" the German asked once. None of the MI6 men spoke. Murchenheim sat back as best as he could, with his handcuffs and aching groin, and faced the reality of a lengthy prison term, probably in solitary confinement. How had Kalil failed? *How much will they get out of me*?

Early the next morning, the men woke from their spray-induced sleep. Some wandered outside to discover the armory gone, a vast crater marking the explosion site. They searched the fortress quickly and discovered their leader, one guard, and the prisoners missing and made the call to Kalil. Panic set in, and Kalil first ran for cover before trying to find out what happened to his pet terrorists. All stones he was able to turn over produced no information. He traced them as far as the Greek military installation, but it was a blank after that. That told him whoever grabbed the Klaus family was a covert group, possibly NATO or INTERPOL.

Kalil was, by nature, an anarchist. He sought only that which best served his purposes. For years, he worked for Communist governments, mainly Russia, but Cuba, China, North Vietnam, and even North Korea paid dearly for his services. When the Communist governments of East Germany and Russia fell, he found himself unemployed, ready to retire and live a life of luxury.

That was when his current employer approached him, seeking to use his ties to known terrorist cells, especially those that had successfully gone to ground in the past ten years. Kalil knew them and trusted none of them. Yet the money had been too good to pass up. Hiding in one of his safe houses, he pondered his employer's reaction to losing their money launderer. Klaus had to die, and if possible, his family with him. As far as Kalil was concerned, that was not a negotiable option. He was compromised.

Men like Kalil planned for such contingencies, and even as the Greek police delivered his wife and children safely home, his evil plots were carried out. Late that night, the house blew apart and burned fiercely, killing Klaus and his family, two policemen, and a policewoman.

Jim was on his way to Cairo when the call woke him up. Cecilia watched his face, unable to hear the voice on the other end of the phone. Her husband's eyes went from bleary to stone cold in a flash. Even though she knew no threat was there for her, she shivered. Whoever had brought on that look was in deep trouble.

CHAPTER 9

Jim put the receiver down and quietly told her what had happened to the Klaus family. Cecilia felt a rush of emotions, struggling for control as she processed the information. She wanted to cry for the children, and she wanted justice for the criminals responsible. Anger, hatred, sadness, and shock all fought within her mind. Jim took her hands and then wrapped her in his arms. She had experienced it first-hand with the loss of her family. Worse, the murderer who killed her family showed her the pictures before he attempted to kill her.

Cecilia cried for the Klaus family then. Holding her tightly, Jim felt helpless and fought down the rage that built inside him. Whenever he didn't know how to meet Cecilia's needs, it made him angry because he hated feeling helpless. Lately, he'd been thinking a lot about the theologian's claim that God was omniscient, omnipresent, and almighty. He somehow knew this was true despite the apparent evidence against those claims.

There was a huge gap between the knowledge of an almighty God and man's free will. God is good all the time. Jim knew this to be true because goodness was part of God's nature. How did a God who was good all the time allow a cowardly terrorist like Kalil to exist and to kill? Knowing that Kalil was no worse in the area of sin than himself didn't help Jim at the moment. That was the reality.

Therein lay the answer. God's Son died for every sinner, and in His goodness, God was patient.

So, am I offending God by killing terrorists? It was a thought Jim had never entertained before. While his mind wrestled with these weighty issues, he simply held Cecilia, falling by error into the very posture she needed most. His strong hand gently rubbed her heaving back as she wept, and he said nothing. Under this care, her sobbing subsided, but Jim's mind still wrestled with his problem.

Wade can analyze his way through anything! I'll ask him what he thinks. Eventually, Cecilia's regular breathing told Jim she was asleep again, but he held her tightly. The light touch of her hair against his face and neck, her breasts pressed firmly against his chest, and the silky softness of her cheek pressed against his own filled him with a sense of wonder. He never thought he would experience love, the love of a wife and family, but he had it now.

Aroused, he did not seek to move her to satiate his desires but held her until his arm went numb and his own eyes finally slid closed again. Only then did he move away from her, but only far enough to release his arm. She reached out for him in her sleep, and between sleep and wakefulness, he searched for and found her hand, and both of them slipped into dreamland.

In the morning, she was more than willing to accept the physical expression of his love. Later, he smiled down at her in the shower, and she knew exactly what he was thinking.

"Shall we tell the boys what we just did?" she asked teasingly.

"Uh, no!" Jim replied, his face burning.

"You've taught them so many things. Perhaps you should teach them how to please a wife. You're very good, you know!" she said, her eyes large and luminous as she pressed herself up against him. Watching him, she almost giggled at his discomfort.

"I, uh, I, uh, think they should learn about that on their own," he mumbled lamely. He grinned suddenly. "I'd like to see them face that challenge like I did." She laughed.

Contrary to popular belief, many soldiers in America's military were men of strong moral fiber, some Christians, some holding

Christian principles. Jim was a virgin when he went to his wedding bed and was embarrassed that he had been so unprepared. Like many couples, if the truth were known, they did not succeed in having sex the first night. Apparently, if Cecilia was being honest, he had improved. He grinned, thinking about that.

"Most instructors don't teach a thing until they've completely mastered it," he mused quietly while shampooing his hair. "I'll have to practice a lot before I can call myself a master."

"Hmmm!" she said, standing on tiptoe to kiss him lightly. "That sounds like fun! But you must not schedule it like you do your other training! That would be a disaster. No, we'll have to find another way of . . . training." This time, she did giggle.

"Blast it, woman!" Jim snapped in mock anger. "Training is hard work. There is no fun in mastering a skill, only relentless practice and hard work!"

"Yes, Captain, but the skills that come naturally, you merely have to practice regularly to ride the crest of perfection," she said, quoting him. "Concentration and practice will produce perfection!" she added, finishing his lecture to his men recently.

He rinsed his hair, slapping her on the bottom before turning off the water. Feeling quite ready to face the day, he hurriedly dressed in his work uniform, fumbling here and there because he was watching Cecilia put her uniform on. She noticed and did a little dance across the floor.

"Having problems getting dressed, dear?" she asked all too innocently. His face turned red, and she laughed. Catching her up in his strong arms, he kissed her thoroughly and put her down. For a moment, she rested her forehead against his hard chest.

"If you mussed me, I'll make you wait for your breakfast!" she said breathlessly, stepping away. In a few minutes, they went to the dining room, where Jim received his mug of iced tea and left for the foredeck to welcome the day. He saw in passing that Andrea, John, and Wade were already up there, their coffee cups missing from the table. Sighing, he made his way to the foredeck.

All three of them turned just too innocently to stare at him. He could feel his face burning, and unable to stop it, an embarrassed grin appeared on his lips.

"Heavy duty this morning, Captain?" Andrea asked, and all four of them burst out laughing. Nothing more was said for a few minutes while they contemplated the dawn sky. It looked as though it would be a pleasant day on the Mediterranean, but one never knew for certain.

"You must be starving, Jim," John suggested lightly in the quiet. They all laughed again.

"As a matter of fact, I am!" Jim said.

As they entered the dining room, Jim automatically counted heads. Nearly half his crew was there, and he knew the other half would arrive in the next few minutes. It gave him a sense of pride to lead a crew of men like this. None had to rise this early. Pleased by how the day began, he approached the table.

The smells coming from the galley were tantalizing, and his hunger awoke anew. He followed Andrea to the buffet and helped himself to a spinach, mushroom, and bacon omelet, several pieces of crisp bacon, some sausages, and a bowl of fresh fruit. Balancing plate and bowl, he carried them to the table where Cecilia was already halfway through her breakfast. She learned early that men like Jim eat quickly, while she chose to take her time, so she got in the habit of starting ahead of him in the morning. He kissed her lightly as he sat down.

"My, my, aren't you rosy-cheeked and glowing this morning!" John complimented Cecilia, laying his napkin on his right leg. He looked down at it for a moment and grinned. It never made sense to him that a napkin, no matter what kind, never covered a man's lap. As he'd learned not to drop food on his pants, it really didn't matter; the humor of old habits amused him. Then he looked up at Cecilia, saw her blushing, and laughed delightedly.

"I think it's safe to say that our Captain will be in a very good mood today!" he grinned wickedly at both of them, saying it loudly enough for the whole room to hear. Chuckles and chortles could be heard, and blushes were seen around the room, and Jim felt his face burning again. It was getting to be a familiar feeling.

He watched as the other men of his team came wandering in, and he quickly consumed his first course of breakfast. Even the arrival of Finn didn't dampen his good nature this morning as he talked with those around him. Doc and Millie invited Finn to eat at their table. Jim wondered if they were taking him under their wing. Cecilia touched his hand, and his attention was suddenly totally upon her.

CHAPTER 10

Zeke came into the dining room with a file of papers in his hands and sat down uninvited at the captain's table. Across the room, Jim noted Finn's frown and sighed. He looked at Zeke and could tell the man had something important to share. Everyone at the table got quiet; indeed, most of the dining room waited to hear what Zeke said.

"Have you ever heard of René Aumont, Ferdinand Brel, Anne Chanté, Nadia Duse, or Jacques Piaf?" Zeke asked without preamble.

"I've heard of Anne Chanté," Cecilia admitted; her eyes suddenly filled with concentration. Jim looked over at her, knowing her eyebrows would be drawn almost together, and found her absolutely adorable at the moment. Zeke cleared his throat.

"Uh, boss, could you please pay attention?" he said quietly. Everyone grinned, and Jim turned to look at Zeke blankly.

"I was, Zeke. I am!" he said, turning back to study Cecilia. She blushed and giggled, and then she quickly kissed Jim.

"Isn't Anne Chanté one of the inheritors of the Chanté fortune? Her grandfather created the Chanté beauty aids company, didn't he?" she asked.

"Correct. She is the only survivor," Zeke said.

"It seems to me I remember her being part of a radical

environmentalist movement in college. She got arrested, and it created quite a stir in the family," Cecilia reminisced.

"Very good!" Zeke said with a grin.

"Didn't we come across the name Jacques Piaf in our last mission for Admiral Runion?" Jim asked, referring to his days as a Navy SEAL commander.

"Good memory, Shep," Zeke nodded in the affirmative.

"So, who are the others?" John asked, impatient to move along.

"René Aumont is the filthy wealthy son of Thomas Aumont, who founded Aumont Industries and made millions in the insurance industry. René hired a brilliant, if unscrupulous, CEO to take the company even further up the financial ladder of industry, then sold the whole thing suddenly two years ago for an amazing fortune and life-long dividends from the stocks he retained. No one understood why he would sell, except that he got an amazing price for the company and outstanding benefits.

"Ferdinand Brel is the only living son of Newt Brel, who founded Brel Drilling. That company contracts with oil companies that need to drill through the ocean floor for oil exploration. Dad turned it into a multi-million dollar business, and Junior sold it when he inherited it. It seems he doesn't share his father's love for drilling on the ocean floor.

Nadia Duse is an unknown now, though I have my all-seeing eyes looking her over as we speak," Zeke finished.

"And what is their connection to our friend Kalil?" Jim asked quietly.

"They call themselves The Committee of Five, and they own Kalil lock, stock, and barrel," Zeke announced. "Over the past five years, Kalil has been quietly building five small to medium-sized terrorist cells. I've been looking over the financial records of the Committee, and it appears that they recently hired the services of a master thief who was only caught once because a greedy girlfriend turned him in. She disappeared when he was released, but no one is sure if he killed her for her betrayal or if she is afraid that's what he's going to do. He's been celibate since then. They also hired the services of a defrocked priest who once ran the Vatican library. He was dismissed from that position because of theft. Not a savory character!"

"Okay! Now I remember!" Jim said suddenly. "Jacques Piaf was connected to the Chechen rebels and an Al-Qaeda group helping them. He was never our direct target, but his name came up twice."

"Full points, Shep!" Zeke exclaimed with genuine admiration. "I'd forgotten that. I'll get on to Admiral Runion post-haste and get the records."

"Great. Do we know where these five terrorist cells are located?" Jim asked.

"In Italy," Zeke said in reply.

"Can we assume they're going after the church or something the Vatican has?" John mused.

"If Jacques Piaf is involved, we'd better plan for the worst and assume nothing!" Dorf interjected quickly. "He was usually involved in something quite complex, if I remember."

"I'll go into the Scotland Yard system to see if they have anything on Piaf. INTERPOL might have something, too," Cecilia offered quietly.

"You can get into the Scotland Yard system?" Zeke asked, his eyebrows raised. "I'd have known if you logged on! My system gives me a regular list of people that log onto that site!"

"Not if I logged on with my aunt's password through her router," Cecilia said coyly.

"I didn't think of that!" Zeke said with a sheepish grin. "You're using her password for INTERPOL, too, aren't you?" he added.

"Why Zeke! How dare you ask a woman to reveal her secrets!" Cecilia said in mock dismay. Zeke laughed at that and shook his head.

"Uncle Zeke is going to be watching you very closely, young lady!" he warned, wagging a finger at her. Zeke looked over at Jim, and his eyes widened in surprise. Jim was fingering the blade of his Ontario Navy Knife, running his thumb along the even silver line of the edge cut into the black finish on the stainless steel blade. Jim looked up suddenly.

"Uh, what was that Zeke? I was distracted," he said. "Did you say you would watch my wife very closely?"

"I was just saying that I have to go change my underwear; thank you very much!" Zeke joked sarcastically as everyone laughed. Jim slipped the knife back into its sheath. Cecilia shook her head as the men around her laughed at the interchange. It was a typical male moment, but she enjoyed her husband's part in it. That was unusual.

"Boys and their toys. Boys and their toys!" she said. Jim just grinned at her.

The levity of that morning carried the crew through the mundane duties of life aboard a steel ship in a saltwater environment. Finn received another lesson about the team that morning, during which they spent two hours training. It happened to be hand-to-hand combat, and he was amazed to see many of the non-combatant crewmembers learning and working right along with the fighting team.

For himself, he had been trained in some combat, but watching these men move made him nervous. They seemed to flow into motion like mercury, every motion fluid flowing as if from a dance choreography. Even Dorf, the giant he was, could get down in the Chinese splits and slide up into a standing position as easily and gracefully as any ballet dancer. Finn watched Zeke and realized the man was deadly with his hands and feet. But the Captain and Mark Drumheiser somehow seemed to be level above the other men. Then, he noticed that Cecilia was practicing with the non-combatants. Shocked beyond belief, he watched her throw around Seaman Stankus, whom most of the crew simply called "Cuss."

Just before lunch, Finn received a call that made him sit at attention quickly and sent a shiver of anticipation through him. It was from the famous Dr. Alistair Gregg, a distant relation on his mother's side and noteworthy current temporary curator (on loan from Oxford) of the Cairo Museum of Antiquities. The call came through the ship's satellite phone system.

"Captain Shepherd's office," Marvin said primly, answering the phone on the second ring to ensure the caller would know he was busy. "Please state your name and business."

"Hello? Who the blazes *is* this? This is Alistair Gregg calling for Captain James Shepherd. Go find that pirate wherever he is on that steel monstrosity he floats around the seven seas and tell him I need to talk to him!" Alistair insisted, his voice breathless in his own excitement.

"Dr. Gregg, this is Lieutenant Junior Grade Marvin Finn speaking. I'm Captain Shepherd's administrative assistant. I believe we know each other," he added hopefully.

"Finn! Young Marvin Finn, Dame Agatha's boy?" Dr. Gregg said after a moment of thought.

"Yes, sir!" Marvin said. He was instantly pleased that Dr. Gregg remembered his mother.

"Didn't you graduate from Eaton?" Unfortunately for Marvin, he didn't hear the humor in Dr. Gregg's voice, and Dr. Gregg didn't remember what a prude his nephew was.

"Er, yes, sir. My father came down from Eaton if you will remember," Marvin said stiffly after a pause.

"I was just ribbing you, boy. Grow a thicker skin, lad! Now, where's that pirate of a Captain you so aptly serve?" Alistair said, irritated.

"I'll put him on, sir," Finn said. He pushed the speaker button on his desk. "Captain, sir, Dr. Alistair Gregg is on the phone for you."

"Hello, Alistair!" Jim's voice boomed over the receiver as Finn hung up his line.

"Where are you? I need you here quickly!" Alistair said immediately.

"Well, I'm fine, and so is Cecilia. How are you?" Jim teased with a grin, hitting the speakerphone button as Cecilia entered his office.

"Oh! Yes! Yes! Nice to hear that, dear boy! Cohabiting as husband and wife happily, I'm sure! Sorry, and all that, but where are you, for goodness sake?" Alistair said, blustering. Finn heard the conversation clearly now, not even pretending to work.

"What's up, Alistair?" Jim said.

"Hello, Alistair, it's Cecilia. It's so good to hear your voice," Cecilia said on top of his question.

"Oh! You're there too! Good. Good. I need both of you right now. Are you going to tell me where you are or not?" Dr. Gregg added peevishly.

"I'm about twenty-one hours away from you, Alistair," Jim said, calculating the distance to Cairo from their present position.

"Excellent. Come for tea tomorrow, at three o'clock. Oh, and congratulations on adding my nephew, Marvin Finn, to your crew. Now slap that tin can you're sailing on the rump and get here! Bye now," Alistair said, hanging up abruptly.

Jim looked at Cecilia, and they burst out laughing at the antics of their busy little friend. Dr. Alistair Gregg was always in a rush until he got to a site to study. His energy was boundless, and every student who had an opportunity to study under him fought for the position and loved every minute of his instruction. He was among the few history professors who believed history was a living and exciting study.

"Marvin, would you please ask Wade and John to meet me in CIC?" Jim said as he got up from his desk.

"That was Dr. Alistair Gregg!" Finn said from his desk. Jim could tell he was excited.

"Yes, and he's invited us to tea tomorrow, so press your best dress uniform. You're going with us," Jim replied with a grin.

"Oh, but he didn't invite me!" Marvin argued.

"Of course he did!" Cecilia stated. "I heard him clearly."

They walked out of the office and made their way to the computer room. Zeke was at work at his station, his hands busy with a keyboard, and the monitors that took up three walls flashed different information. One thing Zeke could do was multitask. He could tell you without seeming to glance at what each monitor was showing. His skill with this system never ceased to amaze Jim. He looked up as the two of them invaded his domain.

"Hi, you two!" he said by way of a cheery greeting. "I was just about to head down for lunch," he added.

"Hold that thought. We'll join you in a minute as soon as John and Wade get here. Dr. Gregg was just on the phone, and he wants to see us, so I'm sure he's on to something," Jim said. Wade came in first, then John a few seconds later.

"Sharky said you wanted to see us?" John asked, coming in the door.

"Alistair called. He's on to something," Jim announced in answer to his question. "We're heading for Cairo. Cecilia, Finn, and I will need the chopper for transportation inland. Have Team 1 ready to transport us and watch our backs." He added.

"Meanwhile?" Wade asked, knowing there was more to come.

"Team 3 takes the launch up the locks with the rest of Team 2. Jacques Piaf has offices in Cairo." Jim answered.

"Oh! Fun and games!" Zeke said, rubbing his hands.

They all went to lunch together, and Jim told the crew their destination. Most of the crew cheered, having met the good Dr. Gregg and his researchers twice before. Finn was pleased that the crew seemed to like Dr. Gregg and felt more disposed to like them. Most of them had he any way of knowing, cared not a whit if he liked them or not. Fortunately for both parties, that knowledge was not public. The conversation at lunch centered on Dr. Gregg.

Again, the crew's excitement level was heightened, and they carried out their duties with panache. Bring It Up arrived to drop anchor off of Port Said, depending on which map one read, in pristine condition. John and his teams left in the launch as soon as the anchor was secured.

Team 1 readied the CH-53D Sea Stallion helicopter for its upcoming flight. The CH-53D Sea Stallion is designed for the transportation of equipment, supplies, and personnel during amphibious operations. This one was slightly modified and improved somewhat from the original design. It could carry forty-five passengers instead of fifty-five, as initially designed. Those forty-five passengers rode in much more comfort than before. This bird could also carry 6,363 kilograms of cargo or supplies.

Dorf and Mark conferred with Master Chief Warner and

Inchworm about the engine and its performance when three new GE T64-GE-416/416A engines arrived. Before they were put on the bird, Inchworm added a few extras and exchanged a few parts for aftermarket improvements, and the Sea Stallion could now speed through the skies at 136 mph, 33 mph faster than before. Dorf and Mark were the usual pilots for any helicopter flights, though several other crewmembers were cleared to fly the Stallion.

Jim helped Cecilia up the steps into the belly of the huge helicopter, and they sat down in the newest seats, which were added for passengers adapted from a luxury jet. Both of them appreciated the latest additions and sighed at the comfort. Finn followed them and looked around the chopper with a critical eye. He'd flown in a few, and the improvements were much appreciated. He joined the captain and Cecilia and buckled his seatbelt as Team 1 took the bird into the air.

CHAPTER 11

The institute had a small landing pad for helicopters that was rarely used. Occasionally, a piece would be uncovered and lifted to the museum by helicopter, but it happened so infrequently that the field often fell into disuse. Dorf looked at the windsock as he brought the CH-53D Sea Stallion in for a landing, adjusted, and paused above the pad for a few moments for as much sand as possible to blow away. He didn't like sucking sand into his turbines, and neither did Master Chief Warner. When the pad was relatively clear, he dropped the wheels and shut down the engines. As the blades slowed, the sound level dropped to allow for a normal conversation.

Although it was only a few blocks walk, Alistair sent his limousine to pick them up. It was a restored 1932 Lincoln he'd found residing in a garage at the institute. No one seemed to know to whom it belonged, so he claimed it. Jim arranged for Calvin Beardsley to restore the old car, and though it cost twice what a new Lincoln limousine might go for today, he felt it was well worth the expense. He thought so again as he settled into the comfortable air-conditioned interior. Beardsley insisted on air-conditioning, although in the original model, it didn't exist. Jim was glad for the modification.

Dr. Alistair Gregg lived in a small bungalow on the institute grounds and was looked after by a competent Egyptian manservant he called Mr. Levi. Their relationship was very formal, and Levi was devoted to Dr. Gregg. Dr. Gregg looked upon him as he would one of his students and treated him accordingly. Both men seemed happy with the arrangement.

Mr. Levi drove the limousine and escorted them into the sitting room. This was the only room in the house not cluttered with documents, books, artifacts, and scrolls. In two other rooms Jim had followed Dr. Gregg through, there was only walking space between the piles. But in this house, Dr. Gregg could instantly put his hand on any piece of information from the past.

Dr. Gregg rose to meet them. He was a dapper man, thin and wiry of build, with white wispy hair and gentle twinkling blue eyes. He wore glasses to read, but otherwise, his eyes were still strong. From long years in the Egyptian sun, his face was weathered and brown, and he had strong hands. Genuinely happy to see his guests, he treated them all to his high-wattage smile and energy.

He kissed Cecilia's hand, shook Jim's hand heartily, put hands on either side of Marvin Finn's shoulders, and kissed him on both cheeks in a traditional Mediterranean fashion. Finn blushed deeply.

"Marvin! It is so good to see you, my boy!" Dr. Gregg said. Jim guessed correctly that Alistair meant that. Family was far away, and he saw them rarely, keeping them close to his heart by saving the letters he received and keeping a photo scrapbook of their pictures.

"Thank you, sir. My mother sends her greetings," Finn replied.

"And how is her music career going these days?" Alistair asked. Dame Agatha Finn was a concert pianist with the London Philharmonic Orchestra. Her skill on the Steinway was legendary in London. Alistair looked at the others.

"All my relatives are musicians!" he said. Both of my brothers and all three of my sisters rose to stardom. George and Thomas both play in the orchestra with Agatha. George plays the first violin, and Thomas plays the oboe. Bethany and Charlotte play for recording studios. Bethany plays keyboards, and Charlotte plays the tenor saxophone quite well. I believe she plays in Jazz clubs, much to our mother's dismay!" he added with a grin.

To Cecilia's delight, he sat them down and served tea and cucumber sandwiches. Jim felt foolish holding the dainty morsel in his calloused hands, though he enjoyed each bite. Mr. Levi, knowing Jim did not drink hot drinks, served him a glass of iced tea with two slices of lemon neatly perched on the lip. He sipped his tea and sat back with contentment.

Alistair questioned Marvin about the family, and for nearly twenty minutes, Jim and Cecilia learned a great deal about the two men's shared family. Part of Marvin's desire to excel was exposed to Jim in a way that helped him see the man more clearly for who he was. At last, however, the last sandwich was gone, and Alistair put aside his teacup, and Mr. Levi cleaned everything up.

Alistair sat forward, pulled a thick folder from a nearby table, and held it on his lap. For a few seconds, he merely stared at it, letting one hand run down the cover in a pensive gesture that was exquisitely revealing. Then he looked up at them, and his eyes took on the intensity Jim saw so often when the man was researching or digging up some great moment of history.

"I've found something rather extraordinary," he began. "You know how I love digging through the archives for things that have yet to be studied? I unearthed an unmarked crate while looking for information on a dig interrupted by the Second World War I. Curious, I pried off the lid.

"The crate belonged to a Waffen-SS Haupts-charfürer Nikolas Bormann. I believe he was here near the end of the war, just as the British finally took control of Cairo, and I believe he was killed in the fighting that ensued. He meant to ship this crate to Berlin and even left instructions in the crate for that event. The crate was sealed and set aside for further study in the confusion, but it was forgotten!"

Alistair paused and then opened the folder. "Bormann was traveling with Johann Honecker, a historian and archaeologist. Honecker was here as part of the team searching for the Ark of the Covenant. On the way to Cairo, Johann picked up some astounding information, if true.

"Honecker claims that there is a huge historical trove beneath the rocks that buried the monastery in Alleghe, Italy. Lake Alleghe came into being in 1771 when a landslide blocked the course of the Cordevole. That's the river that divides the Dolomites into its eastern and western zones." Dr. Gregg produced a segment of a map of the Marmolada region of Italy with Seula to the north, Pale Di S. Martino to the south, and Civett and Pelmo to the east.

"This trove contains important information about the church from its inception until 1771. The Diocese of Belluno-Feltre, and before that Bellunum, maintained a monastery along the river near the present-day site of Alleghe. This monastery was nestled against the mountain and actually contained a building that butted against the mountain wall where a cave entrance was located. The priests are said to have established secure storage inside that cave system.

"The monks of that time were accustomed to keep perishables in the cool recesses of the cave. When Attila came through, the most precious articles of the church were hidden in the caves behind a secret entrance the monks had created at the cave opening. Emperor Henry III created the Bishops of Feltre and gave them the title of Count of cities and vicinities. Their authority was almost constantly assailed by the Counts of Camino, by Ezzelino da Romano, the Scaligeri, the Carrara, and finally by the Visconti themselves. In 1404, the city fell into the power of the Venetians.

"St. Victor, the martyr, lived in the monastery about A.D. 170. Fonteius was the Bishop of Feltre who took part in the Council in Aquileia in A.D. 579. Drudo of Camino (1174) was the first bishop of the united sees of Belluno and Feltre, the latter being the bishop's residence.

"Angelo Faseolo, in 1464, who was appointed on many legations in connection with the Crusade against the Turks, visited the monastery. Honecker claims he found evidence at the church of SS. Vittore e Corona, on the slopes of Mount Misnea. The Crusaders of Feltre erected that church after the First Crusade. According to those records, at the beginning of the Second Crusade, headed by Louis VII from 1145-1147, a great wealth of documents, treasures, and holy artifacts displayed in the churches were stored in the two highest rooms in the cave. It is said by many that once treasures went into the caves, they rarely came out again.

"Then, the rooms were filled up during civil wars and other uprisings. Once something went into that room, it was usually left there, according to Young Johann's records. He was certainly convinced that those rooms held treasurers from the church in historical documents and church finery.

"After the lake buried the monastery, the church mounted two major efforts to recover her goods. One of those was in 1957 when an Italian salvage team was hired to seek an opening beneath the lake's waters. After two crewmembers were killed trying to move rocks, the search was abandoned.

"I believe that the honeycomb of caves in the Marmolada may lead to the storage caverns. It is my educated opinion that I know of a salvage team that might be able to accomplish this exploration and find that treasure trove!" Alistair finished dramatically.

Jim was looking at the map and seeing the names of three towns where Kalil hid terrorist groups. Caprile, Agordo, and Primiero were all within minutes of Alleghe. The Marmolada was a well-known vacation spot, too. An idea began to form in his mind, and he took a few minutes to think about it while Alistair fussily arranged his file folder and put it back on the table. It was Cecilia who broke the silence since her husband was obviously deep in consideration.

"I see why you believe God has blessed your efforts in fighting Terrorism," she mused quietly so that only Jim would hear.

Jim grinned at her and then looked at Alistair, sitting completely relaxed against the back of his chair, his fingers steepled under his chin. Jim pulled his satellite phone from his belt pouch as he spoke.

"I'm calling Ken Worthington," he explained to Alistair. "He's the company attorney and our expert on real estate. I'm going to ask him to find some real estate for us to purchase in or near Alleghe."

CHAPTER 12

"**K**en Worthington!" Finn sputtered. "Sir, his fees are outrageous! I sent a letter of complaint about his last bill stating that fact!" Jim didn't answer immediately as Ken picked up on the second ring.

There were a dozen of these phones around the globe, all secure and designated for the Team's use. Jim pictured Ken seated at his desk, probably having just put down two phones to pick up this one. His voice sounded as though he were across the room, not across the world.

"This is Ken," he announced unnecessarily. His voice always sounded joyful, and Jim guessed that was because the man loved what he did. He was a retired attorney who started and ran banks and invested money that made huge windfall profits more than seventy-five percent of the time. The other twenty-five percent of the time, his investments still paid off handsomely, but not in the "windfall" category. He was working on that. Jim smiled at the sound of his voice.

"Hello, Ken, this is Jim," he said.

"And how is my favorite pirate of the seven seas?" Ken asked with a grin.

"Who are you calling a pirate, you robber baron?" Jim replied evenly. Ken had the word "robber" in his email address, which only his closest friends used. He often took advantage of the government's inadequacies in regulating finance and considered himself a modern-day robber baron.

"How is married life treating you?" Ken asked.

"I still can't believe she loves me," Jim replied honestly.

"Oooh! The honeymoon goes on! Enjoy it. So what's on the agenda for today?" Ken asked, getting down to business. "I've got two bank presidents on hold right now. I figured what you had would be much more interesting," he explained.

"Right," Jim replied. "I want to purchase some real estate in or around the town of Alleghe in Italy. Uncle Andrea is going to retire, and he needs a retirement business to run to keep him young."

"Is he really retiring?" Ken asked. Jim smiled, knowing that Ken had easily read between the lines.

"No. This is a cover, but eventually, he will, and it would be nice to have something like this in line for him. It's all going to be in his name, and it needs to be a legitimate cover," Jim answered.

"Can I get in on this investment?" Ken asked as he typed.

"Wouldn't have it any other way!" Jim replied honestly.

"Okay. I'm booking a first-class flight to Rome as we speak." Jim could hear the click of the keyboard.

"Why not fly into Venice? It's closer," Jim suggested.

"Wow! Venice! Okay, I'm connecting now to Venice. In three days, I'll have a property that will make the company a huge profit over the years," Ken said lightly. Jim didn't doubt the boast at all.

"Call me when it's all arranged," Jim said. "Give Emma a hug from her favorite pirate Captain and tell your wife I said the new addition to the house looks great."

"How did you know she was doing an addition?" Ken asked, surprised.

"Empirical deduction, my dear boy!" Jim said mysteriously. Ken hated anything to do with household tasks, fixing things, or building. On the other hand, his wife loved everything about it, especially the interior design at the end of the building process. The fact that she mentioned the desire to add to their house when they'd met a year ago was something Jim did not divulge.

"Okay, my flight leaves tomorrow. This is going to cost you a fortune. I'm interested in seeing what my next bill does to your new administrative assistant! He's something! Boy stood on a burning deck and all that, eh?" Ken said with a laugh.

"You read all that in his letter?" Jim asked, surprised.

"I knew you didn't know about it, or it would never have left his desk. He seems like a good kid who wants to protect the company, and that's not a bad thing. Gotta go!" Ken said.

"Bye. Talk to you in three or four days," Jim replied, hitting the end button on his phone and putting it back in his pouch. He was smiling in delight and winked at Cecilia, and then he began to rub his hands together with excitement.

"Sir!" Marvin said, alarm in his voice. "A trip like that and real estate! Worthington will cost the company a fortune!"

"LT, one of the things you don't know about is the early formation of this company. Ken Worthington helped us set it up and doubled our investment in the first year. In the second year, he doubled it again! He has the Midas touch and is worth every penny we pay him. He has earned as much, if not more, than our collective treasures! Never complain about Mr. Worthington's charges again, lad," Jim cautioned.

Finn looked crestfallen, and Jim guessed correctly that he would mope over his mistake for the next few days. He was a perfectionist and hated any signs of imperfection in himself. Sighing, Jim looked at Alistair and caught a look in his eyes that told him Alistair knew just what kind of man the boy had turned into. They grinned at each other.

"It will take about three months to get everything ready and in place. What kind of a team do you have?" he asked the professor.

"Ah!" Alistair sat forward, picking up another file folder with one sheet of paper between its manila covers. "Thomas Moore is working for me for the next three years. Lisle Mirelle is here, working on her doctorate. She has her dissertation to complete. Heidi Van Haaten is also here, working on her MS under Thomas. Adley Ferinc is also working on his doctorate. And, of course, there is Mary Ann and Barbara. They're still with me. Oh yes, Dr. Richard Persons has asked for permission to join me for a year of study abroad. His university is paying all his expenses."

"Eight of you?" Jim asked as Marvin wrote down the information.

"Well, I was wondering if I could bring Mr. Levi," Alistair suggested. "He's never been outside of Cairo, and he does take good care of me."

"He's more than welcome!" Jim said enthusiastically.

"Finn, write this down, please," Jim dictated. "Nine from the institute, nine from the Live Oak retreat, and thirty from *Bring It Up*. We'll need transportation for forty-eight from Venice to Alleghe. Cecilia can help you with the details."

"Three months! I'd better get my team working on the research!" Alistair said, bounding to his feet. He shook everyone's hand and stood at the door as Mr. Levi loaded them in the car for the trip back to the helicopter.

Jim enjoyed looking at the pearl-white skin of the helicopter gleaming in the afternoon sun, with the aqua and burgundy stripes and letters glittering against that white background. The ship's logo stood out clearly on both sides, along with the aircraft's registration numbers. Bring It Up was written above the registration SS53BIU, which they chose for the craft.

Anyone watching saw the crew quickly prepare for takeoff when the limousine appeared. By the time they departed from Mr. Levi, the rotors were already beginning to turn. They hurried into the air-conditioned interior and sat down. Minutes later, they were on their way back to the ship. Jim put a headset on and listened as Dorf talked to Cairo air control before speaking himself.

"Anything to report, Lieutenant?" Jim said.

"No, sir. Just another average day," Jim smiled at Dorf's rejoinder. Just another average day meant that at least three different sets of eyes were put on the helicopter when it landed and took off. "Same as four days ago," Dorf added, letting Jim know that four individuals were seen watching the CH53D. Military men often used simple codes to mask information they knew could be compromised.

"It would be nice if we could have two days together," Jim said after a moment of thought.

"Maybe, but not today," Dorf told him, noting that no two men seemed to be working in tandem.

"Hey, boss, you see those four cars that pulled away when we took off?" This was Mark speaking. "I swear one of them was my high school Volkswagen Beetle!"

"I didn't see them," Jim admitted. "They all follow each other out of the institute?"

"No. Two were parked outside the institute, and the other two nearby. Once they were on the road leading out, though, they all went in different directions," Mark replied.

It was an innocent conversation, and for that reason, anyone listening to their frequency would probably ignore it. Just to confuse anyone listening, Jim talked to Mark about Beetles and their upkeep most of the way back to the ship. Cecilia and Finn conferred about his family for part of the trip, then sat silent.

CHAPTER 13

Two days passed while they sat at anchor just off Port Said. Daily practice to hone their rescue skills and team training kept the men busy, for each man had duties in different parts of the ship to attend to as well. Jim kept a sharp eye on the crew, as any good Captain does, making suggestions, complimenting the men who were going above and beyond what their duties called for, and encouraging those who seemed less than motivated.

It may have surprised Jim to learn that his men loved and respected him. Unlike many Navy Captains, he did not reprimand unless it was merited and spent time talking to each man. His men may have been surprised to learn that he kept notes on those conversations and reviewed them often, even praying for many of them. He prayed for each man on his crew every day because he believed in the power of prayer. He also believed in the men of his crew.

Discipline never slacked off, even when he could easily have given the men a break. He knew they wouldn't take the break and expected his constant attention to detail. Life on the ocean was routine on the best of days, he reminded himself often. On the third day, the routine changed. An emergency call came from a container ship where fire doors failed to operate because of electrical problems caused by the fire.

Bring It Up Coral was equipped for this type of emergency and Jim ordered the anchor up as soon as the call was completed. They were the closest help and nearly thirty minutes away. Marvin sent a telex message to Lloyds. He might have raised an eyebrow to know how relieved they were that *Bring It Up Coral* was closest to offering aid.

Pushing the two GM EMD 20-645F7B diesels to the limit, the ship cut through the choppy waters at a respectable twenty knots. Several crew members prepared the GPH fire pumps and three fire monitors on the deck. Other crew carried firefighting supplies to the deck, already dressed in their newest firefighting suits.

Jim stood on the bridge and looked through his Zhumell signature waterproof binoculars as they approached the burning ship. Every crewmember of that ship and the captain were at the bow, pressed against each other to stay as far from the heat as possible, using the bow spray to cool them down.

"Prepare the gangplank for a bow rescue," Jim commanded into his headset. The work on the deck of his ship paused for a moment as the men listened to his voice, then continued. Four crewmembers broke away from the fire gear and moved to the port-side extendable gangplank. Fortunately, the seas were not too rough for such a rescue.

Andrea had the wheel, and he brought the ship in perfectly, holding it in place as the crewmembers rushed down the plank and away from the flames. Then, the interior fire crews ran up the plank carrying as much equipment as possible, returning for another load before heading below decks. While they were moving about below decks, the monitors on *Bring It Up Coral* were pumping 2,200 gallons of foam per minute from the two GPH fire pumps. Firefighting didn't happen often, but when it did, the crew was ready and expertly trained. Flames on the deck were quickly extinguished.

Below decks, the two fire teams worked in tandem. Marvin Finn had one team under his command, and John commanded the other team. Orders were given, everyone lending a hand at the dangerous task, and slowly, the men moved through the bowels of the ship. Sometimes, they used the equipment provided by the ship, and sometimes, their own equipment was all they had. Step by step, yard by yard, they fought the fires raging below until all of them were black from soot and smoke, and the last blaze was smothered. Working quickly had been critical to the ship's future, and the men heaved satisfied sighs of relief when the last flame was extinguished.

It was hard work, taking a little over four hours. Jim and the rest of the crew listened as the battle raged, a rescue crew at the ready should they be needed, while Andrea kept their rescue ship at a safe distance. At last, the weary men appeared on deck to the wild cheering of their own crew and the crew of the container ship. Black smoke still poured from hatchways and windows, vents, and doors melted or twisted by the heat.

Once the fire crews were back on board Mark and Dorf led their team down to sound the hull. This involved opening fire doors and sometimes overriding the system to do so. They were thorough. There were two seams opened by the intense heat and buckling of the deck and bottom plates, but after careful consideration Mark declared that the pumps, if they still worked, could stay ahead of the water.

The pumps didn't work, so Master Chief Warner and Inchworm went on board to see if they could fix the system. Half an hour later, the pumps were working, and the water in the bottom slowly began to sink. Mark and Dorf continued checking the hull until the water was low enough for the repair crew to seal the leak. Expanding foam, specially designed for such instances, was liberally sprayed into the seams until only a tiny amount of water seeped through.

At last, only Dorf and Mark remained on the wounded giant of the sea, and the tow team attached the bollard pull cable to tow the crippled ship. Lloyds wanted the ship taken to Naples, where it originated, and Jim asked Smitty to set a course for that port and to inform him of wind and weather conditions along their path. Nearly an entire day went into saving the container ship, twenty-two hours to be exact, and it was a tired crew that gathered in the dining room for a late and well-earned dinner.

Jim addressed them just before the buffet was opened. He commended his crew for their bravery and expertise, and told them they would have three days leave in Naples barring any emergency calls. Then he told them what their bonus would be, and the men cheered. Marvin Finn was both pleased and honored that the company would reward their efforts immediately. He got on well with the men at his table that night for perhaps the first time. They saw him work, and respected him for his abilities and willingness to work as hard as any of them.

Later that evening, Ken Worthington called to tell Jim he had just finished purchasing a villa, winery, vineyard, orchard, farmland, and about nine hundred and ninety acres of mountain. The total acreage was just over four thousand. According to Ken, the vineyard needed work but could be productive in a year or so. The winery was working, and the family now owned its own label.

The villa was bigger than the Live Oak mansion and had all the potential and more for the Team's unique needs. Ken also informed Jim that he was now contracting to build a ski lodge and vacation center on part of the acreage and that work for that project would begin in three months or less. He was working on the permits and legal issues the following day. The villa would be completely remodeled in four months and ready for everything.

Jim thanked Ken and smiled at his enthusiasm for his work. They were building something together, and if Ken was this excited about it, it would surely be a money-maker. They finished the conversation, and Jim hung up the receiver.

"I wonder what Marvin will say when he discovers Ken Worthington just spent about sixty million dollars of the firm's money?" he mused aloud to Cecilia as they lay together in the bed, reading. She snuggled closer, reached up and kissed his chin, then returned to reading her book.

"Just tell him the potential income the place will generate over the next fifty years, and he'll be happy as a clam," she said. He followed her instructions and was surprised that Finn seemed pleased about the firm's potential profit and concerned about Ken's final bill for the whole project. People were just strange.

In Naples, they only enjoyed one day of leave. An emergency call came in for a small cruise ship and a garbage scow that collided.

Both were in trouble. The cruise ship was tangled against the side of the scow, bow to stern, and could not get loose, and the scow was on fire. Jim and the crew found their way back to the ship quickly. Not one of the men doubted for a moment that the captain would give them further leave at the end of this job, so they returned willingly and in good spirits.

Finding the impending catastrophe was a simple matter of heading toward the pillar of black smoke on the horizon. Andrea took the wheel while the rest of the crew hurried about the deck, ensuring the fire and rescue equipment were ready for the moment they arrived.

Passengers would complicate things because they needed to get them off the cruiser and away from the firefighting equipment and rescue crew. Passengers always complicated things.

Abe was busy in the kitchen with his crew, preparing to cater to eighty-one passengers from the cruise ship and its crew of twenty-one. The crew on the garbage scow tug was trying to fight the fire. They were able to keep the flames away from the cruise ship for the most part but could not do much more. Fires of this nature were always difficult and sometimes burned even underwater.

Jim chafed on the bridge, unable to go hands-on in the rescue. He wore his dress uniform so passengers could identify him as the captain. Cecilia, standing quietly beside him, also dressed in her uniform, smiled at his frustration. She took his hand and squeezed it. She knew he would much rather be in the thick of things, working side-by-side with his men.

He put his Zhumell binoculars to his eyes and studied the wreck as they approached. Both vessels were locked tightly together, the ruined side of the cruise ship battered and torn and tightly wedged against the side of the scow. When they struck, the cruise ship caught the anchor from the scow and dragged it, pulling the bow of the scow toward the liner and locking them together. Some steel cable on that side of the scow dropped somewhere in the middle of the collision and locked the middle of the cruiser to the scow. They would need to be very careful when separating the two vessels.

A familiar whistle from a nearby vessel caused Jim to turn and look at it. The Italian version of the Coast Guard sent out a police cruiser to make the report. A moment later, the captain of that vessel hailed the *Bring It Up Coral*, speaking idiomatic English. Jim replied in fluent Italian, much to the captain's surprise and pleasure. Knowing that speaking the native language was appreciated, Jim listened.

"Vessel *Bring It Up Coral*, we are here to assist in any way we can and to make an official report, over, " the Italian Captain said.

"Roger that. Glad to have you with us. Please keep the curious boaters at a safe distance. Once we get the passengers and crew off the cruise ship, you can come aboard and ask any questions you need to ask." Jim replied in Italian.

"You speak our language very well," the man replied. "Thank you. We will do as you ask."

There was a gentle swell to the water at the moment, but the thunderheads, a huge billowing pillar of cumulonimbus with a corresponding band of nimbostratus clouds, dark with water, threatened a storm and drenching. Jim sighed. His ship was not equipped with the type of stabilizers found on cruise ships and there would be sick passengers on the ride to Naples. Being a man of the sea, he tended to have little compassion for those who suffered from that common ailment.

Picking up the phone on the bridge, he dialed the kitchen. Sturdy answered in a cheerful voice, and Jim could hear the banging of pots and pans and the bustle in the kitchen. It seemed that the galley was always busy.

"Sturdy, we have some bad weather coming in. Tell Abe," Jim said.

"Got it, Shep," Sturdy replied in his rumbling bass voice. Jim knew that Abe and Sturdy would take care of everything in the kitchen between them. He hung up the phone with a slight smile.

Moments later, he made his way down to the deck to help the first passengers find their way to the inside observation deck, two levels above the main deck. Cecilia helped, looking quite lovely in her white uniform, giving comfort and encouragement as needed. All the passengers were safely removed from the cruise ship, then the crew. Andrea expertly maneuvered the ship, keeping it in position until the gangplank was retracted, then moved around the two ships so that the fire crew could begin its work.

Once again, three fire monitors, powered by two GPH pumps, sprayed 2,200 gallons of foam per minute onto the flames, smothering them effectively. Because the refuse was garbage, hot spots within it were dangerous. The fire crew kept at it until Master Chief Warner and Inchworm could cut the two ships apart and separate them.

When the Italian authorities approached Jim, the cruise ship was safely attached to the bollard pull. They had been busy with the passengers and crew. Jim saw that Marvin Finn was with them. Finn saluted him smartly, and Jim returned the salute.

"I cannot allow the present crew of the tugboat to continue moving the scow." The Captain of the Italian contingent said immediately. "They are all intoxicated."

"All of them?" Jim asked, surprised.

"Yes! All of them!" The captain replied in disgust.

"I cannot tow both vessels," Jim announced.

"No, no, my friend." The captain said quickly. "We have ordered another tug. I will remain here with the scow until that boat arrives. I came to ask a favor." The Italian said. "Please wait for me to return before you allow the passengers and crew to disembark," he requested.

"Of course!" Jim said. "We will await you in Naples harbor should we arrive before you catch up to us," Jim replied easily. The Italian bowed slightly and smiled.

"Thank you." He saluted, spun on his heels, and headed for the afterdeck to board his boat, now overfull with four prisoners in various stages of the morning after, their hands held tightly behind them by electric ties. For a moment, Jim studied them, wondering how they could have been so careless while working.

"May I ask what they said?" Finn asked as he walked beside the captain.

"Oh! Sorry, LT." Jim said, glancing at the man. "The tugboat crew was intoxicated. The captain must wait until another tug can come to move the scow. He wants us to wait for his return before letting anyone off the ship."

"Well, that explains some things," Marvin said quietly.

"Stupid thing to do," Jim commented.

"Yes, we might have been fishing dead bodies out of the water, sir," Finn replied.

"Thank God for His mercy on this one," Jim replied sincerely.

"Quite," Marvin responded. He was still slightly surprised that most crew members included committed Christian men. Daily, the crew met for Bible study and prayer. The entire crew attended that event, and Finn had to admit he liked the depth of discussion that ensued at each study. He was also glad to be on a ship where men were careful about their language. Swear words were rarely heard on *Bring It Up Coral*. Perhaps the depth of faith also helped in other matters because there was seldom a flare of temper.

At first, he thought it was because of the presence of Nurse Wozniac and Cecilia. Now he knew it was because the men were sincere in their faith and trying hard to live by Biblical principles. Marvin had never given much thought to God and wasn't even sure he believed in God. That was changing as he listened to the men, and saw the reality of their faith. The depth and simplicity of their faith were often deeply moving and, for that reason, very real.

CHAPTER 14

As predicted, many passengers from the cruise ship became ill on the trip into the harbor. There were a few injuries from bumped heads, too, as people rushed to the bathrooms. The corridors on *Bring It Up Coral* were narrow, and electrical junction and fuse boxes were attached to the walls at convenient head bumping height.

Cecilia did what she could, and Sean and Dr. Wozniac moved among the passengers to help. Jim could see in the set of Sean's shoulders and jaw that the whining of passengers was getting on his nerves. He knew it was getting on his nerves. *They've escaped death in a collision at sea, and all they can do is complain about a few bumps and upset stomachs.* Jim turned abruptly, left the observation deck, and went to the bridge.

"Guess we better get ready for the next one," Wade predicted when Jim entered the bridge. John and Andrea were there, Jim suspected, to stay away from the passengers.

"Next what?" Jim asked.

"Fire. Statistics show that these catastrophes happen in threes more often than not," Wade replied easily.

"Maybe the next one will be a yacht full of beautiful women!" John said enthusiastically.

"Did someone mention me?" Cecilia said with a grin, entering on John's line. "Whining get to you, honey?" She asked Jim.

"Was it that obvious?" He asked, alarmed.

"Well, the crew of the cruise ship are all commiserating with us on serving under a tough Captain." She said with a sly grin. "And, right after you left, one of the men moved around, mentioning that we saved their lives and maybe the passengers should whine a little less."

"You're serious!" Jim said, chagrined.

"Aaaarrrgh!" John said, mimicking a film pirate. "Best they be quiet, or they'll walk the plank, they will!" He added, making them all laugh.

"I favor keel-hauling." Wade grinned. "It lasts longer."

"I'll volunteer Mrs. Fisk-Donahue as an example to the rest of the passengers," Cecilia said with some feeling.

"You would, you little minx!" A strong female voice said from the doorway. Mrs. Fisk-Donahue maneuvered her vast bulk through the door and put her hands on her hips in that no-nonsense way women do. "Captain, this woman spoke rudely to me. What are you going to do about it?" She asked, her face full of triumph.

John couldn't help himself. He broke out laughing, doubled over with mirth, and Wade had a huge grin on his face. Mrs. Fisk-Donahue tapped her foot, looking daggers at them. Jim schooled his face so that no emotion showed. The sudden urge to strike this obnoxious woman washed over him the moment she began to speak, and he hoped he was effectively hiding how he felt about her. Cecilia was laughing as well, and that didn't help.

"And you are?" He asked.

"I am Mrs. Fisk-Donahue, daughter of Sir Ronald Fisk and wife of Lord Michael Donahue—that's who I am!" she snapped.

"Ah, Mrs. Fisk-Donahue. I'm Captain Shepherd. Let me introduce you to Cecilia Shepherd, my wife. Let me also remind you that this is not a cruise ship. We own this deep-sea salvage, search, and rescue vessel. By we, I include every crew member on board. We are all partners in this venture. We salvage and save ships and people but do not run a cruise ship. May I escort you back to the observation deck?" He was rather proud of his speech.

"You may not!" the woman spluttered. "I will not return to that uncomfortable room. The chairs do not suit me, as I told your wife. She told me I could sit in a chair or on the floor; the choice was mine. I ask you!" She continued.

"Don't!" Jim said with a tight smile.

"Don't what, young man?" She asked in a dangerous voice.

"Don't ask me," Jim replied.

"How dare you!" She breathed, her face white with anger. "I shall report you to the maritime authorities!" She continued. "I shall make trouble for you, young man! Mark my words!"

Without comment, Jim picked up the phone and dialed the kitchen. As he expected, Sturdy answered.

"Sturdy, I have a discipline situation up here. Would you please come to the bridge and tell Abe you'll be gone for about an hour? He can come too if he wishes." Jim added.

"Is this going to be fun?" Sturdy asked. Jim could almost hear his smile on the other end.

"An object lesson to one of the rescued passengers," Jim replied.

"We'll be right up!" Sturdy said.

True to his word, he came, bringing Abe. Mrs. Fisk-Donahue gasped as Sturdy bent over and entered the bridge. He was the biggest man she had ever seen. Behind him stood Abe, a fellow bodybuilder. Sturdy, at six feet eleven inches, weighed an impressive three hundred and forty-five pounds. At six feet one inch, Abe weighed just shy of three hundred pounds. Both were bulging with muscle and wearing stained T-shirts, not their uniform shirts.

"Mrs. Fisk-Donahue has graciously volunteered to clean the restrooms on the observation deck. See that she is given the proper equipment and make sure she does a good job. Explain the rust problem and how to solve it, too. Point out how corners tend to stay dirty if one doesn't pay special attention. See to it that she does us proud, gentlemen." Jim said evenly.

"I am not!" Mrs. Fisk-Donahue shouted. Jim ignored her.

"If she refuses again, you have my permission to remove her dress and shoes and ask her to do as she has been told. Each refusal will result in the removal of another item of clothing. Once she's naked, if she refuses again, you may strap her. Carry on, men." Jim said, turning his back and waving them out.

His eyes were dancing with merriment as the two giants lifted the woman by either arm and literally carried her out of the bridge, kicking and cursing. Her language was certainly less than exemplary, and John and Wade had huge grins on their faces as they watched the drama unfold. Sturdy took her out of Abe's hands and lifted her until she was face to face with him.

"If you use bad language again, you will chew and swallow a one-inch square of ivory soap for each word, " he said.

Whimpering, she allowed herself to be led down to the bathrooms. Abe and Sturdy made her begin in the men's room. Two hours later, Jim came down to check on her work and found her in her slip, barefoot, with runs in her hose, using a toothbrush to scrub away rust in the women's restroom. Worse, women from the passengers were allowed to come in and use the facility and see her humiliation. Her face was stained with tears.

"You've done a fine job, Mrs. Fisk-Donahue," Jim said, inspecting her work. "When you're finished here, you may get dressed and ready to depart."

"I'm reporting you, you, you monster!" She said.

"In that case, you may depart first. I'll bring your clothes down after everyone is off the ship," Jim said quietly.

"You wouldn't dare!" she squealed.

"I would," Jim said evenly.

"Well! I never!" She spluttered.

"Then it's about time, don't you think? Good day," Jim replied, walking out. True to his word, he delivered her clothes to her after everyone was off the ship. He brought them down himself to her husband, standing outside the limousine that came to collect her and looking harassed. Jim suspected that her husband looked that way most of the time he was in her presence.

"Are you Captain Shepherd?" he asked, pushing Jim away from the car. Jim almost smiled at his urgency to remove him from hearing distance of the vehicle. Donahue cast furtive glances back to make sure his wife did not follow.

"Yes, I am," Jim replied with a smile.

"How did you do that?" he asked.

"Do what?" Jim asked, confused.

"How did you make her clean restrooms?" he asked.

"On my ship, people generally do what they're told," Jim replied without inflection.

"Oh! Well, I suppose that has to be, doesn't it?" The man said, still looking over his shoulder in fear. "She'll make trouble for you if she can." He warned.

"She can't," Jim said. For the first time, Lord Donahue looked at Jim. Whatever he saw, he decided he would dissuade his wife from attempting such a foolish act. There was something implacable about this bluff seaman.

"Good! And good for you, old man." He added, shaking Jim's hand and taking the clothes. He spun away and hurried back to the car. Jim made sure he didn't crack a smile until he was halfway up the gangplank. The smile came easily when Cecilia appeared at the top, ran down, and leaped into his arms.

"This is most unusual behavior for an Ensign," Jim said, holding her tight and listening to her giggle.

"You actually made her clean the bathrooms!" she whispered. "My hero!"

Jim set her down with a grin, and holding hands, they walked back up to the ship. The Italian authorities were waiting at the top, the captain wearing a worried frown.

"I have a complaint here from a Mrs. Fisk-Donahue," the captain said without preamble. "She claims you manhandled her and made her clean the men's bathroom. Is this charge true?"

"Actually, I never touched her," Jim said truthfully. "And no, it's not true. I made her clean the men's and the women's bathroom on that deck," he added, his eyes twinkling with the memory.

"She is, I understand, a grand dame, a woman of some influence." The Italian Captain said with concern. He watched Jim's face and saw no sign that Jim heard the warning in his voice. "Are you aware that she can and probably will make trouble for you?"

"Captain!" Jim snapped, his voice suddenly stern, his eyes like green marble slabs boring into the smaller man's worried brown eyes. "On board my ship, people do as they are told or suffer the consequences."

"But of course!" the captain said, suddenly understanding. He was still worried. "She claims you made her disrobe in public and clean the bathrooms in her under-things."

"I instructed my men that if she refused again to do as she was told, they were to remove one piece of clothing until she was naked. If she refused, they were to strap her," Jim replied, enjoying the conflicting emotions on the little Italian's face.

"Good God!" The man exclaimed. "What did she do?"

"She refused to obey a direct order from the vessel's captain," Jim replied.

"I hope you do not experience greater troubles from this woman. She has a reputation in this city; I must warn you, Captain. I find you acted in accordance with maritime law, but she will press the issue. She hates you. Do consider my warning!" The captain bowed correctly to Cecilia, kissing her knuckles, then saluted Jim and marched off with his men. As he walked down the gangplank, the smirk on his face told Jim volumes about the trouble that woman had already caused.

"What will you do if she presses the issue?" Cecilia asked, curious. She was still fighting the urge to giggle.

"There are two very large women I know in Boston who will be glad to have an all-expenses paid vacation here in Naples. They will visit her and spank her with a strap until she breaks. It never takes long," Jim replied, walking toward his office with Cecilia's hand tucked warmly in his own.

"May I watch?" Cecilia giggled. She had no doubts her husband was telling the truth.

"I don't know," Jim paused, stroking his chin. "I don't want you picking up any bad habits from these women."

She hit him in the chest and then shook her hand, laughing and wincing at the same time. He lifted her, kissed her thoroughly, and put her down. Just then, the klaxon sounded the emergency signal. Jim sighed.

"Blast Wade and his predictions!" he breathed. Both of them ran to the bridge.

CHAPTER 15

"**W**e have a pleasure yacht burning about three miles out. They're returning from a tour of the Greek Islands, and their point of departure is Rome." Zeke said as Jim appeared on the bridge. Smitty was there, too, looking over the paper Zeke carried and getting the coordinates.

"I told you!" John blurted, coming into the room as he heard the news. "It's a yacht full of beautiful women!"

Jim grinned and gave orders to get underway. He put his hand to his throat microphone and pressed the send button. "Dorf, how are we for foam? We have another fire," he said.

"How big is the boat?" Dorf asked, not bothering with amenities.

"Pleasure yacht, seventy-five feet," Jim replied, looking over the paper Zeke had been handing around.

"Got plenty for that. Most of what we'll do will be inside anyway. Do you know how old the boat is?" Dorf asked.

"She was launched in 1925!" Jim said with a whistle of appreciation.

"Oh, we gotta save her!" Dorf said. Like most men of the sea, Dorf loved boats, especially the older vessels built by hand with amazing craftsmanship. Jim, too, loved the older boats and hoped they could save this one.

Once again, the ship raced to rescue those on board the burning yacht and to try to save it. Soon, they could see the smoke, and it was black. Andrea was at the wheel again, and Cecilia stood beside him, turning to watch her husband at work on the deck often.

"The wood is not burning yet, or not much of it. That is the smoke from a fuel or engine fire, perhaps even a fire in one of the flotation devices. They often used Styrofoam for flotation in those days, I think. In some of the older boats they used sealed aluminum boxes filled with air. We will soon see, Niece." Andrea said.

It was a beautiful old yacht made by the Chris-Craft Company. Beautiful teak decks and trim were everywhere, accented by the white paint. At that moment, black smoke billowed from every opening. On the rear deck, a dozen people stood with the crew of four. Cecilia began to chuckle. There were seven Cardinals, all in their burgundy robes, and five nuns.

Rough weather and rain made the rescue daring and dangerous, but the crew managed to get everyone on board *Bring It Up Coral* safely. Vince Hall wasn't so lucky. He was part of Six Team 2, the first to mount the yacht, and a savage wave flipped the gangplank into the air, throwing him neatly between the two vessels.

Knowing enough to dive beneath the crippled yacht, he came up on the other side, swam around to the back of his own ship, and was soon back on deck and rejoined his team on the yacht with nothing more than a few bruises. John led the team into the bowels of the yacht. It was bedding that was creating most of the black smoke, and in half an hour, they had the flames extinguished. They came out, blackened by the smoke and soot, to be hugged repeatedly by the yacht's owner, who was soon as black as the rest.

Six Team 1 went on board to sound the hull and ensure no leaks. Then they hooked the yacht to the towline and, leaving Jack Boswell to steer the crippled yacht, returned.

Since it was evening, everyone was invited to clean up and join the crew for a celebration dinner. Jim passed John as he entered the dining room and smiled. "Well, you got your wish. There were certainly beautiful women on board this yacht!"

John smiled ruefully. "Be careful, or I'll ask them to exile you from the church," he whispered. Jim laughed. Their grandmother often used this threat against anyone who displeased her.

The seven Cardinals were effusive in their praise and thanks to the crew. Jim warmed up to them immediately, especially the oldest of them. Though feeble, he'd been game on the gangplank, laughing as the men helped him over the dangerous gap between the two boats. To Jim's pleasure, they divided themselves among the crew, one to a table, to meet and thank the men personally.

The eldest sat at Jim's table and introduced himself as Cardinal Thomasso Zerbino. He smiled at them and said in perfect English, "You may call me Father Thomas. Everyone at the Vatican does."

"And what do you do at the Vatican?" Jim asked politely.

"I am in charge of the library and oversee the considerable staff we have working there," he answered. Jim knew that the library at the Vatican was state-of-the-art and designed to house ancient manuscripts and preserve them. The library is a wonderful place to work for one such as me, and I do enjoy my duties."

"Are you a church historian?" Cecilia asked.

"I am. I'm as dusty as some of the books on my shelf, but I really come to life when it comes to church history." Father Thomas said with a smile. "Much of our history is quite ribald!" he added with a wink.

"Do you remember anything about the monastery buried under the landslide that created Lake Alleghe?" Jim asked.

"You know something of our history, I see," Father Thomas said, his eyes lighting up. "Yes, I remember much about it. During World War II, a Waffen-SS officer grilled me about that monastery as if obsessed. Him, I told nothing. You, I would be more than happy to tell whatever you want to know, within reason."

"Hauptscharfürer Nikolas Bormann and an archaeologist Johann Honecker were the men asking you all the questions, weren't they?" Jim asked quickly. Father Thomas raised both eyebrows in surprise.

"How did you know this?" he asked, slipping into Italian without thinking. Jim responded in that language.

"I have some of his papers and Johann Honecker's diary," he

replied. "They mention the monastery and the trove hidden beneath the landslide."

"And are you interested in the treasure?" Father Thomas asked carefully.

"I assure you that if I decide to attempt to unearth it, I will work hand in hand with the church, and all recovered artifacts will be returned to that worthy institute," Jim replied. "For us, it is the challenge of getting to the treasure, not the treasure itself, that draws us."

"We tried, you know," Father Thomas said, shaking his head sadly. "Twice. Both times were a dismal failure."

"Do you know a Dr. Alistair Gregg, Father?" Jim asked.

"Of course! In fact, he was just at our library researching the very same thing! He's a renowned British archaeologist. We spent many hours in amiable conversation. His mind is amazing, and what he has tucked away there is fascinating. Why?" Father Thomas replied.

"Because Dr. Gregg is working with us on an idea to reach those storerooms," Jim replied. "We're going to try. Until we notify you personally, would you keep this all a secret? I give you my word that the church will be invited to inventory what we find if God is merciful."

"Of course, my boy. Now, let me tell you about that monastery!" And for the next hour Jim ate and listened, learning more than he dreamed he would learn in so short a period. Father Thomas was animated, occasionally sipping his glass of wine to lubricate his throat and injecting comments about the fine cuisine. He wound down after an hour, and Jim thanked him warmly for the lesson.

Jim visited the other tables and learned that all four nuns were freshly returned from ten years of service in the Congo. He listened to them recount tales of deprivation, starvation, disease, and great evil. Although the women were of an age with his mother, Jim found them quite beautiful, perhaps because of their generous natures and godly devotion.

He met the other Cardinals, all elderly men who had devoted their lives to the Catholic Church. Some were likable, and others were portentous, pontificating, plenipotentiaries as full of hot air as they were of themselves. Life was like that, and every human organization suffered the same. That the church was included came as no surprise to the world-weary soldier. He wondered how God felt about such things and decided that His response would be the same in every case. Saving the lost included everyone!

They arrived in Naples to a bevy of journalists, two television crews, and a host of cheering people. On a day of dull news, the Cardinals' rescue made the headlines and took thirty-second spots on international news programs.

A prominent American news network that Jim often referred to as "The Mental Pigmy Review" sponsoring a talking head Jim called "I. Blathernot" falsely reported that smoking nuns caused the fire. It was typical of that company to spout sensational news that had nothing to do with reality. An electrical short in ancient wiring caused the fire. That, of course, would not be determined for days, and "The Mental Pigmy Review" never waited for the truth.

Their next rescue also made the news because of the event's spectacular nature and an enterprising journalist who videotaped the incident from a helicopter. A small transport ship hauling batteries for electric cars and solar energy cells caught fire, melted, and sank. While the fire moved swiftly toward the eight crewmembers huddled at the stern, Dorf maneuvered *Bring It Up Coral's* stern into position so the men could leap onto a quickly inflated airbag that would break their fall.

All eight men leaped simultaneously, and the airbag, used to raise sunken vessels, caught them all, bounced them around a bit, and allowed them to survive the inferno that swept the stern even as they leaped. Two of the men suffered minor burns, and the others lost hair and had singed clothing. So hot were the flames that a portion of *Bring It Up Coral* was scorched as the ship pulled away. Moments later, the cargo transport sank out of sight as seams burst under the heat.

It was another slow news day, and once again, the *Bring It Up Coral* crew found themselves in the news. What excited them all was that a national science magazine made much of their ability to improvise a way to save lives. Whoever wrote the article did some serious research on deep-sea salvage. Jim suspected some of the quotes came from Wade, and that suspicion was vindicated when Wade confessed. An avid reader of the magazine, Wade made copies of the article and hung them everywhere on the ship where there was a bulletin board. It had been his idea. His commentary at least made the article come to life when it described rescue techniques and the variables every rescue ship faced. Wade rarely made such an audacious show of pride, but Jim felt he deserved it this time.

CHAPTER 16

Jim arranged for Calvin Beardsley and his crew to come to Venice to work on repairing *Bring It Up Coral* and a special project for the company. Beardsley rented a facility to meet his needs, transported his crew and equipment to Venice, and was ready when *Bring It Up Coral* entered Venice Harbor. Here, the ship would be dry-docked and repaired, and under cover of secrecy, that special project would be completed as well.

"You've not been gentle with her!" Beardsley said, looking at the scorched stern and damaged plates. He shook his hairy head in displeasure.

"We're all fine, thank you, Calvin," Jim said with a grin.

"Yes, but you've bloody wrecked yer ship, don't 'e know?" Calvin retorted his mind all on the ship. Then he realized what Jim said, and he blushed.

Jim and John laughed and shook hands with the genius behind their vessel. As they walked toward the office in the building Calvin leased, he spoke to them.

"I've solved that bloody filter problem for the bathyscaphe," he said. "Bloody Kockums didn't want to work with me at first. Chap I know broke into their highest security building and copied the plans for me. When I showed 'em how to fix it, they wanted to buy my plans, but I'd already patented them. They howled like a pack of wolves after a bitch in heat."

"What an interesting comparison!" Cecilia said, coming up behind Calvin.

"Beg pardon, miss!" Calvin said, hunching his shoulders.

Cecilia laughed and patted his shoulder as she came around to join her husband and brother-in-law. She knew Calvin well enough to know what to expect, and her ears only turned red once or twice during the conversation. Jim counted.

Once the ship was settled on the huge cradle correctly, Calvin and his crew winched it out of the water and into the giant building. Calvin hadn't wasted any time. His entire shop had been transported and set up along one side of the building. The ship looked small inside the huge building, and Jim patted her hull affectionately, then wiped the slime and grime on a rag provided by Beardsley.

In front of *Bring It Up, Coral* was a Davis 70' Sportfisherman yacht, also on a cradle. Her gleaming white hull and fabulous interior were waiting for the special touch of the Beardsley team. Jim climbed the ladder beside the boat and wandered through it, admiring the incredible engineering skills of the Davis company.

He climbed out of the boat and watched as his crew unloaded the equipment they would be taking with them to the Villa Orvieto. A Mack Truck cab with a full sleeper attached to a 45' trailer would haul their equipment into the mountains to Alleghe and their new quarters. Lee Roy Brown and Phillip Eustus would drive the eighteen-wheeler. Jim wondered briefly just how aggressive they might be behind the wheel of so huge a vessel. Deciding they could be trusted, he didn't make any suggestions.

Jim liked these two Australians. Formerly of the Australian SAS they were disciplined and well trained. Lunchbox and PU, pronounced *pew*, were the names by which they were most commonly called amongst the crew. Only Marvin Finn refused to call the men by their nicknames.

They were part of a foursome that included Sean Oxton, their leader and the team's second medical officer and first field medic.

Chance Edwards was the fourth. Ox and Chance were, at that moment, hustling to help load the crates that were on the forklift. These would be transferred into the trailer where Dorf, Mark, C.G., and Vince used handcarts to move and stack them.

Another truck sat beside the eighteen-wheeler, looking relatively small. It was a cube van, and Abe and Sturdy were loading the frozen food and perishables into its refrigerated interior. They would drive that truck. Jim watched the kitchen crew work.

Cuss, or Bob Stankus, and Windy, David March, were old hands. Curtis was new; his nickname was Bull. Bull was Abe's newest project. Abe and Sturdy worked at a mission in Boston when they weren't sailing the seven seas with Jim's crew. There, they found men who were alcoholics and drug addicts, men who had reached the very bottom of the cesspool of life and lifted them from its miry murk into the light of Christ's love.

Abe and Sturdy were very devout Christian men, and they led Bible studies on board the ship most of the time. Cuss had been a truculent bear of a man when he first came on board. Flaccid, lazy, and lacking the ability to trust people, he had earned the nickname "Stinky." Now that his attitude was so different, the men just called him Cuss, and he appreciated the change.

Bob had never been wealthy before. March knew what that was about. Both of them were helping Abe and Sturdy now with Bull, and the man was changing daily into a fine crewmember. Jim noted that Cuss was never far from Bull and grinned to see the changes in these men. He was proud of Abe and Sturdy for their work. The fact that his venture provided an opportunity to help someone like Cuss and Bull made it all worthwhile. Few companies, he knew, had the patience or the time to work with such people. He turned from them to look at the other means of transportation.

An older stretch Mercedes sat at the head of the line. It was a 1966 Mercedes 450 that Ken purchased for the Villa. This one was pearl white and looked like it might have just rolled off the factory assembly line. Jim knew a powerful newer engine under the hood provided over six hundred horsepower with an added turbo-charger for increased top-end speed. He often wondered why the Europeans and Japanese could squeeze so much horsepower out of an engine, and America seemed inept in that department.

Inside, the Mercedes was comfortable but not ornate. A true aficionado of this automobile class might notice that the inside dimensions were slightly smaller than the original. That was because this vehicle was fully armored. Before the seat covers were applied, a triple layer of Kevlar was added beneath. A former American ambassador owned the vehicle, and for years, it sat in a garage until Jim's company purchased it.

Beside the Mercedes were four Jeep Rubicon extended 4x4s, each with a four-inch lift kit, hitch receptacles front and rear that could accommodate trailer hitches or the EP Series Super-Duty self-recover winches from Superwinch that rested securely in the rear of the vehicle, next to the Litegrip sport/utility mount holding a shovel and axe upright on one side. Each Jeep had a grill protector and light protection for front, rear, and sidelights. They were white with tan soft-tops and tan trim. Other extras had been added, actually doubling the cost of each vehicle, but well worth the expense.

Each Jeep was equipped with Pitbull Growler tires, and the 16.5 rims were the same color as the vehicle. Jim liked the Jeep best of all, and one of the new ones belonged to him. His, like the others, was equipped with Teraflex shackles that hinged and rotated to allow the springs to attain maximum droop and articulation. That lets them flex and compress with much greater freedom, preventing unnecessary stress.

Three other vehicles stood beside the Jeeps. They were Jeep's newest version of the Grand Cherokee, and they were also set up for serious off-road action if necessary. True, one gave up some comfort of a smoother ride, but the fringe benefits far outweighed that factor. The Cherokees were also white with tan interiors and trim.

Cherokees all sported top racks and rear carriers that fit into the hitch receptacle and lock into place on the roof rack mounting bars with specially designed clips. Jeeps were equipped with the ARB Rear JK Bumper and Tire carrier, complete with specially designed wilderness trail racks. Chains for all four tires were packaged in neat plastic carrying cases and stored away behind the shovel and axe in each vehicle.

Last but certainly not least, each vehicle was equipped with a snorkel for traveling through deep water. They were well equipped and unusual enough to turn every head that saw them, especially in this part of Italy. Each vehicle bore the company logo on the doors, and the Mercedes bore the Villa Orvieto logo that would eventually go on every bottle of wine shipped out of the vineyard.

Jim looked at the logo with interest because Ken Worthington had hired a well-known advertising firm in the area to design the family crest logo for the winery. It was certainly distinctive, with maroon, silver, and gold colors laced together tastefully. Vineyard Orvieto appeared in a plain font, which was easily readable and powerful above the crest design. He liked it immediately.

Finally, at the end of the row sat a conversion van on a Mercedes chassis. In this, Dr. Gregg and his team would make their way to the villa. They were all busy checking the supplies in the trailer the van would pull. Jim knew the huge diesel plant beneath the hood, complete with a propane unit, had power to spare. Inside, the conversion van was decked out in opulence to mask the hi-tech equipment that filled it.

Once everything was loaded, the convoy left Venice. Vince was behind the wheel of the Mercedes, with C.G. beside him, acting as chauffeur and bodyguard. Ken Worthington sat in the back with Andrea, going over the paperwork Andrea had just signed before leaving. Somewhat stunned, he listened as he realized he now owned a multi-million dollar venture, including over four thousand acres of land. Deeply humbled, he listened carefully to Ken.

Jim and Cecilia were behind the Mercedes, and though they would not arrive until after dark, both were excited to see Villa Orvieto. Finn sat in the back seat, one hand holding the roll bar and the other clutching his briefcase. He seemed ill at ease.

"Marvin, you okay back there?" Jim asked, negotiating one of Italy's many traffic circles.

"I don't think I'm cut out for this type of venture, sir," Marvin said after an appreciable pause. "I've lived my whole life, studied, planned, and achieved living at sea. I know about ships, protocol, and maritime law. I don't know anything about land development!"

Jim knew how to manage this, and Cecilia listened with surprise as her rough-and-ready husband sold the entire venture to Marvin. Being analytical, Marvin hated it when anyone came on too strong, talked loudly, exaggerated, or discredited his information. Knowing all this helped Jim.

He provided facts, as many as he could recall, that he knew were accurate. He gave an organized pitch, using logical persuasion and talking softly and slowly. He was specific and stressed the quality of the venture. Finn was allowed to ask questions and encouraged to validate his own research. The conversation took most of the trip, but Cecilia didn't mind.

Arriving after dark did not allow them to see the property Ken Worthington purchased, but the Villa was everything they expected. It was even more opulent than the Live Oaks mansion! Gwyneth Orvieto Shepherd was there in the foyer to greet them. Maisy Ellen Cuthbert and her husband Much were standing just behind her.

Ellie Tyndale, Candy Duff, and Mrs. Duncan were on the first landing in their housekeeping uniforms. Bob Sears was in the Gardener's apartment, located above the massive twelve-car garage, but he came out to the balcony to wave at them and greet them as they pulled up. Margaret, his wife, and Alice O'Keefe were in the kitchen, busy getting evening snacks together for their guests.

Mrs. Shepherd hugged her sons and daughter-in-law and then hugged everyone else. No one minded waiting through the hugs and warm wishes. When the greetings were finished, the crew went to work unloading the trucks. Much took them down into the basement and showed them how to open the specially designed ready room for the team. It lay behind an eight-foot wide, ten-foot-tall section of a vast wine rack that stretched from one wall to the other and was filled with dusty old bottles of wine.

Wade designed the door to open by voice command. Much said

the password, and the wine rack slid silently back, disappearing to the left. Behind it was a vault door that could be opened with a combination dialed by hand or voice command. Much said the password for that door, and it slowly hissed open, revealing a room much like the one hidden in the basement of the Live Oaks mansion.

It was nearly midnight when the crew finished unloading the trucks and putting everything away. Trunks, crates, and boxes were all placed in storage, some in a basement storage area and most of it above the garage next to the gardener's apartment. Quietly, the men made their way through the vast house to the kitchen for something to drink before heading off to bed. They may be bone weary, but they were satisfied with a job well done. It was quiet in the kitchen as the men took their snacks and drinks, finished them quickly, and headed off to bed.

Most of the crew would take quarters in the bunkhouse, a long, low structure situated on a hill almost a hundred yards distance from the house. Once, in more affluent times, the owners of this property kept horses, and the stables and fenced meadows, paddocks, and pens were still there. During remodeling, central heating and plumbing were added to the bunkhouse. The old rough-hewn wooden bunks had new mattresses, and the windows had all been replaced. It would be a comfortable place for the men to stay.

Dr. Gregg and his staff were escorted to the Villa's third floor, where they discovered old-world opulence with all the modern conveniences. Rooms with gilded walls, twelve-foot ceilings, heavy drapes over delightful window curtains to help keep the chill out at night, and smooth wood floors that echoed with every step. Inside the rooms, some originals and copies of masterpieces hung on the walls beside ornate mirrors and well-polished wood furniture.

Each bed was canopied, a massive king-sized structure with down bedspreads and warm blankets. In keeping with the traditions of the housebuilders, the beds were on pedestals. Though they would have dwarfed a fairly large master bedroom in the States, these rooms were designed to leave plenty of space for comfortable chairs by a fireplace, a window seat, and room to move around. Opulence abounded everywhere one looked.

Each room looked out onto a narrow balcony with a set of double doors opening inwards. The balcony was just wide enough for a lawn chair. Alistair looked out at his and wondered if the weather was ever warm enough for anyone to sit out there. A fire danced merrily in his fireplace, but the warmth did not penetrate the whole room.

Cecilia was waiting for Jim when he entered their suite of rooms. In a huge leather chair, almost burgundy in color, she sat demurely in a yellow quilted bathrobe and large yellow furry slippers with the cartoon figure of Tweety smiling up at him. He grinned and leaned down to kiss her before heading in for a shower.

When he returned, he carefully folded his jeans over a chair near the bed, laid his T-shirt over that, and put his socks on the seat. His shoes were ready at the foot of the chair. Cecilia was used to this habit. Jim liked to be prepared for emergencies. In nothing but his boxer briefs, Jim pulled back the heavy covers and climbed in beside Cecilia, who, when she heard the water shut off from the shower, left her chair by the warm fire and crawled into the cold bed.

Jim didn't mind cold beds at all. At this point in their marriage, Cecilia always snuggled right up against him to get warm, which usually led to something else, which was also very pleasant for both of them. Tonight was no different, and Jim thanked the Lord once again for a loving wife and friend like Cecilia. Tired and content, they lay in each other's arms and fell asleep.

CHAPTER 17

Early in the morning Jim awoke to the sound of a bird singing outside his window. Being careful not to awaken Cecilia, he untangled himself from her and slipped out of bed. Padding over the cold floor to the window, he looked out at a beautiful tree, showing signs of budding, and a pair of nesting birds getting ready for the summer, mating, hatching eggs, and raising their young. Both joined in announcing the first rays of morning.

Jim padded into the bathroom and decided it was bigger than his bedroom in the Boston home he grew up in. Grinning at the opulence, he turned on the shower to get instant hot water. Looking around, he spotted the hot water source, one of his time's new and better inventions. This unit heated water as needed. Stepping into the brass and glass shower, he danced briefly while the porcelain tub warmed enough to stand still. He showered, shaved, and dressed in the bathroom.

He took the time to build a roaring fire in the fireplace to warm the room for Cecilia. The heat was unbearable next to the fireplace, but halfway across the room, the temperature cooled rapidly. He hoped it would provide enough heat for her to be comfortable when she awoke.

Walking softly, he made his way out of the bedroom and downstairs to the kitchen. Margaret and Alice were hard at work, and Jim was surprised to see Bull, Windy, and Cuss working right alongside the ladies. Windy looked up with a grin, and Cuss nodded a greeting. Bull looked at him and nodded once.

"Coffee and tea for you and your lady, Shep?" Windy asked, drying his hands on a stained towel.

When Jim nodded, Windy poured a large cup of coffee, using Cecilia's favorite creamer, and added a small silver pot for a second cup. For Jim, he poured a tall glass of iced tea and added two lemon wedges on top of the glass. He put this on a small wooden tray so Jim could easily transport it back to their room.

"Thanks, Windy," Jim said, taking the small tray from his crewmember. He smiled for everyone in the kitchen before carefully carrying the tray back to his room.

Jim padded into the room, put the tray down, and began to open the drapes covering the three sets of windows and the balcony doors. The room was getting warmer, but he put a few more logs on the fire. This completed, he took the coffee to the bed, sat down, and gently pushed Cecilia's hair out of her face.

"Good morning, beautiful," he said quietly when she opened her eyes. He loved the way her irises expanded whenever she looked at him. Stretching with her hands far above her head and her feet stretched out toward the foot of the bed; she arched her back. Jim had been holding his iced tea in his right hand, and when her belly was exposed, he put his hand on it.

"Oh, you're going to pay for that!" She said, slapping his hand away. She slid into a sitting position, and he helped put pillows behind her and then handed her the coffee. When she had enjoyed her first sip, she wrinkled her nose at him. "If you think this is all the payment you need, you're quite mistaken," she announced, trying to look stern and commanding. The effort broke her face into dimpled smiles and giggles, and Jim laughed with her.

"So, what are our plans today?" she asked, sipping more coffee.

"First, we're going to get a look at the property, and then we're going to have a two-day vacation where everyone can explore our new surroundings. After that, we'll begin training for work at this altitude and sharpen our climbing skills," Jim replied, putting his tea glass down to open the double doors onto the balcony.

"James Robert Shepherd! It's too cold for that!" Cecilia exclaimed, pulling the covers up around her and shivering.

Outside, the weather was cool but not cold, and no leaf was stirred in the early morning light. He stepped out to the fence and, leaning over, looked down to the circular drive below. To the west, he could see the main road leading to Alleghe and, to his pleasure, a large and orderly vineyard of row upon row of vines. He walked back into the room just as Cecilia disappeared into the bathroom.

While waiting for her, he studied his notes on the Diocese of Belluno-Feltre and its troubled history. They held their own against their enemies until the late thirteen hundreds and early fourteen hundred when the Visconti rose up against them. Jim understood the motivation all too clearly. The more churches a Diocese controlled, the more money they had to work with. It was sad when religion was indistinguishable from everything else in the world, but because of the sinful state of the heart of man, it was also commonplace.

Dr. Gregg provided a fat notebook full of geological studies, old maps of active and inactive mines, and even some on the caves beneath the Marmolada. Skimming through the notes Jim began to get very excited about their chances of finding the very cave in which the artifacts still lay hidden. Hopefully, they were not underwater. Silver, gold, other metals, precious stones, and such would be unharmed. But any documents would be lost.

Eventually, Cecilia came out, kissed her husband soundly, and the two wandered down the curving steps to the ground floor and made their way back to the dining room. As formal dining rooms went, this one was typical. The table could easily have seated a hundred guests. They sat at the end closest to the kitchen, filling seats as people came. Margaret and Alice, with the help of Windy and Cuss, provided an excellent breakfast buffet filled with fresh local fruit, scrambled eggs, bacon, ham, kippers, and cooked shrimp with the tails removed, chilled, and served with a delicious cocktail sauce. Oatmeal, toast, and fresh biscuits were also available.

When everyone was finally present at the table, Jim suggested a two-day vacation, beginning with a tour of the property. Everyone responded with great anticipation. Several of the guests were snow skiing fans and wanted to try the slopes, which were still covered in powder. Breakfast continued on a cheerful note following the announcement.

On the tour of the property, Jim realized that Ken Worthington had understated the potential of the property. Divided into three parts, it included a working vineyard that needed great care to be restored to full operational status. However, once that care was provided, the earning potential for the vineyard was exceptionally high. New vines needed to be planted, and old ones cleared away. The second part, containing the Villa, lay back at the rear of the property, hidden from the road by trees and low hills. A stream ran through part of the property there, and lush green grass formed a beautiful carpet upon which to walk among the birch trees, ancient firs, and even some great oaks. The property was breathtaking in beauty.

It was the third part of the property that would eventually be developed into one of the most popular resorts in the area. Groundwork was already underway, and Jim could see that the resort offered something for everyone. In the plans, modern meets the old world, a sure favorite. He could almost see the dollar signs shining in Ken's eyes as he thought about the long-term operation of this resort. Coupled with the winery, this property would provide a double punch.

Ken took them through the resort, showing them the plans of how the old world meets the new, with beautiful architecture, mock-ups of well-known designs, and all the modern amenities. Spas, pools, gymnasiums, and international dining experiences all combined to entice tourists. According to Ken, it would be a medium-priced resort, which would appeal to just about everybody.

Later that day, Jim took Cecilia for a walk into Alleghe. Dwarfed by the Dolomites, and especially Marmolada and Civett, shadows came early to the town. Depending on the time of day, either Marmolada or Civett was mirrored in the lake. For a long time, they walked hand in hand along the lakeshore, admiring the views and talking quietly.

On their return to the Villa, they passed a small café. Two men sat together, talking earnestly, but when Jim and Cecilia walked by, they stopped and stared at the pair. Making a mental picture of them came second nature to Jim, and he could feel the hairs on the back of his head rising. There was that something wrong about both of them that suddenly alarmed him.

For a moment, he was startled by the depth of his alarm. Then he felt Cecilia's hand in his and understood. Because she was with him, she was in harm's way. She looked up at him sideways, a tentative smile dimpling her cheeks.

"You're worried because I'm with you." She said quietly. "I can't ask you not to worry because you wouldn't be you if you didn't. But don't let that make you hesitate or change plans."

He grinned down at her, caught her up suddenly, and, twirling her around, kissed her long and hard. "I've been putting you in harm's way for over a year now. Because you trust me, I can. You understand what this takes. You're willing to take risks, even though it frightens you sometimes because you know the score. Thanks."

In the café, both men continued their conversation. Neither took Jim and Cecilia to be anything but what they appeared to be: a loving couple on vacation. There had been something about the man, about how he walked and stared at them, something that made him seem dangerous. But dangerous men did not bring their wives with them. Whatever it had been about the man that first alarmed them, they dismissed quickly as they watched him swirl Cecilia around and kiss her.

Dangerous men usually don't bring their wives with them. But this wife is dangerous in her own right. She's not the same woman she was a year ago. I pity the man who tries anything with her! Cecilia had been training with them for nearly two years and progressing nicely in the martial arts and weapons training. She was a crack shot. Jim knew she carried pepper spray, a Taser, and her H&K Mark 23 pistol in her purse. He tried to stop worrying about her but gave it up as an occupational hazard of marriage.

CHAPTER 18

The two men talking in the café checked the couple out, even though they dismissed them as dangerous. They had remained hidden and safe by being careful. Helmut Adenauer and Eric Von Humbolt once served in the RAF (Red Army Faction) or Baader-Meinhof gang. Thorough in their investigations, they eventually wrote the Orvieto family off as a threat.

The sale of the property was public knowledge, and it was child's play to observe the family in their luxurious home. Andrea Orvieto owned the land, and his sister, the Shepherd's mother, lived in the villa. Dangerous enemies did not travel with their entire families to root out dangerous terrorist cell groups. Such a thing had never been attempted, and they truly believed they were still unknown and safe.

Both men might have been surprised to learn that they were photographed and identified within hours of Jim's first look at them. Even more horrifying to them would be the wealth of information Jim's unit had in their possession about their past and present activities.

Jim was alarmed to find Helmut Adenauer, Konrad Kohl, Eric Von Humbolt, and Gustav Jung, all leading terrorist cells and near his family. Helmut Adenauer was once a close friend of Andreas Baader and his girlfriend Gudrun Ensslin, who were the real leaders of the RAF.

Adenauer's cell was located in Alleghe in a small rented house on the outskirts of town. Kohl's group occupied a home in the hills just outside of Agordo. Von Humbolt's cell occupied an apartment building in Primiero. Jung had his cell in Venice.

Zeke dug up a second house in Jung's name in Venice that he believed might be used as a safe house. According to neighbors, it was seldom used, and when people were there, no one saw who they were. That fact alone told him much.

Organizations that used safe houses often made this mistake. A house that was seldom used, and when used, people remained hidden from view, was a red flag. Zeke knew that effectively hiding someone in a safe house would be much more easily accomplished by hiding that person or persons in a group of people constantly coming and going so that the missing people went unnoticed.

Terrorists in hiding were still terrorists. Once their money source dried up, they found ways to supplement their lifestyle. Each cell developed special skills as master thieves. One cell became an arms dealer on the international black market. Well-trained in counterintelligence tactics and other such skills, they had remained undetected all these years. Their bank robberies and jewelry heists were unsolved mysteries in four countries, but because Zeke could put them on location when those robberies occurred, he guessed correctly they were behind them.

Two months passed as the crew of *Bring It Up* developed their new training areas. With such dangerous terrorists surrounding them, their training became of first importance. Beneath the vast horse barn, they excavated a full basement that became their indoor gymnasium and included an indoor shooting range. Heavy insulation was used to mask any sound from that room, and two tunnels were added to enter the gym. One came from the wine cellar ready room, and the other came from the bunkhouse.

Doing the construction work meant only the team would know it was there. Hard labor was always a good way to stay in shape, and none of the men complained about the work, dirt, or frustrations from such labor. In fact, they came to appreciate each other even more because each man added something to the work that was not only necessary but also added to the effectiveness of what they were doing. Marvin Finn became a little more accepted as he worked with them occasionally, not because Jim ordered it but because he wanted to help in any way possible.

During that time, Andrea decided to invite an old friend to come and run his vineyard. Rosa Cali, was considered one of Italy's foremost authorities on grape growing and was recently retired from the post of manager of one of Italy's most famous wine label vineyards. She agreed to an interview and instantly agreed to come to work for the firm when she saw what she had to work with. Jim thought she might have designs on his uncle and wished her success in her pursuit.

Ken Worthington invited friends from Maryland who recently lost their farm to development land sharks to run the farming end of the villa. Bob and Marilyn Siple made a great first impression, settling in to run the farm and orchard with deep pleasure. Bob claimed farming was all he knew. When he learned that he and his beloved wife would share in the profits, Jim thought the man might burst into tears.

It was awkward having three new faces to deal with. They kept to themselves what they guessed about Jim and his team and did not pry. In time, they would come to learn everything about the company they joined. Zeke ran full security checks and asked Sir Edward to do the same. Admiral Runion was jollied into checking out the Siples.

Jim learned that Bob Siple served his country as a Marine for four years before returning to the farm. His wife didn't even have a traffic ticket in her past. They were devout Christians, respected in their home church, and a perfect match for the company. Better still, both became immediate friends with Gwyneth and her staff, as though they'd known each other a lifetime. Jim appreciated that and knew their secret would remain closely guarded when the time came to bring them into the inner circle.

Rosa Calien also proved to be honorable in every way. She spoke fluent English, French, Spanish, and German, four important languages in the wine industry. For years, she traveled between America, France, Spain, Australia, and Germany and knew the trade inside and out. Jim soon realized he had added great talent to his team and was actually looking forward to the property's developing potential.

It was pretty obvious to Gwyneth and Cecilia that Rosa had her mind set on winning Andrea's heart. They thought it was terrific, and Jim wondered if it would complicate things. Andrea seemed aware that something was in the air and almost appeared resigned to the inevitable. Rosa was, despite her age, still quite lovely.

Jim had no regrets about adding these three amazing people to the company and decided they needed to know everything about the organization to fit in properly. It was always a hard decision because the more people who knew about something, the less able one was to keep it secret. And Jim's team needed the secrecy.

Work on the training areas was finally completed, and the men began to work hard to condition themselves to the higher altitude. After a month, they were running ten miles with eighty pounds of equipment at a respectable pace. Cecilia often ran with them. Finn tried but learned quickly that he was in no condition to keep up with these soldiers. He determined to condition himself rigorously until he was.

Rock climbing appealed to others on the crew, and soon, a shed was erected to hold all the climbing gear and keep it organized and in proper repair. Quickly the walls of the building were filled with brightly colored carabiners, pitons, descenders, wire slings, tubular ice screws, hammer axes, ice axes, mountaineering shovels, climbing harnesses, and black climbing rope. Helmets with powerful lamps sat on high shelves in neat rows, each covering a box of fresh batteries. Powerful flashlights that didn't need batteries were also neatly hung.

Dr. Gregg and his team worked alongside Jim's team, learning to climb. Some already had some experience, but by the end of two months, everyone was proficient in the skills necessary for safe rock climbing. Most of them enjoyed it by then, though a few still found the dizzying heights frightening.

Cecilia was one of them and marveled that Jim could casually stroll to the cliff's edge, plop himself down with legs dangling over the edge, even leaning out to watch birds nesting on the cliffs. To her, it seemed that he was without fear, and she correctly guessed that much of his life involved such risks that sitting at the edge of a cliff was hardly a challenge in courage. It took her every ounce of courage merely to stand within a foot of the edge of a precipice.

Spelunking was always a risk. There were hours of discussion about sending a small team in first to explore the cave system. At last, through persuasion and cajoling, Jim agreed to allow both teams to go in together. It was not an easy decision, and knowing the risks made it one of the toughest Jim had ever faced. Still, he knew the training that had been going on for two months and was confident both teams were capable and ready.

Finally, after weighing all the data, Jim decided it was time to enter the cave system. More training was no longer necessary, and all the equipment was in place. His teams were ready and straining at the reins to move on the project.

Two days before entering the system of caves, Jim sat with Smitty, Dr. Gregg, Sparks, and Zeke, looking over the geological surveys and satellite images. There was, it appeared, a pathway all the way down to and below the lake's surface. At least imaging indicated that this was the case.

Smitty, Sparks, and Zeke were excited about the GPS refinements they developed. A GPS wouldn't track in the cave because it couldn't link with a satellite or receive a clear signal. The three of them solved that problem by devising a system using a radio beacon, radar, and a sophisticated computer program that would allow them to pinpoint their exact location from a series of stations installed as they went.

Small plastic boxes containing surprisingly sophisticated technology would communicate with the central station at the cave entrance and provide an exact longitude, latitude, and altitude reading based on the data from the GPS satellite feed. The relay stations were designed to indicate the various changes in those positions, keeping the system accurate to within one meter. They'd been testing the devices in the rooms and tunnels beneath the house and barn and found them extremely precise after only a few adjustments.

Jim clapped all three men on the back and told them how proud he was to lead them. Under his praise, they turned sheepish, but he could tell, nonetheless, that they were pleased. Such was his leadership that these men could rise to their full potential, and they knew it. Once more, he caused their loyalty to him to rise another notch, for such is the quality of all great leaders.

Without realizing the full potential of what he had accomplished that morning, Jim left the three happy inventors to supervise other teams preparing for the exploration. Everyone was excited about the adventure, though Jim knew from experience that a few days in a cave would change their mind dramatically. The penetrating cold and darkness of a cave were real enemies to spelunkers. He and his SEAL team once spent a week in a cave, and they all remembered the experience.

At least we'll be better prepared this time. Jim remembered well the cold that seeped into bones, the hard, unyielding rocks that put relentless pressure on the body pressed into them, and the darkness that seemed somehow to possess the ability to shroud the mind as well as the body. Amplified noises and creeping things that loved darkness and dampness were not to be easily forgotten. *This time, we won't be hiding from deadly enemies. Silence won't be mandatory. And this time, I have faith, something I didn't have then!*

Moving everyone to the high camp was accomplished without difficulty, and they spent a night outside the entrance to the caves they planned to use as a base camp. Finally, the day of their exploration dawned, and Jim kept them outside the cave entrance until everyone had watched the sunrise. He wanted that memory for the days ahead. Everyone had risen before dawn to break camp. At last, he saw that everyone was ready for the venture and sighed. It was time to begin.

Jim looked at everyone assembled on the ledge as they watched the sun chase the shadows of night up and down the brown rock formations surrounding them. He was very much aware that twenty-nine lives were in his hands, including Cecilia's. Feelings like this were common for him, and at times, he thought it might get better, but it never did. Whenever he led a SEAL team mission, he knew the lives of his men depended on his ability to lead them wisely. This was different and no easier for him to bear. Now, he had civilians and women to worry about. Sighing heavily, he gave the order to prepare to enter the cave.

He led Team 1 with Cecilia, Dr. Gregg, Smitty, FM, and Zeke. It was his job to check their packs, gear, and helmet lights before they ducked into the cave's narrow opening. Jim took the lead, the powerful light on his helmet penetrating the darkness almost sixty feet before him. This part of the cave slanted down in a gentle slope and gave enough headroom for even Sturdy to stand upright.

Jim noticed that Dr. Gregg was adjusting his communication gear. He smiled at the little man. "It takes a little getting used to. By tomorrow, you won't even notice it." He said encouragingly. He attached a twelve-foot length of climbing rope to Cecilia's belt while he talked. Once she was hooked up, she turned and attached a similar rope to Dr. Gregg's belt and so on to Zeke, who was last in line.

Zeke attached a hundred-foot line to his belt and passed the end to Dorf, who would follow when the slack was taken up. This was a safety precaution. Every team would be divided by a hundred feet of rope in case of cave-ins or emergencies. Adjusting his sixty-pound pack, Zeke took one last look at the sunlight and turned to follow FM down the slope.

FM and Jim carried eighty-pound packs, Smitty a sixty-pound pack, and Cecilia and Dr. Gregg carried thirty pounds of equipment. As they penetrated deeper into the cave, the darkness closed around them, and Zeke passed the first turn with a sigh, losing all sight of sunlight.

Dorf passed the hundred-foot line to Mark to indicate that he should lead. At six foot nine inches in height, he knew he could see over the others and chose to go to the back of his team. Mark waved cheerily and disappeared into the cave, followed by Driver, Sparks, Ferenc Adley, and Thomas Moore. When it was time for Dorf to enter the cave, he handed his hundred-foot line to JR, leading Team 3.

John nodded to Wade to take the rear, and his team hooked up. C.G. followed JR, Vince followed C.G., Lisle Mirelle came next, and then Heidi Van Haaten in front of Wade. When it was time, Wade passed his hundred-foot line to Sean Oxton.

Ox had his three Australian teammates with him. Lee Roy took the rear position. Ox put Mary Ann Lewis behind him, then Chance, then Barbara, then Phil, with Lunch Box bringing up the rear.

The kitchen crew was last to enter the cave, carrying most of the food supplies and cooking gear. Abe took the lead with Sturdy at the rear. Bull, Windy, TP, Mr. Levi, and Cuss were between and eager to go. Abe grinned. The kitchen crew rarely got to tag along on an adventure, and he was looking forward to this one. His men were no less excited to be part of this one, and he was glad they could add to the well-being of the expedition. It certainly didn't show in any overt nervousness if his bulk bothered him in narrow confines. He was confident Jim would find a way every participant could follow.

CHAPTER 19

After an hour of walking through the cave, they reached a level portion where the ceiling opened above them, and the floor was not littered with stalagmites. Here, they halted for a time until everyone caught up. Sturdy, who had been nearly bent double through the last fifty feet of corridor, straightened up with a delighted grin. Jim let them all rest for ten more minutes.

Smitty was busy with his new equipment while Sparks and Zeke huddled close on either side. "We've come about 3.6 kilometers, Shep," he announced. "We're still nearly nineteen hundred feet above sea level. That means we've dropped a little over a thousand feet."

Zeke opened his laptop and turned it on. He brought up the satellite feeds and studied them. "We're going to drop faster now, boss," he said, his eyes intent on the screen. "Better get us moving."

"You taking over now?" FM asked with a grin. "I thought that was Cecilia's job."

Everybody laughed, but Jim took Cecilia's hand and led her to the cavern's end. He looked back at FM. "We'll both take over if you don't object," Jim said with a deadpan expression. John bent over, laughing, coughing, and slapping his thigh while the other men laughed. Cecilia kept her face straight for all of two seconds before her cheeks dimpled, and her cupid bow smile seemed to light up the cave for Jim. Just to make his point, he held her close and kissed her.

"Hope you brought enough for everybody!" Barbara Stafford quipped. "I'll just help myself!" she said, suddenly grabbing FM and kissing him soundly.

"Must be somethin' in the air, Shep," FM drawled, never even raising his eyebrows.

"Oooh! He's good!" Barbara said.

"What, that didn't rate a great?" FM exclaimed, suddenly taking her head in his hands and kissing her soundly.

"I'll accept that rating," she said breathlessly when he finally released her.

"Uh, I think we better get going," Dr. Gregg grinned.

Jim understood why the interchanges were taking place. They were in a large cave, and darkness closed around them quickly, along with the penetrating cold. Most men wore powerful halogen headlamps, and every other person carried a large hand-held spotlight. An almost oppressive silence settled over the group as they moved deeper into the cave. Jim guessed it would be John who first broke the silence.

His guess proved right as his younger brother, always sensitive to the mood of a group of people, suddenly broke into his favorite Broadway song. He had a strong baritone voice but didn't always hit the notes he aimed for. Still, listening to "I Have Often Walked Down This Street Before" suddenly echoing down the chambers before them broke the somber mood. Some of the crew winced at the missed notes but didn't say anything.

"Jeeze, Commander! I didn't know you could sing!" Lunch Box said.

"Is that what that noise was?" Mary Ann Lewis said quietly from behind John. "I thought someone stepped on a stray cat!"

"I retire deeply chagrined," John pouted, making his lower lip quiver expressively as though he were about to burst into tears. On a six-foot-three-inch Marine, it looked pretty comical. Jim found himself grinning, and Mary Ann laughed outright. "And then she wounds me to the quick by laughing at my sorrow!" John said with mock despair.

"You're a Marine! Suck it up!" Lisle said, brushing her hand lightly over his arm.

The mood was better after that, and every time it sank a bit because of the oppressive darkness, John or FM said or did something to change it. They could all hear each other in the cave despite the distance separating them, though at times, the noise of voices was garbled and unintelligible to those farthest away. Until one got used to it, the odd sounds somehow grated on nerves already raw from the dark and cold. By the end of the day, they all felt weary beyond description, and yet they realized they were growing familiar with a world of darkness pierced only by their lamps. Somehow, knowing they were all together helped keep spirits up.

MREs and NASA meals provided proteins and sustenance to rebuild their strength during the lunch break, but Abe and his able crew provided breakfast and dinner. They sat around a portable heater operated off the generator's power and talked for an hour about nothing important while Abe and his crew got dinner ready. Surrounding their camp were halogen lamps on lightweight aluminum stands. When they made their way to their tents, Smitty turned on the "blue" lamps that would light the way to the latrine for anyone who rose in the night. These pathway lights provided just enough light to ensure no one tripped and fell.

Cecilia tested the air mattress and decided it would be very comfortable. Jim was busy zipping their two sleeping bags together, so she inflated the pillows. Their tent was close to the other tents, so they were quiet, preparing for bed and getting cozy in the cool air of the cave. The strange silence seemed almost oppressive at first until Cecilia began to pick out the sounds of dripping water and the whirring wings of bats flying through the cave to various exits for their night's hunting. In a way, the cave seemed to take on a life of its own, both frightening and inspiring.

Jim reclined on the mattress with his arms around Cecilia, listening to the men whispering, Dr. Gregg's group giggling and expressing their thoughts on the passing bat population. At the moment he liked his life very much. This was what every soldier prayed and lived for. Moments together in amazing places without the threat of attack from anything human were few and far between.

He fell asleep listening to the soft sound of running water somewhere ahead of them. None of the drips bothered him in the least, blending in with the other muted sounds in the cave. Their tents were explorer dome tents designed to keep insects, reptiles, and other pests out. He'd cautioned everyone about ensuring no food was out where a bear could smell it.

John's hand touching his foot awakened him in the early morning, and he slipped out of the sleeping bag without disturbing Cecilia. Following his brother, they crept down the corridor to the garbage dumpsite, where Jim was suddenly confronted by no less than six huge brown bears. They were scavenging through the garbage and seemed undisturbed by human presence. Wade, FM, and Zeke crouched behind rocks, watching the bears. Jim noted that Wade and FM were both armed, which made him feel immediately more secure.

It was good to know that the bears were in the caves and seemed shy around humans, though not afraid or disturbed. Often, they cast glances toward the humans, perhaps wondering if their feast would be interrupted. He decided they probably wouldn't pose a problem when one of the younger bears began to pad its way toward the camp. The bear paused near the tents, sniffing the air, and turned away to rejoin the others. When they picked through the garbage, the bears left in another direction, seeking other food. Once they were gone, the men cleaned the garbage area and put everything in new bags.

The next day progressed well. Some choices led them to dead ends but were soon set right, and every two hours, they stopped to rest, drink, and eat something. Jim warned everyone of the presence of the bears, and they were careful to bury their snack garbage each time in the sand when they could. Deep sand was deposited in some areas by water running through the caves many years before.

Sean made the rounds, ensuring everyone drank enough water, took their salt supplement, and checked for blisters or other foot problems. Jim's team knew the drill, but Dr. Gregg's team hadn't quite picked up on the importance of drinking enough water. Sean chastised them and made them drink their canteens dry before he would allow any to continue. Some complained, but he wasn't about to hear it, and his demeanor soon silenced the complaints and brought compliance.

Although one never got used to the oppressive darkness, they enjoyed the second day much more, discovering several beautiful caverns and even deposits of precious gems. By evening, everyone was ready to stop for the night. When Sparks set up the outer defenses that night, he included a shock fence to keep the bears from entering their little tent compound. There was no sense in taking any chances. Jim approved.

Once again, they gathered around the heater to eat and talk about their trek. Tonight, the talk hovered around how close they were to their objective and what obstacles they might face. At that moment, they were following an underground river, and its waters rushed by a few yards beyond their circle of tents, a pleasant sound even inside a cave. Jim and most of Dr. Gregg's team believed this river would lead them to the chamber they sought.

"There is mention of an underground river in a few of the documents we were able to study at the Vatican," Dr. Gregg mentioned as he and Jim discussed their options. "The chamber we seek is above that, reached by a fissure in which they carved steps to help negotiate the steep incline. My educated guess is we'll find the entrance into the church, blocked by the landslide, of course, and from there be able to discover the room."

"What if the landslide collapsed the cave behind the church?" Jim asked.

"Then the fissure will be hidden beneath the surface of an underground pond or lake." Dr. Gregg said conversationally.

"So we may need to make a night probe," Jim replied, his eyes thoughtful.

"A night probe?" Dr. Gregg asked.

"That's what a dive in a cave is called," Jim replied. "We brought the equipment to make a night probe."

"But that means none of my team will be able to get inside the room!" Dr. Gregg exclaimed forlornly.

"Not to worry, Doc," Jim replied, patting his diminutive friend on the shoulder. "We'll excavate an opening from that room out over the lake and get you in that way." Alistair nodded. Earlier that day, the men had excavated an opening large enough to get everyone through a tight spot, working together in pairs until even Sturdy could walk through the opening.

Remembering the care they'd taken in that job, he felt better. These men knew the risks inside a cave. When they were excavating that opening, only the men working there stayed close to where the picks and hammers chiseled away the stone wall, lest a cave-in trap them. Wade was especially careful to study the rock around the hole they were enlarging to be sure it was safe.

Jim knew he had the tools for excavation and the explosives experts to make it happen without destroying any sensitive materials inside the storage room. He knew because he was one of them. Sparks was working with most of the team and teaching them, and he felt some of them had the ability to become experts in the field. Handling explosives was an essential skill for a soldier. But in a cave, especially close to a cave-in area, there were myriad dangers in using explosives.

That night, a bear tried the outer defenses, waking them all bellowing from the shock. A few minutes later, a deeper roar filled the cavern as an older bear tripped the defenses. The shock was seventy-five thousand volts. Amperage killed, not voltage. At that voltage, a human being would be rendered momentarily unconscious or disoriented enough to be easily captured. The bear felt discomfort and pain. It was enough pain to discourage any other attempts to penetrate the defenses, and the night passed without further event. Even those who rose to use the latrine did not see the bears afterward.

The following morning, everyone was excited because they knew they were close to making a discovery. Most hoped that the room would be untouched by water and accessible. Only a few faced the possibility that it could be hidden forever beneath a watery grave or a pile of rock.

Like many solution caves, this one offered views and vistas that took one's breath away. In one section, they came upon a flowstone drapery of white beneath a bright red group of bottlebrush stalactites surrounded by sandstone. Jim sent Mark up the flowstone to look into a beckoning cavern beyond.

Mark made the arduous climb, his athletic gymnast instincts helping him swing his body in just the proper arc patterns to move from foothold to foothold, handhold to handhold, as he made his way to the top. Shining his light through a small opening, he looked down at a long tunnel barely two feet high.

"Some of us won't fit if we go this way, Shep," he reported, looking down at them from his precarious position. "Hey, Dorf, catch me!" he said, letting go and riding the flowstone like a slide. Dorf moved into place to catch his friend in a tumbling fall. Neither was injured, and they stood together and brushed the dirt away from their clothing as if they had done this every day. Jim grinned and shook his head.

Finally, in the late afternoon, they entered a large cavern, leading them to a small underground lake filled with crystal-clear water. At the far end of the lake, they could see signs of a cave-in. Studying the debris and the still underground lake that had slowly settled over the years, Dr. Gregg sighed.

"The water may have been high enough to reach the storage room," he said sadly.

"I don't think so," Jim said quietly. "These are Baldacchino canopies that form when the surface of a cave pool has receded beneath a growing stalagmite or flowstone mound. In this instance, I would bet on a flowstone mound, water flowing up from beneath but leaving just as quickly as it flowed in. The Baldacchino canopies aren't high enough to reach the storeroom if it is indeed beyond this pool somewhere. If our calculations are correct, we're at least sixteen to eighteen feet below the lowest chamber. I doubt if my men are off by more than half a foot if that. We'll have to make a night probe to see," Jim added.

"Better you than me." Dr. Gregg said, smiling. He'd put his hand in the lake and felt the icy waters, shivering dramatically as he wiped away the wetness.

They set up camp around the pool, the lights showing the water almost perfectly clear and accenting it against the red sandstone surrounding it. Behind the sandstone was solid rock. Some walked out on a shelfstone, a ledge or projection extending from the edge of a cave pool, or attached to a speleothem dipped in a cave pool. These almost always formed from calcite when material precipitated on top of a cave pool, much like rafts, attaching themselves to the side. This one was thick enough to support three or four bodies, which told them that long years passed in its forming.

That night, the bears did not approach the camp. Most of them were accustomed to the darkness outside their sphere of light, and it no longer weighed on them as it had. The air inside the cavern was cool and fresh enough to suggest openings or fissures they had not discovered to allow the passage of air up and out of the cave system. The appearance of several thousand bats streaking by the lamps confirmed that suspicion.

CHAPTER 20

No one ducked for cover or screamed; even the women were used to this phenomenon. They watched the bats pass without comment, amazed at their sheer number, aware that the tiny flying creatures had no interest in humans. They were interested in insects and a delicious supper, and then they retired once again. It was close to the time when they would bear young. Jim wished them a happy evening of hunting and a large amount of food.

"If I wake up as a vampire, you're the first one I'm biting, sweetie." Mary Ann said to Lunch Box, sitting down beside him.

"How many black fellers you seen as vampires in the movies, dearie?" Lunch Box asked sarcastically. "Vampires don't like dark meat," he added with a grin.

"I always thought a tall, strong black man would make the perfect vampire," Mary Ann retorted, suddenly leaning in and biting him playfully on the neck.

"He could hide better in the shadows!" Barbara said, looking at Lunch Box.

"Hey, boss, can you get these two Sheilas to leave me alone?" Lunch Box said, fending Mary Ann off playfully.

"Sorry," Jim replied. "I've got my woman. You're on your own."

"Oh, thanks!" Lunch Box whined playfully. Jim grinned. Lunch Box was a handsome black man with a happy nature, even for a soldier.

With that bit of levity, the evening meal broke up, though there was an extended discussion about black vampires. Those with garbage detail took the garbage out to a place where they could bury it and returned without seeing any bears. They slept soundly, Jim waking only to the sound of the bats returning, knowing it was near morning. Though he could not return to sleep the final half hour allotted for that activity, he contented himself with holding Cecilia closely until the alarm on his watch brought her to wakefulness.

Watching her come awake, he realized again how fortunate he was to have her by his side and kissed her gently. She arched and stretched, smiled at him, and then lay back against the pillows. Her eyes studied him with their usual intensity, as though she needed to satisfy herself each morning that he was actually there. Finally, she touched his hand. He knew this was an invitation for them to begin their day in prayer. Dutifully and willingly, he bowed his head and began the day correctly.

Later, gathered around the heater, he listened as Abe shared from his vast knowledge of the Bible. They were just finishing II Samuel, the life of David, King of Israel. This morning's lesson was from chapter 23, and the account of the thirty mighty men caught and held everyone's attention. From preparing the night before, Jim knew who his favorite was. Benaiah, the son of Johoiada, a valiant man of Kabzeel was his pick.

Benaiah wasn't one of the three or the greatest, but he was right up there at the top, and Jim liked him for that. An experienced soldier knew there was always someone out there who was better, stronger, faster, smarter, or more highly skilled. A good soldier never had aspirations of greatness. Those got in the way sometimes. Good soldiers trained, worked hard, and kept their edge, hoping for the best. If they came out victorious, they lived to fight another day. It seemed to Jim that Benaiah was much like that.

Jim liked the fact that there were thirty mighty men, not just one, or three, or five. Thirty was a good number, and he knew from experience that thirty good men could seem like hundreds. Looking around the circle, he noticed how Abe kept everyone's attention, even Dr. Gregg and his team. For his part, Jim was convinced that these daily Bible studies were keeping everyone sane in the darkness. Danger lurked around every corner, but spirits were still high. Twice, that extra level of sharpness and attention saved them from near tragedy.

After breakfast and Bible study, it was time to take the next stage of their exploration. Excitement ran high as preparations were made. Knowing Jim would lead the night probe, Cecilia was nervous but bravely hid it behind a façade of cheery comments. Jim knew and hugged her, nearly reducing her to instant tears.

Making a night probe was dangerous in any circumstances. Jim chose John and Wade to accompany him on the first dive to map out their route if other divers needed to go down. The water was fifty degrees, and they could stay down at shallow depths in their thermal suits for sixty minutes. Anything more increased the risk significantly. Jim was no fool. He decided they would stay down forty-five minutes, no more. John and Wade nodded soberly at his announcement.

Safety lines were attached to their belts, and another line was attached to Wade, the third diver down. The team could pull them out if anything happened or use the rope to find them if necessary. When it came time to turn back, Wade could use the line to speed up their return, giving them more time for exploration.

Jim grinned at Cecilia and gave her a thumbs up just before turning over in the cold water and disappearing under the shelfstone at the far end. They could see his light for only a brief moment before it disappeared. Jim stayed low, close to the bottom, and watched for any stalactites that might puncture his tank or snag his airline above. Such dangers were always present in a night probe.

Staying low posed no problem here because sand was at the bottom instead of silt. Fins easily stirred up silt, so the divers behind would be in a fog. John could see his brother clearly, and Wade could see them both with his powerful dive lamp. The passage through to the next cave was only sixty feet in length. Jim watched the top of the tunnel just disappear and slowly rose until his head broke the surface. Rising slowly was necessary because one could meet a stalactite, sharp edges smashing the facemask and injuring the eyes.

Using his dive light, he looked around and saw that this cavern was filled with debris from the landslide of 1771 at the far end. There were no less than eight fissures on the inside wall, and from where he was, they could not see any steps, though a pathway did wind around to connect all eight fissures. A natural set of steps, formed by nature, led them up and out of the pool. Once they were free of their tanks, they tied off the safety line and tugged it four times to let the men on the other end know they were feet dry.

Unpacking quickly, they pulled out their shoes and put them on, then carefully checked their gear. All three men knew they were near the entrance to the storage chamber so long hidden. Experience taught them that moments like this were worth savoring. Discoveries of this kind always impressed upon them the wonder of history uncovered. After a moment or two of introspection, Jim motioned for them to follow and rose to his feet. It was time to explore the fissures. Catching grins of anticipation on his friend's faces, he knew they were ready.

In the fourth fissure, they encountered crudely carved steps leading up toward an arched opening. Watermarks went to the second from the top step and stopped. Breathing a sigh of relief, Jim climbed the final two steps and stopped to stare in wonder at the storeroom of the old church. Monks had fashioned a worktable at one side, with shelves above. Books, wrapped in tattered and dried oilcloths, were carefully stacked on the shelves.

On another wall, a set of shelves had been erected. Those shelves were thick and strong and bore old chests and trunks, some with locks still hanging on the hasps. Years of dust covered everything, and the only signs of occupancy were the tiny footprints of rodents, probably rats, none of which seemed fresh. The bones of an owl lay on the worktable above rotted feathers and skin, showing the bird died there.

"In the old days, they kept owls in libraries to keep the mice from chewing papers and books," Jim said quietly. "That fellow must have been trapped in here after the landslide and eventually died of old age." There were a multitude of round pods or pellets containing the indigestible bits of food owls dropped around their feeding grounds. The men studied these for a moment. Interested enough to pull them apart and study what was inside, they huddled over the one they were examining.

"He fed well while he was here," John said, noting the pellets sticking up out of the dust.

"You history types know the weirdest things!" Wade commented.

"There's something odd about that wall section between the bench and this wall," Jim said, pointing.

"I think it might be a door," Wade said, looking at it. The three of them made their way across the floor, staying close to the wall, carefully stepping lightly because of the dust rising from their steps.

"It seems to have stayed dry enough in here," John said hopefully.

Jim gave way to Wade to check the door. After about twenty minutes of studying and trying different things, he found an old rope underneath the work table. Shaking his head, he gently pulled the rope. It broke immediately.

"Nuts!" He said with disgust. He held the broken end for them to see, then turned his light into the hole. "Humph, there seems to be a ring at the other end." He came out from beneath the table with his hair full of spider webs. His wet suit was covered in dust. Brushing the cobwebs away, he stood up. "We'll need a bar with a hook at the end to open this if it still opens," he announced.

"How about a spear from one of the spear guns?" John asked.

"That would work!" Wade said with excitement in his voice. Without comment, John ran out of the cave and returned with a spear that had been removed from his spear gun. He held it out to Wade. Probing the hole carefully, Wade managed to grasp the ring with the barb of the spear and pull slowly but with increasing pressure until, suddenly, the ring gave way. There was the clanking of chains as an ancient windlass turned to open the door.

The windlass was in the next room, and they studied the mechanism with interest for a few moments. "Seems someone was familiar with ships," Wade suggested, straightening after looking over the apparatus. "This is very similar to the windlass used to raise and lower anchors from the early cargo ships. The counterweight was a stone lashed with hemp, one piece passing through the chain. "We'll have to replace all the ropes, perhaps with nylon chord, so that the doors continue to work," Wade instructed. They turned from the windlass to look over the room.

This one was filled, much like the first, with a workbench, shelves, books, shelves with trunks and chests, and a few items resting on the floor along the wall beneath the workbench. Another door beckoned to them beyond that, but Jim ignored it for a time, returning to the open door and beginning to scrape the dust away from the floor.

"What are you looking for?" John asked.

"There were three fissures before the one that led us up to the storeroom. I think each one accessed a separate cave," Jim answered as he continued brushing away dirt. There was nothing to find. He studied the wall and found it only after careful agonizing scrutiny.

"They closed the wall!" He said suddenly. "They used mud, like a stucco coating, over stacked rocks!" His knife flaked away the coating to reveal the rocks. Wade busied himself with the ring for the next door while Jim pushed the rocks out to tumble into the next room. He couldn't see them land, but he could hear them. The last room that had been so carefully sealed up proved similar, though it was much larger, a little higher than the others, obviously the recipient of newer artifacts, and filled with treasures from the past that had little to do with the church.

Looking along the wall of that cave, Jim noticed light shining through a narrow hole about sixty feet down. He carefully made his way to a head-high fissure through which he could see the lights in the cave that held their camp. He saw FM standing at the shelfstone, loosely holding the safety rope in his hand, deep in discussion with Cecilia.

Jim keyed his headset and spoke to FM. "Hey, would you mind

talking a little less to my wife and paying a little more attention to your job, FM?" he said. "Hey Zeke, what are you entering into that computer?" he said to Zeke.

"I'm the one who is supposed to be watching!" Zeke said. "How did you know what I was doing?" he asked, mystified.

"He's just guessing." Sparks said, not taking his eyes off his work.

"I heard that, Mr. Sparks. Are you about done rigging that explosive?" Sparks looked up. Jim thrust his arm through the hole and waved, and everyone laughed.

"Jeeze, boss, I thought you'd become clairvoyant or something!" FM complained. "Now I'm disillusioned! I was ready to believe you were in tune with some great spirit or something!" Everyone laughed at FM's expression, and Jim found himself laughing too.

"Well, get your disillusioned rear over here and help Sparks make this hole bigger," Jim said lightly.

"Uh, Shep, did you notice the underground river flowing right beneath your arm?" FM asked. "That water's cold!"

"We'll need a bridge, then," Jim said through the hole.

"Don't ya just love the way he says that?" FM asked no one in particular. "Like we're just gonna pull one out of our pockets and 'hey presto!'" there's your instant bridge, boss!"

"I expect you to do a little less talkin' and a little more workin', Mr. Miller!" Jim said through the hole in the wall. FM threw up his hands and stalked off in a mock temper to find the makings of a bridge.

Expecting the need, Jim knew that several of the men carried a little extra weight in inflatable rafts that could be used to mount a lightweight yet strong bridge over which people could traverse the underground river safely. FM, of course, knew all this but liked playing the fool and getting people to laugh at his antics.

Marines and Navy SEALS are trained to adapt, and in a relatively short period, a much larger opening appeared as parts of the cave wall burst and crumbled into the underground stream. Using two rafts, they formed a pier on either side of the river, and the third raft served to ferry people from one side to the other.

Dr. Gregg was the first to arrive, followed by the members of his team and Jim's unit, who had the equipment to provide light in the caves for exploration, cataloging, and study. Jim's men would help, lifting heavy artifacts and holding them patiently while the experts studied them, photographed them, and cataloged them.

Jim and Cecilia moved among the artifacts and records with great respect, learning what they could. Dr. Gregg already agreed that the church's treasures would be turned over to the Vatican out of respect for that worthy organization. The Vatican, in return, would allow some pieces to be displayed in various museums and provide a healthy finder's fee of ten percent of the total value of the find. However, many artifacts did not rightfully belong to the church.

Sharky stood looking around silently, and Jim could almost see the money signs in his eyes as he guessed the value of their find. Finn was quick with figures and knew the company's operating costs better than anyone else but Jim, John, and Wade. In the last room, they uncovered treasures from civilizations that had influenced and plagued the Diocese of Belluno-Feltre. It was here that history became the real truth, primary sources describing the events of that particular time. To Jim, it was like looking through a mirror into a time past and seeing it unfold through the eyes of those who lived it.

Yet the church's prejudice against particular groups was also evident. Many Illuminati things were located in the corner of one of the storerooms. Books confiscated from people during the Reformation lined shelves; some of them were obviously respected and cared for, and others were left to rot through time. Treasures were seized from families that had been excommunicated, and church officials confiscated their lands, houses, servants, cattle, and worldly goods.

Cameras flashed, and people talked in low, muted voices, echoing around the cavern, making it difficult to hear any conversation unless you were right in the middle. Laptop keyboards clicked as notes were entered and photos downloaded and labeled. Groups broke at various intervals to eat or drink, but they were hurried breaks. Only at dinner time did the entire group stop and rest.

The crew stayed beneath the ground for five days until Dr. Gregg was satisfied that every piece of history had been examined, photographed, and cataloged. Hands were raw from constant washings in the cold water. Shoulders and backs were weary from lifting heavy chests, books, and other artifacts about. Despite those discomforts great finds had been made.

That night, they sat around the heater and ate quietly. Dr. Gregg was the only one who seemed inclined to talk. He seemed awed that a diary written by a German archaeologist was the catalyst that led to the discovery of this treasure trove of historical artifacts. No one really knew who Johann Honecker was or what he had ever done. Yet his words inspired their venture. History, if one took the time to study it, was filled with what some called random events, and those who knew better called God's purpose.

In the morning, Jim allowed everyone to rise at their leisure. Being among the first to rise, he enjoyed a sumptuous breakfast with his wife and sat talking to Alistair, John, and Wade about some of the things they'd discovered. The discussion was intense because Alistair didn't want to turn some of those things over to the church. As people rose and joined them, the discussion continued far into the morning until a consensus was reached.

Before bringing the church to this place, certain items would be removed and stored at the estate and studied more carefully. Those from the Illuminati and Reformation would not be turned over to the church. Everything else, including the treasures confiscated from families excommunicated, would remain in the church's possession.

That day, they moved those items they were claiming out. Teams would return with proper equipment to move them up and out of the cave safely. Once that task was finished, they gathered around the campsite once more and spent a day resting. To many, one day didn't seem like enough, but it was soon over, and they slept one last night in that part of the caves.

Tired and satisfied, everyone began the arduous climb to the cave entrance in the morning, following Smitty and his GPS unit. Everyone was in one large group, no longer needing the safety lines and distance. Wade talked to Jim and Dr. Gregg about using a suspended cable and a basket to bring things up to the surface while they endured their second day of hiking toward the entrance. FM and Inchworm made comments and suggestions while everyone else listened.

Jim listened to the conversations going on behind him as he followed Smitty. The constant clinking of climbing gear, the hollow thudding of footsteps, and the creaking of leather and cloth against cloth all seemed to melt together with the other sounds of the cave. No one lagged, and Jim kept the pace easy. This was an uphill climb, and he didn't care how physically fit he was; the climb took a toll on everyone, including himself.

CHAPTER 21

Three days later, they finally arrived at the cave entrance, pausing there long enough to allow their eyes to adjust to the bright afternoon sunlight. It was a festive party that hefted the gear and packs and made their way back to Villa Orvieto. Even the steep climb down the Marmolada did not discourage those already bone-weary. Everyone was looking forward to sleeping in a bed and eating something other than camp fare.

Jim listened to the talk around him, his mind racing as he considered the logistics of moving everything down to the villa. He knew that Wade and others were also contemplating the task ahead. Again, he marveled at man's ability to adapt to any environment and create what necessity demanded.

Standing next to a radiant Rosa, Andrea and Gwyneth met them at the door. Most of the staff and the rest of the crew were there, too. Jim's team had the discipline to clean and store everything before breaking away to shower and prepare for dinner. Some suggested that Jim join Cecilia rather than working at putting everything away, to which he merely smiled and kept working. He would never ask his men to do something he was unwilling to do himself. They knew why he did the work and respected him for it.

Dinner proved to be a celebration feast, and the kitchen staff chased Abe and his crew out when they offered to help, telling them they were part of the celebration. Jim sat next to Cecilia, listening politely as Dr. Gregg recounted their trek through the caves and the discovery of the storeroom to Mrs. Shepherd. Dr. Gregg was an amazingly interesting storyteller, a skill honed to perfection after years of teaching, and everyone enjoyed hearing it. Jim saw the entire expedition through the eyes of his elder friend.

"There's romance in the air!" Cecilia whispered into Jim's ear toward the end of the meal. Her eyes were drifting between Dr. Gregg and Gwyneth and Andrea and Rosa. Jim followed them and smiled lopsidedly.

"With you nearby, there's always romance!" Jim replied in a whisper, kissing the lobe of her ear. "Are you speaking of Andrea and Rosa or Mother and Dr. Gregg?" He added after the kiss.

"You never miss anything!" Cecilia said that secret smile she had when she knew her husband was getting intimate. "Most men wouldn't notice that kind of thing." She added.

It was true. Jim observed people and had learned early to read their body language. Now, it was second nature to him, and he missed little when it came to reading how people were reacting to one another. Dr. Gregg was definitely interested in his mother, and she returned the interest. Rosa had her eyes and heart set on Andrea, and Jim could see that Andrea felt much the same for her. It would be interesting to watch the chase.

Jim didn't get to think much about that since Cecilia managed to capture and hold his undivided attention for the remainder of the evening. In the morning, he lay beside her, watching the sunlight play through the cracks in the curtains and dance in the air of his bedroom. He was in love, deeply committed, and knew everything about his life had changed. Realizing that his days as a soldier were ending, he found that he didn't regret the change. He rose, showered, and brought coffee to Cecilia, then waited to escort her to breakfast. The day would be busy, but as long as she was at his side, he knew the day was somehow better. Knowing God was like that. Just knowing

He would be there, watching, loving, caring, made every day different and better. His relationship with Cecilia taught him that.

At breakfast, the discussion centered on the logistics of bringing the treasures from the storeroom to the surface. Since keeping a find of this magnitude secret was virtually impossible, the teams decided to invite the Vatican to send a representative or a team to accompany them into the cave for the extraction efforts. Jim made the call the morning after the first artifacts reached the light of day, calling from his spacious and comfortable office in the villa.

Not knowing the proper procedure, he called one of the rescued Cardinals in residence and, after fencing with a secretary, spoke to the aged man. Three days later no less than all six Cardinals rescued from the burning yacht and an entire team of experts arrived from the Vatican to take residence at the villa, local hotels, and the local monastery.

News spread, and by the following day, the little village of Alleghe was bursting at the seams with reporters. During the days of recovery, expectations and excitement ran high. Eventually, the entire collection from the long-lost treasury was exhibited to the Cardinals and their experts in the villa before packaging and shipping preparations began.

For Dr. Gregg, this was yet another astounding accomplishment in his career, and Jim and the crew were more than happy to let him have the limelight. He mentioned his three successes with the *Bring It Up* crew and hoped to work with them again on his next venture. Claiming that the crew of *Bring It Up* had what it took to succeed in any such venture, he was quite adamant and sincere. When reporters asked what the next adventure might be, he held a finger up to the side of his nose and winked at them.

"That is a secret for later." Was all he would say on the subject.

Kalil stood at the rear of the crowd and watched. Whoever these men were, they did not appear to be a threat to him. Soldiers did not bring their wives and mothers into battle. He knew of the plans to build the resort and watched the work at the vineyard. It was all serious work and moving along at a pace that astounded him. Only Paul Klaus had developed things this quickly. Secretly, he was pleased they found such treasures. It would be interesting to steal them when his terrorists raided the Vatican. The obvious military nature of this team had bothered him, but he was slowly changing his mind about them.

Convinced of his safety, Kalil turned away from the crowd and walked to his rented Mercedes. He did not notice the camera cleverly concealed on the stone fence that followed him. At his desk, hidden behind the bookshelves in the library, Zeke watched Kalil with interest. They now had photos and a paper trail to follow with the rented Mercedes. Watching the man drive away Zeke noticed another car pull out and follow. Working quickly with his camera, he got photos of the men in the car. Kalil was being very careful.

Plans to move the artifacts to the Vatican took a few weeks to organize. Finally, however, the final crate was loaded on a truck, and the convoy set off toward Agordo and the winding road down through forest and mountain to Vatican City. Jim breathed a sigh of relief and gave everyone a few days' break.

Taking advantage of the time, he and Cecilia explored much of the Val Cordevole, taking in the sights and visiting towns and villages. Occasionally, they went on foot, but most of the time, they enjoyed the journeys in the Jeep. Caprile, Cencenighe, Canale D'Agordo, Caviola, and Falcade were nestled along a winding forest-lined road that ran between the Marmolada and Pale D' S. Martino to the east and west, and Mount Civetta to the north. Each town or village seemed to suddenly appear out of the forest, as if by magic, seemingly untouched by the march of time.

Local handicrafts were very much alive in these towns and villages. Most were based on woodcarving and ironwork, activities that left their mark on place names such as Fusine (kiln) and Forno (furnace). The sounds of artisans sawing, drilling, chiseling, and hammering in their workshops were so common that even the deer and fox lingered around the village boundaries undisturbed.

They hiked up to Mount Pelmo to see the footprints of dinosaurs set in a natural museum on a large slab of rock fallen from the side of the mountain. There were paintings and statues to see everywhere they went, many of St. Christopher. It was a refreshing time for the entire team, and Jim returned each day to hear stories from the men on their visits, skiing, and climbing experiences. At last, however, the time came for the team to brainstorm over the intelligence Zeke and Sparks gathered over the past days.

Once the entire team was gathered at the conference table hidden behind the library shelves, Jim called for quiet. If anyone was surprised at the instant silence, no one said anything. Jim grinned at the men and spoke.

"I'm just going to let Zeke cover himself with accolades for his intelligence gathering," Jim teased.

"Gawd! He's already insufferable!" Lunch Box moaned quietly.

"I'm going to pretend you didn't say that, Aussie!" Zeke said with a deadpan expression on his face. "As our esteemed Captain says, I have indeed gathered a great deal of intelligence." Zeke got serious as the information he had appeared on the computer screens in front of the men.

"Kalil is working for the Committee of 5 in a bold three-pronged attack. He is planning to rob the Vatican and burn the library!" Zeke announced dramatically. Everyone paused for a moment before Sean spoke first.

"He'll have every police agency in the country, in the world, looking for him!" Sean said.

"Exactly!" Zeke said. "That is indeed his plan. Though his tame terrorist cell doesn't know it, they are scheduled to be sold down the river so that the police agencies can chase them down and catch them. None of them know this, and only one other person in the entire crew knows the full plan. Kalil is playing this very close to the vest but carefully planning each step. This is one canny planner!"

"He wants all eyes turned toward the Vatican!" Jim said, putting it together. "So what are the primary and secondary targets?"

"As usual, our Captain is first to see the whole picture!" Zeke said.

"Suck up!" Sparks commented to his brother.

"A promotion would be nice," Zeke replied without rancor. "As I was saying, before the name-calling got out of hand, the captain is correct. "The primary target is a series of oil pumping platforms in the Mediterranean. The Committee of 5 intends to shut down oil production in the Mediterranean. Their secondary target involves the oil rigs in the Atlantic, starting with those in the Gulf."

"Do they have the troops and technology to carry out this plan?" Jim asked.

"Not really, but their plan might have worked if no one was wise to it." Zeke replied. "They intend to plant charges on the platforms under cover of darkness, two platforms each night, until they are all set. Then, from a central location, they will detonate the charges. They plan to have everything in place for the night of the Vatican gig." Zeke added.

"And what does the Committee of 5 get out of this?" Jim asked.

"They're environmental terrorists with an agenda. They corporately own about a million acres of land along the shores of the Mediterranean, most near the oil pumping stations. Their idea is for the fallout from the disasters to make pumping oil illegal in the Mediterranean, and while property values are down, to purchase as many properties as possible, giving them a monopoly of oceanfront property. They want to become major players in international politics around the Med."

"Let me guess," Jim said, sitting back in his chair and looking intently at Zeke. "You had a look at their computer files?" He asked.

"Once again, you go to the head of the class, Jim. Uncle Zeke is watching you! How am I doing on that promotion before anyone else comments." Zeke said, looking ferociously at his brother and sticking out his tongue. Jim paused, looking from Zeke to Bill and around the table, making everyone wait for his answer.

"You almost made it to Ensign," Jim said with a straight face.

"I am an Ensign!" Zeke said.

"Not if you keep dragging this report out, you're not!" Jim said with a laugh. "Besides, most of our Ensigns know not to stick out their tongues." Cecilia stuck her tongue out at Jim immediately. "Perhaps not," Jim said with a mock sigh. "I'll have to see if Barbara and Mary Ann can give charm lessons."

Everyone laughed, as Jim intended. He understood the need for comic relief in the midst of dealing with terrorists. Comic relief was welcome and relieved the building tension in the room as the bad news unfolded. This plan was slick, and but for the intervention of God, it might very well have been carried out, including the death of many workers on the platforms at sea.

"Yes, I did look at their most private computer files," Zeke admitted.

"How the devil do you do that?" FM asked.

"If you're connected to the Internet, I can, given time, unearth everything you have stored in files," Zeke said easily.

"Even encrypted files?" John asked with interest.

"Yes," Zeke replied without inflection. He acted as though it were an everyday occurrence, simplicity in itself. Perhaps for him, it was.

"Most people use codes that are familiar to them. I can usually find a password by using a combination of birthdays, anniversaries, addresses, and even phone numbers. Only Nadia Duse and Jacques Piaf use unusual passwords. However, I've written a program that lists letters and numbers used most at startup, and then analyzing them, I can usually find the password within a few hours." Zeke added by way of explanation.

Jim allowed Zeke to finish his explanation because all the men needed to know facts like that. He knew about the program Zeke wrote because they often used it to break into files in government systems. Once Zeke had finished his explanation, he picked up the report again.

"This group really wants political clout, and they know the fastest way to gain that is to control something beneficial to the government or be a major financial power. This guarantees them both. It's really quite brilliant. Twisted, but brilliant. The one thing I haven't mentioned yet is that they control the nanotechnology used to clean up oil spills. It's a German company, very advanced in the industry, but under the thumb of Nadia Duse."

CHAPTER 22

"**S**o, they basically come out of this smelling like roses," C.G. snarled.

"If nobody is the wiser," Zeke said with a smirk.

"Which group is doing what?" Wade asked.

"Jung is leading the group assigned to the Vatican. He's found a defrocked dissident priest to help with layout and security. The priest used to work in the library. His leftist views made front-page news a few years ago when he hid a terrorist who tried to kill the Pope. The Pope was not amused," Zeke commented sarcastically. "Nor was the defrocked priest quiet in his denunciations of the Vatican."

"Von Humbolt's group will hit the oil platforms in the east Mediterranean, Kohl's group the platforms on the north shores, and Adenauer's group the platforms along the south shores. They're being trained carefully in the use of cortex underwater. Some of them are getting crash courses in electronics too because the command for the detonation will be hardwired into the electrical system controlled by the deck's computer system," Zeke leaned back.

"Ideas?" Jim asked quietly after a pause.

"We're going to be spread pretty thin protecting the oil rigs," John mused. He'd been busy writing while Zeke was talking. Jim thought he might have devised a plan for saving them already but didn't press him. He merely nodded and waited.

"We can save the rigs if we use both boats and the chopper," John said confidently. "We'll need outside help at the Vatican," he added thoughtfully. For a moment, everyone considered his words.

"Give us the details," Jim suggested, his pencil poised to write.

"Dorf's team takes the south platforms using the chopper. My team takes the north platforms, using the tug. Sean's team takes the east platforms using the yacht. With the tug we park near the center and use the HSB to cover ground both ways. The yacht can tow the Rigid Raider and do the same," he offered.

"Uh, Commander?" FM spoke apologetically, sheepishly raising his hand.

"Yes, FM," John answered.

"We call it dropping anchor, not parking," FM corrected with a straight face.

"It's the same thing, though, isn't it?" John asked innocently.

"You bein' a Marine and all, I just thought you might not know," FM replied, waving his hand negligently.

"Hey! Once I'm feet wet, I leave that nautical jargon to the navy geeks," John replied, as if serious. Everyone laughed, once again welcoming the release of the tension. "Okay, for you Navy guys, we drop anchor!" John said, making quotation marks in the air as he said, "Drop anchor."

"Who do you have in mind to help with the Vatican?" Jim asked. "That is, if they allow us to suggest help and if they believe us." The six Cardinals they'd rescued might help with that.

"Oh, they'll believe us. We just gave them a major treasure trove they thought was lost. I'm sure we can convince them with our evidence that they will need help," John replied. "You might rope Dr. Gregg in to help you with that," he added thoughtfully.

"And the help?" Jim asked.

"I think we should go to Admiral Runion for that. A SEAL team could probably handle everything for us. I'd opt for a Marine, but we're so important. All the Marines are probably tied up fighting somewhere," John's facetious remark brought gales of laughter.

"One marine as opposed to a SEAL team?" Sparks said with a snort.

"It works out to about the same thing," John said, looking at his fingernails as if distracted. Again, Jim appreciated John's ability to bring humor into the situation.

"Yes, but the enemy might have a young woman, and then the Marine would be helpless!" Cecilia said quietly into the ending laughter. The room roared as she patted Jim's shoulder, and he blushed.

"Too bloody right by half!" Lee Roy Brown guffawed, slapping the table. "I think you should opt for a GIGN team for the Vatican," he added as the laughter died. Jim listened as he smiled at the distracting comments. That had been a good idea.

"Reasons?" Jim spoke quietly, his voice even, looking at him expectantly.

"These Committee of Five blokes are in France, right? Let the Frogs handle the bloody wankers at the Vatican. They'll never connect them to us. Besides, GIGN units are well-trained, and they work well with others. They did for SAS," Lunch Box replied.

"Bloody! Wankers, mate?" Sean raised an eyebrow, elbowing Lunch Box. "There's a lady present!"

"Sorry, Cecilia," Lunch Box said earnestly. She knew the men rarely used bad language and was a bit surprised to hear it coming from Lunch Box, but she understood the intensity of the moment. She smiled.

"Wankers describes them quite nicely, Lunch Box," she said. "Apology accepted for the other expletive."

"Oh great!" Jim sighed, shaking his head. "Now she's talking like you Aussies!"

"Aussie, Aussie, Aussie, ooh rah!" the four former Australian SAS men shouted as one, raising a fist in the air.

"Getting back to business, I think your idea works, Lunch Box," Jim said quietly, grinning at the Australians. "I'll get on to Sir Edward and ask him to invite GIGN to the party. The rest of the plan is good too, though there is a high element of risk in separating the teams."

"Did you have something in mind for my team?" Jim asked his brother with a slight smile. He thought he knew what John would suggest, but this was his idea, so he let him explain it fully.

"You gentlemen get an all-expenses-paid trip to the Vatican!" John said. We have to make sure that none of the cells can communicate with Kalil. I'm sure he'll be close by."

For a long moment, he looked at his men, his face deadly serious, his eyes searching each of them. Others in the room might have felt some discomfort, but not one of the team members felt any. Jim read in their eyes the resolve to go ahead, and at last, he nodded.

"We leave at three hundred hours," Jim stated, carefully stacking the papers in front of him with deliberate motions. "Get everything packed. Only the four-man units go."

"Aye, Captain!" Wade said, snapping off a salute as he rose to his feet. The other men followed suit, some nodding and some saluting. Jim grinned at them as they exited the conference room to get their gear together. As the last man left, he silently prayed for their return.

Cecilia waited for her husband to rise and kissed him lightly on the cheek. He cocked one eyebrow at her, and his stormy green eyes softened as they gazed into her intent hazel eyes. Today they were more blue than green because of the top she was wearing. She smiled shyly, a tiny dimple appearing on her cheek.

"Just letting you know I approve," she said simply, raising her shoulders in a shrug and then leaning forward to kiss him lightly on the lips. "Do come back in one piece!" she added, tugging at his fingers. He grinned down at her.

"I intend to," he said. As he turned away, she saw in his eyes that look that sometimes frightened her and always excited her. He was in his "soldier mode," and she knew better than to try to distract him. Mentally, he was preparing himself for the battle to come and to lead his men to victory with extreme prejudice. At that moment, she felt that same prejudice. These men were lawless villains of the worst sort, anarchists, most of whom made their point by killing innocent women and children. She knew their sort intimately. Even worse, one of them was planning to betray his own men.

Watching Jim flow across the floor, his footsteps smooth and somehow menacing, like those of a stalking tiger, she shivered slightly. She was married to a very dangerous man. Smiling slightly, she gathered her things and followed Jim out of the library. As she strolled down the curving steps in the main foyer, he was already out of sight.

Sixteen men quietly gathered their gear into black waterproof bags in the weapons room hidden so carefully beneath the old barn. Jim watched Zeke, Frank, and John squatting to his left as they checked each weapon before it went into the bag. They were hardened professionals and knew the drill. Their focus was intense as they checked and rechecked everything. Life depended often on a soldier's detailed preparations. Like him, none of them missed a detail.

Jim's team would travel in two vehicles. Jim put his bag in the back of his Rubicon, and Frank Miller crowded in next to him to add his equipment. Besides Jim's white Rubicon was Zeke's black Hummer H-2. He and Smitty already had their gear stowed. Together, they checked under the hood before leaving the vehicles and heading into the house. Each team would relax until it was time to go.

Behind the villa was a wooded area next to a stream. Among the trees were hammocks, and Jim went there after a light lunch to rest. He took a book written by one of his favorite authors, and he simply sat and read for a while. Then he napped until the dinner call. Opening his eyes at the sound of the bell, he sighed, stretched slowly, and sat up, swinging his legs over the hammock's edge and allowing gravity to do the rest.

Giacomo Pirandello, the second chef, loved to bang away at the triangle outside the kitchen door. It was his way of calling everyone in. Reminding him of the many American western movies he loved so much, he twirled the metal rod around and around with gusto. Satisfied that no one could miss the noise, he hung the rod behind the triangle and returned to work.

Salvatore Ariosto was head chef at Villa Orvieto, and he glanced up as Giacomo returned. He grinned at his friend. "It is well that I was not baking the soufflé, no?" he exclaimed, putting his hands up to either side of his head as though protecting his ears from loud noises. Once in the past, the bell ringing had collapsed a perfect soufflé.

"Si!" Giacomo nodded vigorously. "Old people, they become so aggravated when things do not go as they planned!" It took Salvatore a moment to realize that Giacomo was talking about him. He flipped a spoon of peas at his partner, and they laughed. Both loved working for Senior Orvieto and his polite friends from America. Their antics were frowned upon by the housekeeper, who bent to pick up the offending peas from the floor with a stern look. The two men winked at each other and laughed again. As the housekeeper threw the peas away, she smiled at the two men.

For the team, the mood at dinner was anything but somber and reflective. They were soldiers riding the crest of the wave of perfection, trained, skilled, and ready. None of them really thought much about the upcoming mission. Instead, their thoughts focused on enjoying the company and a fine meal before an early self-enforced curfew. Each of them knew the importance of having good memories to take into the bleakness of battle. It helped bring balance.

Bill Franklin sat between Windy and Cuss and watched and listened from his end of the huge dinner table. It was, he reflected, the first time in many years that he felt a part of something, alive, fulfilled. There was a sense of purpose to his life. He owed much of what he felt to these men who surrounded him and the soldiers he worked with. Most of them treated him with respect, a fact that continually amazed him. They knew about his past, the alcohol abuse, and yet they treated him as though he were an essential part of their work. No one ever mentioned his past or even looked at him as if he were somehow damaged. They respected him!

He knew they were about to venture out on a dangerous mission. Coming from a background of a lifetime of service in the Navy, he was familiar with such men. This team was like others he had seen. Like all human institutions, the Navy turned out good men and men who fell far short of the expectations and standards set by tradition and current command. His experience with such men was extensive.

Some of the SEAL teams he'd been around had been rude, mean-spirited, and demanding. Most of them were like this team.

Jim's unit was tight. All the men trusted each other. And though they were dangerous and deadly soldiers, they were also men of principle. Their code was the highest code, and they followed it carefully. Saying that they believed in God and Country meant something to these men. They believed in God and followed the basic Judeo-Christian principles of that belief. When it came to their country, it was simply patriotism.

But there was something more. The four Australians were part of the team, and though their allegiance was to their native land, they were a part of what this team was doing, too. No less patriots, they were serving a higher cause. Bill knew that as long as terrorists haunted society, men like this would stand against them, and he was pleased to be part of that.

After a fine meal, the team rested in various parts of the villa for an hour or so. Some gathered around the billiards tables in the game room, while others sat at leisure in the library reading. Still, others sat around small tables playing various games. The usual cries of success, frustration, and laughter at both echoed in the house's halls. At seven o'clock, they rose and turned in for a short night of rest.

CHAPTER 23

FM sat quietly as Jim drove the winding mountain roads toward Venice. Heading for the Vatican meant going in the opposite direction of the other teams. They were going to Venice. Frank thought Italy was a beautiful country with a lot of old-fashioned charm. He would have preferred to talk, but Jim, he knew, was one who liked quiet and wanted to think. He contented himself with looking at the scenery and letting Jim get on with his thoughts.

Zeke and Smitty were chatting away in the Hummer. Their talk was primarily technical, and most of the journey was taken up with a discussion about surveillance equipment and the possibilities for improvement. They were practical geniuses, and their talk centered on things that could be done more than on dreaming and impractical ideas. Zeke drove, and Smitty scribbled on a scratch pad, drawing plans and schematics and making cryptic notes that only he could decipher.

Jim's team arrived at the Vatican using the simple cover of tourists, entering with a large group and breaking away only after following the group for about half an hour. The Cardinal Jim remembered most fondly from their former rescue met them in a hallway near the library as they moved away from the group. No one noticed the four men disappear from the main group.

The elderly cardinal walked slowly and listened carefully as Jim described the impending danger to the Vatican treasures. If he was alarmed it didn't show. The name of the defrocked priest drew an irritated tisk from him, nothing more. He led them to the security chief, who introduced them to the GIGN team that arrived earlier that morning.

Jim immediately liked Francois Beaumont, Captain of the GIGN team. Looking over the men, Jim decided they were on a par with his own. Soldiers were quick to see the strengths and weaknesses of other military groups. Since everyone on Jim's team spoke fluent French, they conversed in that language for some minutes before the Italian security chief cleared his throat. The Vatican's police force would be called upon to help, and it was their turn.

He led them into a conference room and listened as Jim outlined the upcoming attack. Gustav Jung and his terrorist cell were not to be taken lightly. Jim shared what he knew about the terrorist, and the GIGN Captain nodded in appreciation. They had little on the terrorist but had been briefed about the American unit and their information. His expectations had been high, and Jim did not disappoint.

The Vatican, of course, had its own crack troops. Jim knew a little about their training and deferred to the Italian security chief in a manner that promoted an atmosphere of cooperation. The GIGN Captain watched and learned. Twice before, he worked with the Vatican security forces, and both times, he found them proud and uncooperative. The American seemed to be an expert diplomat and an able leader. *Perhaps it is how he defers and listens, even when the ideas do not fit his plans. He is a canny one. And he is not arrogant, like many American officers I have met, though perhaps he has more reason to show pride than others. I can learn from this man, and in the end, I think my unit will be the better for it.*

Of course, he knew his own country's opinion about America and Americans. Experience taught him that his country was wrong, very wrong, when it came to judging America and its people. Lately, his work had been with the very people his own country welcomed with open arms, a people who followed a religion of blood and hatred.

The Islamists were quick to cry for peace, but many of them wrote peace in blood and preached sedition and prejudice. Like many such people on earth, they were as quick to kill each other as opposing enemies and adherents to different religions. Beaumont was almost ashamed to admit he was a patriot of his country. Yet deep down in his heart, he knew his patriotism would never wane.

Jim smiled across at him as if reading his mind and sensing his discomfort. "I'm honored to work with you, Captain," he said sincerely.

"A friend of mine in Solenzara said you were an honorable man and that I might learn much working with you," Captain Beaumont said quietly. "He met you once and remembers that meeting with fondness. You made quite an impression and a good friend."

"You embarrass me," Jim said in perfect idiomatic French, moving smoothly into that language. "It is I who met an honorable and courageous man. Governments often make tragic errors, but it is men who must live together despite them. Is this not so?"

Zeke grinned at his Captain while FM and Smitty nodded their approval. He'd gone to the heart of the issue. Captain Beaumont noted their interchange and relaxed even more. These Americans both respected and appreciated his team. Jim's following words cemented their friendship and mutual trust.

"Gustav Jung must never know that Americans played a part in this. I am purposely turning the attention of the Committee of Five toward the GIGN. When the time comes, and we take them down, I will repay your trust by inviting you to spring the trap. It is your country that will try them, after all. GIGN will gain much honor, no?" he said.

"So, you will not carve the notches into your pistol?" Beaumont asked with a grin. "So many claim that is what Americans do best."

"Some do," Jim replied seriously. "Many in my country shame me by their actions and prejudice. You and I are patriots, and there is no room for us to seek glory, and the men who serve here at the Vatican are much the same." He included them with a wave of his hand. "My own country would probably welcome this committee of five with open arms and hail them as political heroes. But we will see that they are properly punished for their crimes, not for us, but for the sake of our countries and peace."

"Yes, it is as you say," Beaumont agreed quietly, nodding. "Let us proceed."

Jim outlined the plan for the three-pronged attack planned against the Vatican. Jung divided his men into three groups with special assignments, attacking from three different sides. Two groups would cross the wall while the other would enter through St. Peter's Square.

They were communicating with encrypted radios, hand-held units, with one hundred and twenty channels to choose from. Jim knew the frequency they would use and the pattern for changing frequencies. He did not explain how he knew, but no one doubted his word. Cell phones would serve as backup communication. He pointed at Zeke. "This is where our computer expert asserts his genius." Zeke had been waiting for his chance to speak.

"This disk," Zeke explained, holding up one of several computer disks, "works with your cell phone tower relays. Anyone using a cell phone will have to dial three fours to use his phone."

"I have heard of this technology," Beaumont and Security Chief Schumacher said in unison.

"We can effectively monitor their radio frequencies as well and interrupt their signal so that they cannot communicate with each other by radio," Zeke added.

Chief Schumacher was an old campaigner with sixteen years under his belt as head of the Corpo della Guardia Svizzera Pontificia. The Swiss Guard prided itself on keeping the Pope safe. Jim knew they were conversant with modern military strategy and techniques and dedicated and well-trained soldiers. He also knew they were not on the same level as the GIGN troops or his own. Chief Schumacher also knew this.

"I will place myself and my forces in your capable hands, Captain Shepherd and Captain Beaumont," he stated. Both soldiers nodded. Jim's next words cemented his relationship with Chief Schumacher and Captain Beaumont.

"We will share command, sir. It will be my honor," he said.

Beaumont received his next surprise when Jim turned to him and asked him how he saw the mission. Captain Beaumont considered his options for a long moment, then outlined a plan of action that seemed suited for their needs. Jim listened carefully and nodded in approval. Twice, he made a suggestion. Beaumont realized that Captain Shepherd had all the qualifications necessary for anti-terrorism. The tips were beneficial. Chief Schumacher knew the terrain and pointed out important obstacles and danger zones. Within half an hour, the three men had outlined a plan.

"May I suggest that your men wear the same uniforms as the GIGN?" Beaumont required after a pause as the two men considered their plan. "That way, no one will know they are Americans. All four of you speak fluent French. You, especially, speak the language like a native."

"That works for me," Jim agreed. "Two of my men are the technical wizards for this setup. Frank Miller and I would like the opportunity to be in on the actual takedown."

Hours later, waiting in the cramped recess of an underground drainage system, Jim and Frank exchanged looks. They were part of a five-man team, crouching in the darkness, remaining silent. Jim eased his H&K MP5SD forward an inch and nodded once to FM. In turn, FM raised a thumb to signal that he was mentally and physically ready. The other three GIGN members nodded that they, too, were ready.

Because it was a night operation the GIGN provided black uniforms to go over the body armor Jim and his team brought. Captain Beaumont was interested in the Kevlar leggings and sleeves, something his men didn't have issued. Their gloves were different, too, but gloves were more a matter of preference. The black masks were tight and uncomfortable.

FM put a hand down to check his Beretta M92F 9-mm pistol. The strap was buckled across his hammer to keep the gun in the holster until he needed it. With the H&K MP5SD, he didn't think he would need it, but it was good to know it was there. The pistol was for a last resort and close in fighting. Like the other men squatting in the damp drainage tunnel, he wondered when the action would start.

"I have movement over the west wall," Zeke's voice suddenly sounded in his ear. Zeke was in the Vatican's command center, communicating with everyone.

"I have movement over the north wall." That was the voice of one of Beaumont's men watching that entrance point. Then Smitty's voice sounded.

"Enemy movement in St. Peter's Square!"

It was time. Jim moved silently to a spot where he could look above at the grill. Footsteps, very quiet yet audible, came close and then passed over the grate. Seconds later, Jim led his men up and out of the tunnel. They were behind their enemy and had the element of surprise. Helpful also was the fact that those audible footsteps shielded their own.

Cat-like, the men padded after the terrorists. When they were in position, Jim suddenly leaped forward and put his MP5SD against the back of Jung's head.

"Do not move, do not make a sound, or you and your men will die. You understand, no?" Jim commanded in a whisper.

Jung turned his head just enough to see that his men were indeed in the same predicament. He saw the GIGN insignia on the uniforms, and his eyes widened.

What the hell are the French doing here? How did they get onto the Committee of Five and our plans? Damn! I wonder if Kalil is compromised! He didn't want to think of the alternative that Kalil had sold them out. Immediately, he discarded that idea. Kalil would have waited until after they burned the library to sell them out if he were going to do that.

Jim quickly used enforcement ties and a gag to restrain his prisoner. He keyed his microphone. "Unit one has Leader Jung in custody." That, he saw, rocked Jung, the man looking at him with fear and curiosity.

"Roger that, unit one. Unit two has a lieutenant and followers in custody. Explosives neutralized," Beaumont's voice replied.

"Unit three has the main group in sight. They are waiting for the signal to attack," one of Beaumont's men reported.

"We will join you in a moment," Beaumont said in reply.

Jim turned Jung and his men over to the Swiss Guard without comment and hurried with his men to join Beaumont in taking down the main group. Jung's plan was for them to launch an all-out attack on the night watch while the other groups set the explosives and went to work on stealing the most valuable objects. As plans go, it was daring and might have worked successfully.

Moving carefully, Beaumont's men surrounded them in the darkness and, at his signal, suddenly rose. Each GIGN man had his laser sight pinpointing a kill shot on one of the terrorists. Confusion reigned for a moment among the terrorists, then one of them raised his gun. The soldier covering him dropped him with a three-round blast through the head. In the silence that followed, Beaumont spoke.

"No one else has to die tonight. Drop your weapons, step back with your hands on your head, your fingers interlaced," he repeated the command in Spanish, German, and Italian. Jim was impressed with Beaumont's skill in each language and grinned behind his mask. His eyes were on his man, and he saw the gun begin to rise. Dropping the man with a three-round burst before his enemy's trigger finger could tighten, he moved his target to another man, picking one of the few that looked like they still wanted to fight.

"Resistance is futile," Beaumont urged quietly. "Gustav Jung is already in custody. So are the men assigned to the explosives detail. Drop your weapons, step back with your hands on your heads, your fingers interlaced." There was that something in his voice that told the terrorists that resistance meant sudden and violent death. They'd seen two of their number die already.

All but one complied. Two MP5SDs spat into the night, and six bullets tore most of the man's head off. It was the end of the battle for the others. Even those contemplating pulling a knife cooperated sullenly. They were bound and turned over to the Swiss Guard. Once Italian authorities were roused and brought to the Vatican, Jim knew that the prisoners would be treated harshly and according to his instructions. The Rome police department was very protective of their Pope.

In an anteroom of one of the smaller chapels, the men stripped away their battle gear and relaxed for the first time in hours. Jim sat on a stool, cleaning his weapon, and wondered how his other teams were faring. There was so much that could go wrong. He wasn't there to provide help, and that rankled the most. Sighing, he let it go and concentrated on his equipment.

Beaumont came to thank him for his participation. Jim gave him a Bring It Up business card with his secure satellite phone number.

"Sometimes our laws hinder justice. If such a time should ever arise, I would be honored to help you," Jim said simply. Beaumont looked at the card and smiled.

"Many things can happen on international waters; is this not so?" he commented, showing almost all his front teeth in a wicked grin.

"It has its advantages," Jim replied soberly.

Kalil was close to the Vatican, close enough to hear even the suppressed gunfire from the balcony of his hotel room. His smile was satisfied as he listened to the short bursts. The battle did not last long. *So much for the Swiss Guard.*

Leaving the balcony, he entered his room and stretched out on the bed. An old army blanket made of wool covered the bedspread, and his own pillow caressed his head as he lay back. It was a trick he used to avoid leaving any DNA evidence. Law enforcement had become very sophisticated in the late years. A hand-held mini-vac lay ready to use in his suitcase. He would vacuum the bedspread when he folded his blanket in the morning.

In the morning, he expected excited news about the attack and robbery and waited expectantly in front of the small television set in the room. Nothing about the Vatican was in the news that morning. Kalil wondered if Jung had performed so well that no one knew yet. He decided to wait until noon in Rome.

At breakfast in the hotel's dining room, he listened to see if anyone was talking about the Vatican but heard nothing of interest. Checking out of his room, after carefully cleaning every surface he might have touched, he wandered about the city. He was close enough to Vatican City to know if police cars rushed to the scene, and by noon, he was worried. This close someone would know! Someone would talk! He listened in vain.

Choosing a small establishment with a television to eat lunch, he took his seat. Again, no news from the Vatican! Worry pushed its ugly head to the surface. Something was very wrong. Finishing his lunch, he left the establishment and hailed a passing taxi. Forty minutes later, he purchased a one-way ticket to Madrid. Keeping careful watch, he saw no one tailing or showing undue interest in him. Satisfied he was undetected, he gave his boarding pass to the flight attendant and walked on the Air Italia flight.

Earlier, during the darkness of night, Von Humbolt watched from the rented yacht, anchored about a half mile from the last oil rig on his schedule. He could trace the bubbles from the diver's tanks on the surface using his night binoculars. They were nearing the oil rig, and it was the moment when they were most vulnerable. Anyone looking down from the rig could see those bubbles.

Carefully, he lifted his binoculars and studied the rig. There were three guards posted, but none were looking toward the water. All three were seated in a lighted tower on the rig's north corner, playing a game, probably cards. His attention went back to the divers. They were near the base of the rig now. Von Humbolt nearly soiled himself when the cold steel barrel of a pistol pressed against his head, just behind his right ear. A hard voice with a markedly Australian accent spoke softly, so softly he was sure it would not be heard more than a foot away.

"Twitch and the other half of your head is fish food," Lee Roy Brown said softly. "Hands on the back of your head, fingers interlaced!"

Von Humbolt obeyed, letting the binoculars drop on the cord around his neck. Strong hands pulled his arms down behind his back, the grip almost frightening in its power. Handcuffs snapped on his wrists almost simultaneously, making this man a law enforcement professional.

"What's the charge, sir?" Von Humbolt asked in English, his accent heavily German.

A kick to the back of his leg dropped him to the deck with a cry of pain, and his ankles were quickly tied with plastic restraint ties. Restraint ties were added to the wrists, and the handcuffs were removed. Then, another set of ties fastened his hands to his ankles. The position was uncomfortable, and Von Humbolt grunted.

"You must think me very dangerous," he said hoarsely.

His hair was grasped, and his face turned painfully upward to look into a black face heavily painted in military paint to blend into the darkness. Cold brown eyes bored into him, and a moment passed before the man spoke.

"If I thought you were dangerous, I'd have shot you. I could have dropped you with one shot, but you're not worth a bullet. You're a terrorist, a bloody coward," Lee Roy slapped a piece of tape over Von Humbolt's mouth and let go of his hair. He patted the back of his head. "Now, don't go anywhere." He said with a grin. "We wouldn't want to lose the head of this terrorist cell!"

Less than a minute later, the three crewmembers of the yacht were dumped unceremoniously beside Von Humbolt. For an hour, they lay there waiting, ears straining to hear anything other than the lapping of the water against the yacht's hull. Cramping brought whimpers of pain and groans of agony from them occasionally. At last, the sound of divers climbing onto the rear platform brought them hope. They would be discovered and rescued. Their hopes died.

"Got all three, I see." It was the voice of the man who had captured Von Humbolt.

One of the divers began cursing, and Von Humbolt heard the sound of a fist striking home. The diver was silent after that. *What happened? How did anyone know? Who betrayed us?* Von Humbolt was left with his thoughts. They were not comforting thoughts as he contemplated prison.

Someone started the yacht and moved it to the base of the oil rig. Other voices could be heard now, the language unfamiliar to Von Humbolt. Rough hands lifted him and carried him to a crane-operated elevator. He found that all of his men were there, trussed as he was. The divers looked pretty rough, sporting black eyes, swollen noses, and jaws, and one had a bloody ear.

"We've been following these blokes from rig to rig, disarming their devices. A GIGN unit will be here presently to transport them for trial. Don't let them loose for any reason. If they have to go to the bathroom, that's just tough! Got it, mates?" Sean said to the crew leader on the rig. The man nodded, towering over Sean by almost twelve inches. He looked like he could handle any problems. Sean grinned at him.

"Feel free to let them know how you feel about being blown up by a couple of creeping cowards," he suggested with a wave.

Konrad Kohl tried to fight. Somehow, someone had crept onto his boat and right up to him. The moment the pistol pressed against his head, he spun and tried to take out the shooter. Something exploded against his face, and he flew across the deck, landing hard, stunned and disoriented. Before he could recover, strong hands turned him over and trussed him like a chicken for roasting. Tape was slapped across his mouth.

"Jeeze, Wade. Hope you never decide to hit me that hard," a distinctly American voice said as one of Kohl's crewmembers suddenly fell beside him, similarly trussed. C.G. was grinning as he said it. "Gotta go back for the third bird," he added, turning back to go down into the bowels of the fishing boat.

Beneath the surface at the base of the oil rig, John and Vince watched the three divers approach. They were invisible to the approaching divers because their bubble-free diving units gave off no telltale signs of a diver's presence. Staying as still as possible in the dark water, they remained invisible to the enemy divers.

Vince took the diver to the left and John, the diver to the right. In their hands, they held a small device that punched through the dive suits and injected a serum that produced instant unconsciousness. Both divers went limp. The middle diver didn't notice immediately, and by the time he did, he could not help them.

Vince neatly cut his airlines while John snared his right hand with a nylon chord and wrapped it tightly against a metal pipe. Then John grasped his left hand so that he could not insert any of the detonators into the explosives wrapped around his body. The diver struggled until he lost consciousness. John let him go and hauled him to the surface while Vince dragged the other two.

Wade piloted the fishing boat near the oil rig to help with the pick-up. Reaching down, he hauled two divers onto the platform while C.G. hauled the other one up. In a few minutes, they had them trussed, taped, and lying next to Kohl. He glared at the men working silently around him. *Who are these men? How did they know about our plans? Who betrayed us? Could Kalil betray us? No, he's too cautious. It must have been one of the Committee of Five. But who?*

Crew members from the oil rig boarded to take charge of the prisoners. John told them of the GIGN troops that would be collecting the prisoners. Meanwhile, they were not allowed any freedoms or even access to a bathroom. They were to remain tied up and taped until the GIGN took possession.

"Feel free to let them know how you feel about being blown up while you wait," John offered with a wave of his hand as he stepped off the oil rig deck onto the elevator. Kohl began shaking at that point.

CHAPTER 24

elmut Adenauer watched the helicopter set down on the oil rig down on the oil rig. He read the *Bring It Up* insignia on the side, but it didn't register anything with him. Turning to call for one of his men to check the registration, he found himself staring into the business end of a Beretta M92F pistol. A face, arm's length behind the gun, painted to blend into the night, looked almost ghostly. The bright white of the eyes and the lazy smile were almost disarming.

"Just twitch the wrong way or say something out loud, and I'll be obliged to send the back half of your head all over the dashboard and windshield of this fine vessel. That would be very messy, wouldn't it?" Jack Boswell said lightly. "It's a nice boat, so let's not mess it up with bits of your brain matter."

Adenauer might have moved or shouted, but the silencer on the end of the pistol told him this was a professional. Not to mention that the man had come onto his bridge without making a sound. Wisely, he raised his hands.

Boswell's other hand moved forward, and the world went berserk and black for Helmut. It was a stun gun, and Boswell aimed it perfectly at the side of his neck. Adenauer was out for the count. Trussing him quickly, Jack kept his ears open for any problems below.

Mark Drumheiser was down there dealing with the other two. He grinned when Mark suddenly appeared at the hatch.

"I had to kill one of them," Mark said matter-of-factly. His eyes were sad.

"On the radio?" Jack asked.

"Gun. Must have heard the grunt from the first one I took down," Mark answered. He dragged the dead body over to the side and dumped it unceremoniously into the ocean. It was no less than the man deserved: an unceremonious burial at sea. He had no patience with terrorists, especially the kind that killed indiscriminately with hidden explosives. Jack noticed that the body sank quickly.

"What did you weight him with?" he asked.

"Extra weight belt from a diver's suit below," Mark answered.

"Too bad we can't do that to all of them," Driver mused. "Think of the money it will cost to keep them alive in prison all those years! We could save the French government thousands of dollars," Helmut Adenauer listened to their accents and placed them as Americans. *What is the American military doing in this?* He had no time to think of anything else.

Suddenly a spout of water geysered into the air, followed by a hollow thump that lifted the boat and slapped it down again with a loud thwap. Jack and Mark looked at each other in horror.

"You go," Driver said. "You're a better diver than I am."

Mark nodded, heading to the rear platform to gather his gear and slip it onto his back. He was quickly swimming toward the oil rig when the first body floated to the surface. Jack saw it and spoke into his microphone.

"I think one of the terrorist bodies just surfaced to your left," he said. His face was bleak as he wondered what Mark might find beneath the now calm surface.

"I see it," Mark said, coming to the surface and swimming toward the body. He could tell from the discoloration in the water that the explosion shredded this one. As he reached the body, a head broke the surface. Mark breathed a sigh of relief as his friend Dorf ripped off his dive hood and mask. He was shaking his huge head as if disoriented. In his arms, he held Bill Kline. Mark saw Bill's head lolling limply to the side.

"Can you hear me?" Mark roared, pulling his mask off.

"Barely," Dorf admitted thickly. "That blast nearly tore our heads off. One of the legs took most of it, but Sparks seems unconscious."

Mark put his mask on and looked under the water. Both Dorf's legs seemed okay, so he deduced Dorf was talking about being behind a leg of the oil rig when the blast went off. That probably saved his life. He helped his huge friend back to the boat and then helped lift Bill to the platform. Driver was pulling off his mask and checking him for damage. There was no blood coming from his ears, which was a good sign, and he was breathing, which was also a good sign. His breathing was not labored and seemed rhythmic and even, another good sign. Still, a blast underwater was deadly.

"What happened?" Mark asked Dorf as the giant removed his diving gear.

"One of these geniuses had the detonators already attached to the explosive. There's a tricky current down there, and it banged him against some crane debris. Looks like a crane fell off the platform sometime in the past. It's pretty corroded and covered with sea life, so it's been down there for a while. Anyway, the silly bugger blew himself and his two buddies to hell. All the explosives were wired to go simultaneously," Dorf said thickly. He looked anxiously over at Sparks, still lying on the deck.

"Is he going to make it?" he asked.

"He's probably going to have a really bad couple of days, but I think he'll pull through all right. We'll get him to Sean as soon as we can," Driver said. "Can you still fly?" he added.

"I'll fly, Dorf can copilot," Mark said. Let's get this rig over to the boys waiting on the platform."

Good to his word, Mark started the boat and brought it neatly to the suspended dock. At the end, an elevator waited to take them up. Dorf had Sparks over his shoulder and was carrying one of the terrorists by his belt. Men from the oil rig hastened onto the boat to take the other prisoners.

"There's a GIGN group coming to pick them up," Mark informed them, ensuring Adenauer heard. "While you're waiting, you can let these men know just how you feel about being blown up," He added with a wicked grin.

Just then, Sparks moaned, then vomited and coughed. Dorf lifted him down to the elevator floor and looked into disoriented eyes, relieved to see they could finally focus. He grinned.

"Thanks for the chunk shower," he commented wryly.

"Huh?" Sparks queried, shaking his head and digging at his ears. "I can't hear you," he said.

Dorf shook his head and pointed at the mess on the back of his wetsuit, gesturing animatedly with a finger. Sparks grinned and shook his head, wincing as he did so. It was obvious the blast had done some physical harm.

"Sorry," he said hoarsely. "Did any of them survive?"

Dorf shook his head, and Sparks waved a weak hand as if to say, "Idiots!" Mark nodded his head in agreement, catching Dorf's eyes. This one had been close. Had Dorf and Sparks not been behind the leg of the oil rig, the sound waves would have killed them. They'd all been there before and remembered the firefight along the River of Death. Kevlar's body armor and divine providence saved their lives several times in that encounter.

You never get used to near-death experiences. You only know that they will come in this line of work. It could have been me this time. Sparks experimented with his arms and legs and slowly pushed himself up, glad for Dorf's huge hands helping him. *I wonder how the other teams are going. I hope they don't run into an idiot like we did!*

Kalil tried desperately to reach his units in the Mediterranean, using cell phone numbers and radio calls. None were answered. Having access to one of those phones, Zeke traced the call neatly. He knew that Kalil would not stay put long. Once he was unable to reach his terrorist cells, he would disappear.

Kalil did not wait a full day in Madrid. Unable to reach any of his contacts, he bought a one-way train ticket to Paris. A train offered many stops to change plans if necessary. He took a sleeper car and noted carefully everyone who boarded with him and shared that car. On high alert, he watched everyone suspiciously. One could never be too careful!

Next to him, at the far end, a husband and wife and two small children made their way into their car with some difficulty. On the other side of him were three girls, possibly college students, giggling as they entered their cabin. No one looked the least suspicious. Further on was a businessman, close to retirement, obviously Spanish, with flip charts showing growth charts and what looked like a sales bag and some computer equipment. On the other side of him, in the last cabin, was a little old lady, possibly English, with her lady attendant hovering over her.

Kalil might have been surprised to learn that every occupant of that car worked for Sir Edward and was there to learn everything possible about him. Feeling secure and safe, Kalil entered his cabin to work until dinner. Try as he might, he could find no answers to his questions.

CHAPTER 25

Listening to the news, Kalil became very concerned. Reports of the terrorist attacks on the oil rigs and the Vatican were now running simultaneously. Somehow, the press knew there was a connection, even what that connection was. His unit had been compromised. Someone talked. Feeling very insecure, Kalil made his way from the train station in Paris to the airport. He used all his skills, changing cabs, doubling back, and constantly checking to see if anyone was following. During his trip to the airport, he saw the occupants of three of the cabins on his train but did not connect them to any danger to himself.

The businessman was first, obviously making his way to his conference in a white limousine. People tailing someone did not use such flagrant and visible means! Passing off the businessman as of no concern, he next saw the young couple and their children in a taxi, pointing at the various sights as they traveled through the famous city. Then he saw the old lady and her nurse in a cream-colored Bentley.

Things often happened in threes. He smiled as he reached the airport. Feeling entirely secure, he made his way to the ticket counter and bought a ticket to Cairo. Once on the plane, he settled down in first class. He did not recognize the pretty flight attendant, now speaking perfect Arabic, as one of the three college girls on the train.

She had already changed her eye color through special contact lenses, and a wig completed the quick change to a very different person. Her accent finished the disguise perfectly.

In Cairo, he hired a car to drive him to Jordan. While passing through Jerusalem, the vehicle was stopped. Kalil found himself suddenly surrounded by Israeli troops, all pointing guns at him. Then he saw the four Mossad agents. Swallowing nervously, he kept his cool. He had papers, and they were near perfect. This should be only a minor glitch in his plans. After all, he had done nothing in this country for a long time. Taking a deep breath, he concentrated on relaxing and remaining unthreatening.

His hopes sank immediately as the foremost Mossad officer leaned down and looked into the car. "Ah, Mr. Kalil, welcome to Jerusalem! There are a great many people who want to know a great deal about you!"

They know my name! I'm a ghost! No one knows that name. I buried it eighteen years ago! "I'm afraid you're mistaken. My name is Ishmael Mir. I am a businessman from Morocco," Kalil lied easily.

"Oh, I don't care if you call yourself Ishmael Mir, Thomas Ghandiri, Emil Tobin, or Kalil. They're all the same man, now, aren't they?" the Mossad agent asked with a smile. "My name is Ira Lehman. You may have heard of me, yes?"

Kalil's shoulders sagged. The head of the Mossad addressed him as if he had been a naughty boy. *Who betrayed me? Was it Aumont? Was it Brel? Only they would have the audacity! But why? Or was it a leak from someone once in the KGB? I will find out who, and they will die a most unpleasant death!*

"Your prisons will not hold me, cursed Jew!" Kalil spat. He didn't like the smile on Ira's face.

"Perhaps. Perhaps not. Either way, by the time you get out, your plans will have come to naught. Your money source . . . what do they call themselves? Oh yes! The Committee of Five! It will have dried up. Eventually, you will find another source of money, as you did with Paul Klaus.

"Killing him is what gave us our final clue to your identity. Only the old-school Russians wasted such resources without remorse. You had his wife and children! You got your precious notebook so cleverly encoded! Yet you still killed him just to protect yourself. It was that act that set the intelligence community working on identifying you. I believe we are much better than you thought we might be, my friend. You thought yourself safe, but never have you been safe from us.

"Now, would you kindly accompany my men?" Ira stood back, and Kalil slowly got out of the car. He wanted to kill Ira Lehman right then and there, but there were three Israeli pistols pointed at him, along with the weapons from the Israeli police gathered around.

Ira smiled at him as though he had read his mind. Discomfited, Kalil was cuffed and pushed into a waiting car. His mind was spinning, trying to make sense of what had just taken place. *How do they know so much? No one read that book except Klaus! Or did Murchenheim talk? The cursed Red Army Faction were always more trouble than they were worth. Anarchists! Idealists! Fools!* It did not occur to Kalil that he was the greatest fool.

Jim answered his secure satellite phone on the second ring. It was Ira reporting that Kalil had been picked up. Captain Shepherd was in the Command Intelligence Center on board *Bring It Up, Coral*. They were pushing the huge diesel engines to their stops on a run to Basin D'Arcachon.

"Hello, Ira!" Jim acknowledged his friend and colleague.

"We have the fox," Ira said lightly. "He seems to think that anarchists and idealists are fools but seems to have missed the fact that he made his bed with them."

"So, for him, it is money. That is how he measures his power. Many of the old Russian schools are that way. Money is their god," Jim replied flatly.

"Yes. But money is not a good god. An impotent god is never a good god," Ira said with conviction.

"We're on our way to Basin D'Arcachon," Jim informed him. "The Committee of Five will all be in Bordeaux to attend an international conference on sudden climate shifts, otherwise known as 'global warming.' I expect they will be very cautious since they know their plans have come to naught."

"Are they still riding that old horse?" Ira chuckled.

"With a passion. It's come to a complete stop, but they're still kicking and spurring at it in the hopes that the skeletal remains will somehow animate and carry them further," Jim laughed.

"That's a perfect picture, my friend. I will speak with you again when you have them in international waters," Ira said. "Use caution."

Jim put his satellite phone back in the pouch at his belt and smiled at Zeke, who had been busy the entire time at his computer keyboard.

"Think they'll be able to hold him?" Zeke asked, not looking up from his work.

"Doubtful," Jim answered. "It would be like trying to put one of us in a prison. Eventually, we'd find a way to escape."

"And where do you think he'll go when he gets loose?" Zeke asked, looking sideways at Jim.

"Right for our throats," Jim replied with a strange, hard look, suddenly turning his green eyes stormy.

"Swimming in those waters, one can encounter a very deadly current," Zeke said with a wicked grin.

"The ocean is full of deadly currents. We're just one of them," Jim replied with an answering grin. His eyes were now as cold as an open grave. As Jim exited the Command Intelligence Center, Zeke shivered. *Glad I'm not going up against the captain! Any man who goes up against Jim Shepherd is fish food!*

Jim went up to the observation deck and stood for a while, just enjoying the sea air and the sense of a steel deck beneath his feet again. He loved the sea, and whenever their work took them ashore, he missed it terribly. Wade came up on the deck, looking for him, and for a moment, the two men stood side by side, saying nothing.

"John wanted me to tell you we have a conference with the team in twenty, Jim," Wade said after a long pause.

"Thanks, Wade," Jim replied.

Wade nodded and left the deck. When they were at sea, most of the men did not salute and used names or nicknames instead of rank. Even though he had thawed considerably, only Marvin Finn insisted on saluting and using rank. Jim smiled as he watched Wade glide off the deck, a big man, stalking the deck like a tiger, fluid in motion, power exuding from every pore as he moved out of sight. It was such an honor to command such men as these.

Jim went down to the medical wing and found Sparks out of bed, dressed, and arguing with Millie about attending the meeting. She had her short arms crossed beneath her ample bosom, and her brown eyes flashed with anger. Across the room, her husband Charles was doing his best to hide a smile. He winked outrageously at Jim and turned away so his wife would not see the chuckle that escaped. She heard it, though.

"Charles Lyle Wozniac, I'll deal with you later!" she snapped.

Jim schooled his face to show no emotion and walked over to the pair. "Is there a problem, Aunt Millie?" Jim asked just a shade too innocently. Behind him, he heard Charles snort. Inwardly, he winced.

"This young scallywag has decided he's attending your meeting, Captain," she announced with some heat. "He should not be up and about yet!" She looked so comical standing there, her arms crossed, her tiny body filled with authority.

Jim looked at Sparks and saw his clear green eyes dancing with laughter, though his face remained smooth. Tiny nurse Wozniac, only five feet four inches, facing off six foot one inch Bill Kline was funny enough. Jim smiled just slightly. As Captain of the ship, he had to deal with many unusual circumstances.

"Perhaps he can walk as far as the conference room, sit there, and then return after the meeting. Would that be alright?" Jim asked.

"Oh, get out of here, the both of you!" Millie said, grinning despite her anger. "This whole crew is incorrigible!" she said, stamping her foot.

Jim grabbed Sparks by the arm and moved him out of the hospital wing. They grinned at each other as Millie's voice rose again with that authoritative pitch as she addressed her husband. Sparks sighed as he stretched his legs.

"How do you feel?" Jim asked.

"Right as rain, now," Sparks said. "The first two days were the worst, and the headache disappeared yesterday."

"Still, it was a near thing. You sure you're okay?" Jim replied.

"Shep, I'm good to go," Sparks said with energy.

"You'd say that if you were wounded, bleeding, missing both legs and dragging yourself through a swamp," Jim grinned.

"Probably," Sparks admitted. "I had a good teacher," he added.

"Kissing up to the boss?" Zeke joined them in the corridor, grinning at his twin brother.

"Never hurts to kiss up to the brass," Sparks said with dignity. "In this man's navy, you need the brass on your side."

"Get the wife on your side, and you've got it made," Zeke retorted with a snort of laughter.

"The wife prefers to be called by her name!" Cecilia had joined them unobserved, slipping her hand into Jim's as they walked behind the brothers.

"My humblest apologies, Mrs. Shepherd," Zeke said, turning, bowing, and tipping his hat. Cecilia grinned and then laughed aloud.

"Millie is right. You men are incorrigible!" she said.

One by one, the team filtered into the conference room. Windy, Bull, TP, and Cuss were putting pitchers of tea, soda cans, and bottled water on trays on the counter that ran the length of the room. Glasses rattled in their plastic carriers, and large bowls of ice were already present. Sturdy brought in a fruit tray, seeming to shrink the room by his very presence, then just as quickly ducked his head and exited through the door.

Windy and TP took positions on one side of the conference room while Bull and Cuss took the other. They knew the men on the team and served them drinks without being asked. This was a service they didn't have to perform, but they took pride in doing it, and Jim didn't discourage it. Occasionally, in these planning sessions, one of the kitchen crew gave them a key piece of the plan. They might not be fighting men, but they were intelligent, and Jim respected that.

What that did for the ship's morale was incredible. The entire crew worked together better because every man knew he was respected.

Even Bull was catching on. Truculent as he was when he first joined the crew, he was unwinding fast under the tutelage of Windy and Cuss. He even smiled now and addressed the other members of the crew, including officers, with respect and without fear. That was the most significant change in the man. He no longer suspected that the men of the crew were laughing behind his back, and he was learning to trust. The latter would come in time.

Zeke moved around the room and sat down at his space, plugging his laptop into the system that would allow him to download all his files to the other laptops online. Every team member had a PowerBook G5 in front of them, enhanced and designed for maximum efficiency. In only minutes, Zeke signaled that he was ready to go. Taking their cue, the men opened their laptops and pushed the start button.

Zeke designed the screen-saver program, and each computer had in the background for just a moment a cartoon caricature of Zeke looking at them through a telescope, his one eye huge in the lens. His favorite saying was, "Uncle Zeke is watching you." None of the men even cracked a smile at the familiar figure as pictures began to appear on the screen. Five snapshots of Renée Aumont, Ferdinand Brel, Anne Chanté, Nadia Duse, and Jacques Piaf, all recent photographs, now filled the screen.

"This is the Committee of Five," Zeke said. "The next picture is the floor plan of the convention center in Bordeaux. This convention center has a central security booth, and video feeds everywhere except the bathrooms and dressing rooms behind the stage. I've been able to watch our five friends and discovered that they meet for an afternoon drink near the end of the day. All five of them have ordered the same drinks for the past two days. Security at their meeting is still high with a team in place to keep them secure."

"We could slip something in their drinks!" Lee Roy Brown suggested quickly. "Something that would make them easy to handle," he added, looking around the table.

"We could fake a fire, set off the alarms, and nab 'em when they're runnin' out," Driver offered after a short silence.

"Why don't you have some dignitary invite them to a private

session, someone who would appeal to their vanity? That way, you could take them quietly, and no one would be the wiser?" Windy spoke up. "Surely there is someone they would be happy to meet with?"

"Hey! Yeah! I like that!" Wade said enthusiastically. "But who would all five of these people want to see together?"

"Well, Chance looks a lot like Mike MacCaully, head of the Earth First faction in England. We could make sure the real MacCaully takes a long nap that day and try that," Windy answered.

"Windy, you're a genius!" Jim said, slapping the table. "This will work!"

"Have you thought about the legal aspects of this?" Windy asked cautiously.

"Go ahead, explain," John encouraged him. All the men turned their attention to Windy.

"Well, they hired some terrorists to do some very bad things, and we have evidence in the money trail and any confessions, provided they're obtained legally. All they're going to get from our "enlightened" countries is a slap on the wrist," he said calmly. "Somehow, that doesn't seem adequate under the circumstances," he added.

CHAPTER 26

"**W**e've thought about that," Jim said quietly. He looked around the table, remembering the debates he and the team shared over the last few days in the war room. They spoke of little else while cleaning their weapons and checking their equipment.

"We are capable of holding a trial and exacting justice because we don't have the oversight of so many military units. We've even done that." For a moment, Jim looked over at Cecilia. The man who had nearly killed her now lay in a nursing home, a vegetable, helpless and unable to communicate. It was a fitting punishment for his life of crime. Worse than life in prison or a quick death penalty, he lived with an active mind, hating every moment of his existence yet unable to do anything about it.

"Jacques Piaf will go to Ira Lehman and the Mossad. The other four will be turned over to Sir Edward's lot. They will probably not be in prison long, but they will pay something for their crimes," Jim answered.

"And they'll know who we are," Zeke said softly.

"No, they won't!" John said with a huge grin. "Whoever does the grab will be in GIGN uniforms we "borrowed" from the Vatican job. We're going to "borrow" a yacht too. Sir Edward fixed it up this morning. It's a GIGN yacht that they're retiring because it's been compromised. Since everyone doing the grab will speak impeccable French, no one will be the wiser!"

"Chance doesn't speak French like a native," Sean pointed out.

"Chance isn't going to get to speak!" John grinned. "He's going for the ride, too, pretending to be a prisoner. Wait until you see the make-up job we have planned for him!" Wade was grinning widely, and so was Zeke. They'd been busy typing comments to each other on their units and were excited by the idea.

"Just when were you blokes going to tell me about this?" Chance asked, trying to keep his face schooled to displeasure. The tiny smile playing around the corner of his lips won the day. "Good night, you're all rotters!" he said emphatically.

"And Jacques? What happens to him?" TP spoke up before he realized he had put his thoughts into words. He relaxed when everyone treated it as just another question from the group. Following the investigation, he knew all the names well and knew what these terrorists had accomplished, planned, and even some things that were yet to happen.

"Ira has some plans for Jacques. The Mossad is very good at making people talk. Jacques will be an open book by the time Ira is done with him. We'll know his Russian contacts, and we'll know all about Kalil, who, by the way, has escaped. What Jacques doesn't know will be filled in by the contacts Ira grabs," Jim replied.

"Sorry, boss!" TP waved a hand. "I didn't mean just to blurt that out."

"We all value your input, Tom," Wade said easily before Jim could speak. Jim waited and then added his opinion.

"TP, every man on this ship is as important and valuable as the next. You've learned that very well, and I'm proud to have you on my team. Don't be afraid to speak up. You never know when your idea or comment may save us all or make our job easier. In these sessions, no one is out of line when they speak. In fact, I would be put out if you had a good question or idea and didn't speak it."

TP grinned and nodded. He was learning that. Not one of the crew members ever brought up his drinking, which led to his early retirement from the Navy. If they talked at all about his wife's betrayal and leaving him while he was at sea, it was with respect for both of them. At his last review, Jim asked him how he was dealing with his feelings now that alcohol no longer played a part. He'd been glad to be able to answer that his friends on the cooking crew were helping day by day, and for Jim, it had been enough.

Sir Edward had everything in place when the team arrived at the port. Jim arranged for the infiltration team to leave in stages, just in case anyone was watching the ship. He went first, with Chance, in a rented Renault, a nondescript vehicle that looked like many others in that part of France. It was dark brown with a tan interior. Both men took turns driving, and neither thought the car was well made.

"Bloody thing handles like a drunk platypus!" Chance mumbled after negotiating a series of tight turns through a small village.

"Have you seen many of those?" Jim asked innocently.

"Oh sure, boss!" he replied with his usual grin as they slid around another corner on wet paving stones. "They're always in and out of the bars in Perth!"

After several route changes, they merged onto the Rocade A630, crossing the bridge into Bordeaux. Their destination was the Hotel Sofitel Bordeaux Aquitania. It was described as a four-star hotel on the borders of the famous wine-producing region and the Arcachon basin, on the banks of the lake of Bordeaux, next to the Trade Fair Grounds and the Conference Center. It was an ideal location, only ten minutes from the center of the city. The restaurant "Le Flore" was of top quality. Fifteen meeting rooms that could handle up to 1,200 delegates and a nearby golf course made it a favorite of business people, especially in the wine industry.

Mike MacCaully occupied a room on the non-smoking floor. Getting into the room was no problem for pros like Chance and Jim. Chance, actually an inch taller than MacCaully, could easily fit into his clothes. MacCaully was not powerfully built like Chance but heavy enough for his clothes to accommodate the difference in build. Chance thought his taste in clothing was quite good.

They didn't touch anything but the glasses in the room. Each glass was coated with an invisible agent that would react with any liquid, putting MacCaully into a deep, untroubled sleep for seventy-two hours. They left the room, entered their own across the hall, and waited for MacCaully to arrive.

A quiet knock on the door brought Jim out of his chair to look through the peephole. His eyebrow raised slightly at the face waiting in the hall. He opened his door with a smile and ushered in Captain Francois Beaumont, GIGN. Beaumont was the GIGN team leader at the Vatican.

"You are surprised to see me, no?" Francois smiled, quietly stepping through the door.

"Did Sir Edward send you?" Jim asked, closing the door and following Francois into the room.

"Ah! You have a formidable friend there! Oui! It is as you say. Today, you will deliver to me a great prize, and I will help you, no?" Francois replied, beaming at Jim. He was certainly in a mood to be expansive. Jim smiled.

"Any help is welcome," Jim replied.

"Good! Now, you will send your team to this address, where they will dress in the proper uniforms," he handed a piece of paper to Jim. "Then, when we have arranged to seize this Committee of Five, we will escort them to GIGN vehicles and your GIGN boat! All is arranged!" Francois said.

"When you say all is arranged, does that mean your superiors know what is happening?" Jim asked quickly.

No, my friend! No one knows! Only I know at this present juncture. Sir Edward informed me that you have gathered much evidence against these conspirators. It will be, as you say, a coup for me! I may even get a promotion!" Francois answered, his eyes twinkling. "We keep this under wraps until all is accomplished."

"I'm in your debt, Francois," Jim said with a smile.

"Ah! This I know! And, when the time comes, I will call upon you to settle that debt, no? But until then, we keep it between ourselves." Jim shook the outstretched hand. "I am sure some of my superiors are on their payroll, no? I must be careful."

Francois left the room, and Jim grinned at Chance. "That was a stroke of luck for us," he said.

"We're making some good friends in the right places. They understand what we're doing and why. Perhaps one day they'll have a team of their own for their own country," Chance replied.

"Yet the more people who learn about us, the more we become exposed. I think it may be time to go on another treasure hunt to keep us out of the public eye for a while," Jim mused.

"As long as we stay on the ocean, we're pretty free from trouble," Chance said after a moment of thought. "Even if people know about us, they can do nothing unless we give them evidence. So far, we've been very careful not to do that."

Jim picked up his cell phone and dialed the team coming in for the snatch. He gave them the new address. John replied that they would be arriving in ten minutes. His voice sounded assured, and Jim smiled as he closed his phone.

A green light on a small black box Chance held in his hand suddenly began to blink, signaling that McCauley had returned to his room. Chance's grin was vicious as they waited. He plugged the earpiece into his right ear and listened through the microphones they'd planted in the suite. It didn't take long until the clink of the bottle against the glass was heard, followed by the plunk of ice cubes going into the drink. Three minutes later, the thump of a body hitting the floor came through loud and clear. McCauley was down and out for the count!

"Time to go, Shep!" Chance said lightly.

They headed across the hall into the suite and lifted McCauley's body easily between them. Crossing the hall back to their room was the only time they were in danger, and as luck would have it, no one appeared from the elevator or exited their room while they were carrying the body across. They would move him back once the snatch was complete.

Chance returned to the room and cleaned out all the glasses, washing them carefully and wiping them to make sure there were no fingerprints that didn't belong. He put on one of McCauley's suits and prepared to await the arrival of the Committee of Five. Jim returned to his room, now holding the black box. The suit would go with him and never be returned, eliminating any chance of DNA evidence linking him to this mission.

"Hey, Shep, can you hear me?" Chance said softly when Jim was seated.

"Loud and clear," Jim replied, talking directly to Chance through an earpiece the man had inserted.

"Okay. I'm going offline now," Chance said, taking the earpiece out and slipping it into a small compartment hidden in the heel of his shoe. He fully expected to be carefully searched by someone before the Committee of Five ventured into his room. The microphones would be turned off during that search so that any sweep for listening devices would turn up negative. Effective as the plan was, it still left Chance on his own, though only for a few minutes. It was a risk. He had been more than willing to take it.

Shortly after the invitation went out, three men knocked on Chance's door. He answered the door and looked inquiringly at the three men, who were obviously the advance security force. The smallest of the three spoke.

"Mr. McCauley. Our employers will be here shortly. Do you mind if we check your room for recording devices?" he requested politely.

"You probably want to check me, too," Chance said, ensuring he mimicked his best Oxford accent. He wasn't supposed to speak much. As the men came in, Jim turned everything off and made his call to the team. They were in position before the security team finished their sweep. Jim watched through his peephole as the men left the room. When they were gone, he switched everything back on.

"If you're listening, Shep, we're in business in less than five minutes," Chance was talking near one of the microphones. Three minutes later, the Committee of Five appeared in the hallway with their three security men. They never made it to McCauley's suite. Jim's team took them in the hall quickly and quietly.

The yacht GIGN provided was a converted fishing boat, probably sixty years old, kept in excellent condition. Jim guessed it was one of the boats they seized in a drug raid because the engines were designed to make this boat about twice as fast as it was originally rated. Other than that, it was practical.

Chance, with expertly applied makeup, sat among the prisoners, his face bruised and bloody. Doc administered a mild sedative to help him sleep so he would not have to talk. Dorf, Wade, John, and Bill Kline were in the cabin, dressed in their GIGN uniforms, their faces covered by sinister-looking black balaclavas. The H&K MP5SDs in their hands were the weapon of choice of the GIGN, and each man carried an FN Five-seveN pistol at his hip.

When they spoke, they spoke perfectly idiomatic French. Occasionally, one of the prisoners would ask a question or make empty threats. Ferdinand Brel was the most abusive in his threats. Jacques Piaf had yet to speak. As for his security detail, they cursed and threatened until Wade jammed the butt of his MP5SD into one man's mouth, breaking teeth and sending the man halfway across the cabin. The fact that Wade did not speak first or after effectively silenced the other guards. They knew they were in the hands of professionals who had been given freedoms rarely enjoyed by law enforcement.

"You are taking us into international waters?" Jacques Piaf finally asked quietly after a long silence.

"It is as you say," John replied quietly. "Your plot to destroy coastland waters by detonating explosives on oil rigs in the Mediterranean and Caribbean has been thwarted. Your use of terrorists to do this has raised questions. And, your plan to monopolize your land holdings along the coast of the Mediterranean will never come to pass. This is all you need to know."

John phrased it purposely as a French policeman would have phrased the statements. The authority in his voice was unquestionable. Zeke grinned, watching through his computer system and monitoring their vital signs. Each statement shocked them, and on three at least, the signs of increased stress were evident. Piaf, however, remained calm.

"He's a dangerous one," Zeke said quietly. Cecilia, sitting next to him, nodded her head. Her fingers were busy with the computer keyboard. She was compiling a complete dossier on the security forces, and what she found confirmed Zeke's appraisal. Both were aboard *Bring It Up Coral*, still anchored in the harbor.

All three security men were wanted in at least three countries under three different names. This was confirmed by their fingerprints, taken while they were unconscious. Her aunt in CID was checking for further warrants. She pressed the communicator button on her headphones.

"Jim, can you come to the CIC for a moment?" she listened for a moment, and then Jim's voice replied.

"I'm on my way." She smiled as he spoke. He rarely used endearing terms, especially when all the men listened in on the frequency. She added the "honey" that should have been there in her mind. Her husband had much to learn about women, but she was patient.

Jim arrived at the Command Information Center, which, in his mind, was the Computer Center, and entered with a smile on his face. He enjoyed interacting with his wife whenever he got a chance. She looked up and returned his smile.

"Hi honey!" she said.

"Is that any way to address your Captain?" Zeke asked with a wide grin. "What if all of us decided to address him that way?"

"I dare you!" Cecelia retorted, sticking her tongue out at Zeke and then turning to kiss Jim.

"Please don't dare them to do that!" Jim said, putting her down gently after kissing her thoroughly.

"Is this Ensign receiving special treatment, Captain?" Zeke asked, his eyebrows raised.

"Absolutely!" Jim replied. "What did you want?" he said, addressing Cecilia.

"What did you want, dear?" she corrected, stressing the last word. "I think that the security force with Jacques Piaf will be wanted in several countries," she said quickly. She showed Jim the reports she'd received from CID and Interpol.

"Ah! These are bad boys. How does Jacques get contacts like

this? Kalil and these boys make me think Jacques is very important. Will you forward this information to Ira, please, dear?" Jim added the dear after a slight hesitation, and Cecilia smiled at him in such a way that he decided he would try it more often. His thoughts were on other matters, but he'd filed away that information for the future.

After Jim left, Zeke turned to her. "Oh, the wiles of women!" he said. "You'll be training him to say 'yes dear' to everything before long!"

"Shut up and type something!" she replied, her face flushed as she sent her results to Ira.

CHAPTER 27

Ira, on board an Israeli military destroyer, received Cecilia's message shortly after it was transmitted. In his quarters, he sat at a small metal desk that folded down from the wall and read through everything she had. Nodding his head slowly, he called his assistant into the room.

"David, we will have three guests to house with Jacques Piaf. They are not to be given any access to the other prisoners. Piaf and his security force will eat and exercise at different times. When we get into port and transfer them to our facility, they will be transferred separately," Ira commanded.

David looked at him for a few minutes without saying anything. Ira often had pauses between commands, so this was not unusual behavior. It also gave David time to think, and by the time Ira nodded that he was finished, David understood that those three were the primary sources of information for his country. He saluted his superior and left, aware that Ira hadn't even looked at him since giving his orders. He was not offended.

An hour later, the yacht and destroyer approached each other. Mark Drumheiser, behind the wheel of the yacht, pulled back on the throttles, bringing the boat to a slow stop, using reverse to stop all motion. A launch, with a full security force on board, was lowered into the water next to the destroyer. Moments later, powerful diesel engines roared to life, and the vessel's pilot brought the boat expertly beside the yacht. Well-trained in such encounters, the men all acted as if they were meeting in person for the first time for the benefit of the prisoner's watching.

Once the two boats were securely fastened to each other, the security detail leaped on board the yacht and went below. They brought Piaf and his security force up first, now shackled so that walking was difficult, especially in the tossing waves. Piaf fell twice, only to feel rough hands yank him to his feet. On deck, he looked across the water at the markings on the destroyer. One look at the identifying numbers and insignia made his heart sink.

"Israel!" he exclaimed. One of the security detail smashed the butt of his rifle to the back of Piaf's head, sending him instantly to the deck, unconscious. The security men looked murderously at their Israeli counterparts and then at the men in GIGN uniforms. Wisely, they remained silent.

Once they were safely aboard the destroyer the detail returned for the other four members of the Committee of Five. These they treated no less harshly, escorting them to the destroyer in silence. Mark watched them as they were lifted from his yacht to the launch, accurately reading the terror in their eyes as they realized that they were being handed over to the Israelis.

"They'll spill before Piaf," Dorf said quietly from behind his diminutive friend. Mark nodded in the affirmative. They turned together to take the yacht to their next rendezvous. Dorf radioed *Bring It Up Coral* that supplies had been successfully delivered. That was the cue to head out to meet them. The six CIGN operatives that would replace them on the yacht were already on board. Cramped in their hiding place, they waited patiently. Remaining hidden, they would appear only after the transfer to *Bring It Up Coral*.

Andrea was at the wheel when the orders came to head out to sea. He answered the order according to proper procedure and, with the harbor pilot watching carefully, took the tug out into the Mediterranean. Once the harbor pilot stepped off the rear platform onto his launch, Andrea opened up the throttles, and the ship plowed through the choppy waters with all the finesse of a battering ram. He loved the sensation of piloting a ship like this.

Kalil watched the ship depart. *Why does that particular ship appear so often of late?* He had checked them out. They were a legitimate and well-known deep-sea salvage and rescue operation currently working in the Mediterranean. Still, there was something that aroused his suspicions. He would wait until the yacht arrived, and he would see.

When the yacht returned, the GIGN operatives were no longer wearing their black balaclavas, covering their faces. They were dressed in regular uniforms, and he recognized two. To be sure, he followed them to their headquarters and, posing as a reporter, asked what they had done with their prisoners. All six stared at him until he became uncomfortable, spun on his heels, and left. He had the uneasy feeling that these men knew who he was. That was a feeling that he had more and more and he didn't like it.

A few minutes later, Jim received word that Kalil was in town and knew about the Committee of Five being taken. He profusely thanked his new friend in the GIGN and promised to be careful. Once he was off the ship-to-shore phone, he sat back at his desk, his eyes unfocused, his forehead drawn in concentration. The safety of his ship and his crew was of the utmost importance.

Marvin Finn, the captain's executive assistant, stepped into his office and found him still concentrating. Finn cleared his throat.

"Sir," he said quietly.

"Lieutenant, please have the team assemble in the conference room," Jim said, looking up.

"Aye, sir," Marvin replied, snapping off a salute. "I've finished those reports and filed everything. Is there anything else you want me to do?" This was added almost as an afterthought.

"Yes, there is. I want you to attend the meeting," Jim replied, leaping to his feet and heading out of his office. Cecilia, listening from her office, followed him out. Marvin returned to his office to call the team to conference.

Jim reached out, almost without thinking about it, to take Cecilia's hand as they made their way through the ship's narrow corridors. She smiled secretly and kept up with Jim's long strides with little difficulty. They were the first to arrive in the conference room.

"Sit!" Cecilia said, pushing Jim toward his chair. When he sat, she began to rub his shoulders. "You're a bit tense," she said, leaning her head down so her mouth was close to his ear.

He inhaled the scent of her hair, felt it caressing his neck, and, on impulse, turned and kissed her. John and Wade entered at that moment.

"I thought a woman's place was in the home," John said lightly.

"I live here, dopey!" Cecilia shot back, her cheeks flushed from the kiss, her eyes dancing with merriment.

"Oh yeah!" John replied laconically. "I keep forgetting."

"It's a sure sign of old age," FM said, stepping into the room as John spoke his last words.

"Stuff it, Grandpa!" John said with a grin. "You're older than me!"

"You're only as old as you feel," FM replied.

As usual, most of the crew joined Jim in the conference room. Only Andrea remained at the wheel. Jim decided that the conference room might have to be enlarged. The room grew quiet as the last person entered.

"There is a very real danger that Kalil will raise a force to attack this vessel," Jim said quietly, his voice carrying to the far end of the room easily. He watched his team digest this, knowing they'd already reached that conclusion.

"Then he's in Barney!" Sean said emphatically. "I take it we get to repel boarders in this instance," he added, nodding his head vigorously and grinning at his friends.

"With extreme prejudice," Jim stated, his eyes suddenly stormy. "We're going to lure him in. Lloyds has asked us to raise a midsized transport ship from the bottom near the tip of Italy's foot. Her engines failed and she foundered on some rocks and went down in about forty feet of water. Sir Edward pulled strings on this one. It's a German vessel, and the cargo may be interesting. A German company was dispatched immediately to recover the vessel, but hasn't entered the Straits of Gibraltar yet. We'll be on-site when they arrive. That could be interesting, too."

"How are we going to play this one?" Dorf was the one who uttered the question that was on all their minds.

"As of now we go into our teams of eight. Team one has the first twelve-hour shift. Team two has the second twelve-hour shift. When you're off duty, four sleep immediately, while the other four are backups if needed. When they're sleeping, the first four are backup," Jim replied.

"We have four divers in the water with weapons. Four men are on deck, with weapons at hand. Two are on watch while the other two tend the divers. Andrea will have the wheel. Master Chief Warner and Petty Officer Rule have the equipment operations and maintenance. I want both of you armed," Jim said, looking at both men.

Inchworm grinned. "Now I know why we always have to qualify with our firearms," he nodded at Jim Warner. "Wipe the cobwebs off your blunderbuss, boss," he said.

That got a laugh from everyone.

Jim Warner, one of the senior officers, smiled back at the younger man. "Oh! I thought I'd just use my longbow," he said, mimicking an aged voice. "The blunderbuss makes so much noise!" his face was serious as he mimicked the aged voice. "They have about the same range if I'm doing the shooting. I could use a crossbow, but loading the thing requires so much effort!"

"You two slay me!" John chortled, slapping the table as he laughed.

"Any sign of trouble and all able hands respond. Abe, make sure your boys are armed and ready," Jim said, nodding at Abe.

"We've been practicing lately," Abe said, nodding at the men lining the wall behind him. "They'll make a good account of themselves," he added in serious terms. "Are we using live ammo or non-lethal rounds?"

"Only the team will use live ammo," Jim replied after a moment of thought. "Non-lethal rounds are effective in close quarters. Those of us with live ammo will try to keep the fatalities minimal," he added.

"Divers will come out of the water on the outside perimeter of the attacking vessel. Try to get on board the vessel and neutralize it," Jim outlined his plan, looking at his men. "The German tug probably won't have any mounted weapons, but you can be sure that Kalil's boat will."

"We want the high ground," Wade said quietly.

"Yes. If the ship that comes out with Kalil's crew is higher than our vessel, we go undercover, luring them on board and into the boat where we can control where we fight. If that happens, I want Doc, Millie, and Cecilia in the war room for safety. If the boat is lower, which I expect, we will have the high ground," Jim said quickly.

"What if they launch a torpedo at us?" John asked.

"I'm counting on it. Our response will be timed so the torpedo gets near enough to look like a hit. The shock wave will toss us a bit, so be ready for that impact. They'll be lured into moving quickly, too quickly to respond to our initial attack," Jim looked around at the men as he spoke.

"Some of you have never experienced that so that it will be a new experience. Just follow the usual drill for impact, and you should be okay. Just make sure your weapons are on safe during the impact!" he added with a grin. "Sparks can tell you why."

"What happened to you, Sparks?" Sean asked quickly, seeing the blush spread on Bill Kline's neck.

"My weapon went off while I was in training," he said almost too quietly for Sean, two seats away, to hear.

"Your bloody weapon went off! Who'd you shoot?" Sean asked. "And speak up, mate. I can barely hear you," he added, enjoying the other man's chagrin.

Kline shot Jim an angry look; then his face cracked into an embarrassed smile. Looking around, he noticed everyone waiting, so he finally sighed and spoke. "The bullet ricocheted off the deck and bit me in the butt!" he said tersely.

"Shot yourself in the arse, did you?" Chance asked, trying to keep the grin off his face. "Must have been bloody awful!" he added, chuckling. "You must have been in Barney with your XO!"

"On his orders, the medic took the bullet out without applying a local just to drive the lesson home!" Zeke said, laughing at the memory. "He yelled like a baby!"

"Well! It hurt!" Bill thundered above all the laughter. His face was now beet red, but he laughed with the rest, remembering a lesson he would never forget.

"Crap! It's a good thing we're using non-lethal rounds!" Bob Stankus said seriously. "They hurt bad enough!"

"Okay! Back to order!" Jim commanded after a moment of comments and laughter. The room quieted.

"I want Kalil alive if possible. He's escaped a maximum-security prison, so he's a dangerous enemy. Don't underestimate him. Whoever he picks to attempt to board us will be professionals. Don't underestimate them. Remember your training! Stay with the basics and execute just like we practice. Use extreme prejudice when dealing with them," Jim added.

"Full body armor under the coveralls?" Wade asked.

"Absolutely. You guys in the water, be careful! You won't have that protection," John said soberly. There were nods from the men, nods of agreement, but no raised eyebrows or signs of fear. Jim watched his men with a warm sense of honor in his heart for such courage.

"Any questions or suggestions?" Jim asked in the short silence that followed John's comment. No one had questions, and for the first time, no one offered any suggestions. Jim waited, and when the silence went on, he nodded to Zeke.

CHAPTER 28

Okay, guys, listen up!" Zeke said. He punched some keys, and every laptop on the conference table showed a Geodetic Survey of the area where they would be working. Italy's version of the National Oceanic and Atmospheric Administration produced the nautical charts for all navigable Italian coastal waters. Zeke waited until everyone had a chance to study the chart, a matter of about five minutes, and then broke the silence.

"The currents in this area are pretty predictable during daylight hours. But at night, they get tricky and, as our stranded cargo ship discovered, deadly. According to the Captain's report of the incident, the ship was literally hurled against the rocks repeatedly, a steady current dragging it back each time. Then, when she began sinking, another current turned the ship around twice, dragged it under, and south of the rocks into forty feet of water. The captain thinks she struck bow first, although she sank stern heavy," Zeke looked around to make sure everyone was following his report.

"Ten of his crew were lost in the violence. We will need our bow thrusters running twenty-four-seven for this job. Can they handle that, Master Chief?" Zeke looked at Jim Warner.

Both thrusters can run at full throttle and produce three hundred horsepower. That's 224 kW for you, geeks," Jim Warner replied with a grin. Petty Officer Rule just finished a thorough check on them. Let's hear what he has to say."

"They are man-made machines, gents, so anything and everything that can go wrong may indeed do just that!" Inchworm said laconically.

"Oh, that's reassuring!" Driver said sarcastically.

"Well, I'm a realist," Inchworm replied in defense. "They check out fine, but you never know. Volvo built them, so they should run just fine. We've used them carefully and, at times, pushed them hard so we know how they hold up under pressure. I'm sure our pilots know what to do if we lose one," he added.

"What happens if we lose a bow thruster?" Windy asked, interested. He knew his question would be treated with respect and answered, and he was pleased that he no longer worried about asking anything.

"We can't hold the ship steady. The current could turn her in either direction. If we have the crane deployed, a cable could be snapped, or the crane yanked off the deck, endangering the divers," Wade answered quickly.

"That's probably not a good thing," Windy said, thinking it all over. "We'll have to pray that nothing goes wrong!" he added with a nod.

"Okay, men," Jim said. "We'll be on station in about twelve hours. Get as much rest as you can and keep your powder dry."

Slowly, the men filed out of the conference room. Zeke hurried up to the CIC. Inchworm and Master Chief Warner made their way to the engine room to ensure the engines ran at peak conditions. Some of the team went to the war room to check their weapons, while others took advantage of a chance to rest. Abe gathered his kitchen crew together and herded them out of the room.

At last, only Jim, John, Wade, and Cecilia remained. They sat quietly for a few minutes, and then Cecilia asked the question that had been nagging at her throughout the meeting.

"Why do you think Kalil is so dangerous?" she asked.

"He's a ghost. No one knows much about him. In fact, if it hadn't been for Klaus, we still wouldn't know anything about this guy. He obviously has former Russian ties and plenty of money, so somebody is backing him, and whoever that is, he or she is savvy. How he managed to fly under everybody's radar is still a mystery and proves he is brilliant. Breaking out of Ira's maximum security prison was a master stroke," Jim replied evenly.

"We definitely have to take him alive," Wade stated quietly.

"If we can," John added ominously. "If we can," he repeated almost in a whisper.

Cecilia shivered, and Jim put his arm around her. "We've faced dangerous men before and will again, honey," he said encouragingly. "We just have to be very careful with this one." She nodded, but he felt the tense muscles beneath her skin.

"Let's hope the Germans and that crew don't show up at the same time!" Wade said.

"Not good, that," John interjected needlessly.

"Kalil will move quickly. He won't want witnesses, and if I am any judge of such men, he will know the Germans are on the way. He'll strike before they get there," Jim said.

"And from what we know about him, he won't be in the boat. He'll be on shore somewhere where he can watch. We'll have someone on the shore to intercept him, or more than one someone!" Wade added. "Whoever we send will have to be very good."

"The hasty blow goes oft astray!" John quoted quietly. "Let's hope he's not as good at quick plans as we are. I suppose it wouldn't be good to think that way," he added, working it all out as he spoke. "If we underestimate him, some of us could die. So let's plan for the worst."

Following the meeting, work went on as usual. Cecilia never ceased to marvel at the work that went into keeping a ship in top condition. None of the men ever complained about scraping rust, painting, cleaning decks, or any other myriad of menial tasks they had to perform. They all knew the score, and they all pitched in. Even her husband took a scraper and brush in hand. She was convinced he did it for morale, but he did it; that was the important thing.

Her own work kept her busy enough that she didn't have much time to worry about the upcoming danger. At morning and evening devotions, the prayers changed significantly. Listening carefully to the prayers, Cecilia was surprised. She noted that none of the men prayed for safety, and she asked her husband about it on the way back to their cabin.

"Honey, we're going into battle. There's nothing safe about that! We all know that. What the men really fear is that in the heat of battle, they'll act without thought and slaughter people who don't need to be slaughtered," he added after a pause. Cecilia realized now why the prayers intrigued her. The men knew the danger of pitched battle and the blood lust, and they were good and decent men, unwilling to shed blood needlessly. It made her feel better about the whole situation.

Even daily training changed subtly. More attention was given to the basics, and the teams competed for the fastest time, highest score, and best response, sometimes winning by the smallest margin. Jim watched them carefully, knowing the danger, knowing they were riding the crest of the wave of perfection, and wanting to keep them there as long as he could.

They arrived at the wreck site in the dark hours of the morning. Locating the wreck using their sophisticated underwater detecting equipment was simple. Wade gave the order to drop anchor and watched the heavy chain unwind from the locker, mentally counting off the fathoms. At seven fathoms, the anchor hit bottom, dragged for a moment, and then dug in.

Only an hour before the change of watch, Wade ordered his two lookouts to the observation deck and led the rest of the men erecting the crane and getting equipment ready for the dive. Lunch Box and Vince shared the watch from the deck, their lenses moving in a slow one-hundred-and-eighty-degree arc. Vince could see the dark rocks of Favgnana and Levanzo, the two islands closest to Sicily. Lee Roy could see Marettimo, the westernmost island of the Egadi. The ship was anchored closest to Favgnana, a few miles from the shipping lane through the Egadi. They knew that when Kalil's men came, they would come from Marsala or Trapani from the island of Sicily. That they would come fast and hard was a given.

Vince watched the rocks just off of Favgnana's shore carefully, knowing that someone would be watching them. The sudden flare of a cigarette or cigar clearly pinpointed Kalil's lookout.

"John, I got Kalil's lookout!" Vince said into his headset.

"Are you sure there's only one?" John asked immediately.

"No, sir. Still checking," Vince replied, his glasses now sweeping slowly over the rocks.

"I've got a boat, no lights, about a half mile off, port side, about eight o'clock," Lunch Box said.

"So, about 190° south by west?" Smitty's voice cut in.

"Hey, you're supposed to be in bed!" Lunch Box admonished.

"I woke up early. So sue me! I've got it on my radar. Give me a minute to turn the spotlight their way, and we'll give them a wake-up call," Smitty replied flippantly. A moment later, the powerful spotlight burst into the darkness, penetrating the blanket of night like a sword thrust, outlining the boat half a mile away.

The lights came on immediately, and Lunch Box could see two men standing on the deck, looking their way. The boat turned away and moved further west toward the shipping lane. Lunch Box could clearly read the name and port of registration on the stern and read them off.

The light turned off, and the darkness settled like a gentle rain falling about them. Vince lifted his night vision scope to his eyes again. The lookout on the rocks stood in plain view, watching the spotlight catch his partners. He turned and moved back into what he was convinced was his secure hiding place. Wondering what the man might have done if he had known he had been discovered, Vince continued to watch.

"I'm pretty sure there's only two men on the shore, and which one is Kalil," Vince said. "Good work with that spotlight, Smitty!" he added.

"I have an incoming boat rounding the northern point of Levanzo, moving fast!" Smitty's voice sounded excited. "It's a high-speed boat. I can see a mounted gun and a gunner," he added.

"How accommodating!" Jim's voice sounded in everyone's headset. "Kalil has called when we're all up and ready! John, Wade, Dorf, and

Mark, in the water, now!" he ordered. Quickly checking his weapons once more, he prepared for the battle.

Zeke hit the button to call all hands to emergency stations, which was the agreed signal that the attack was imminent. Cecilia was already on her way to help Dr. Wozniac, and Millie shivered at the sound. She offered up a prayer for her husband and the crew. When she entered the hospital wing, she found the good doctor and his wife kneeling in prayer. Without hesitation, she joined them. Three heads bowed, and each prayed in turn, asking for protection and that any wounds would not be fatal.

In the kitchen, Abe knelt with his crew in prayer before passing out the shotguns and non-lethal rounds of ammunition. He was proud of his men as they faced the possibility of combat with few signs of stress. The exercise and training they participated in each day had worked wonderful changes in each man.

"Anyone have any worries?" he asked as they assembled to move to their places of assignment.

"Naw!" TP said laconically. "They'll take one look at Sturdy here and probably faint dead away," Sturdy stood one inch shy of seven feet tall and looked impressive, holding the tiny shotgun in one hand.

"I'm a big target. Watch my back!" Sturdy said with a smile.

They moved out, Sturdy leading TP and Bull to the corridor they would guard while Abe took Cuss and Windy to the opposite corridor. The chances were slim that they would see action, but they were ready.

On the shore, Kalil watched as the men of *Bring It Up Coral* dove for cover when his gunner opened up, strafing the deck. Then, they were too close for the .50 caliber machine gun to do any damage. As they came to a stop beside the ship, something sailed through the air and landed in the center of his boat. An explosion followed, accompanied by a blinding flash of light. It was a stun grenade, and Kalil cursed, closing his eyes as the flash momentarily blinded him.

Four men leaned over the side and fired three times each, their Heckler and Koch MP5SD weapons on single-shot settings, and Kalil heard the shouts of pain and surprise. Some return fire, sporadic at best, could be heard, but they were firing at a difficult upward angle. Kalil was still trying to clear his head when shots sounded behind the boat. Divers had come out of the water and were attacking his boat! Kalil watched as the captain dived for the floor and covered his head until his eyes finally cleared enough to see. It only took a few seconds, but it was enough.

Twenty men, all seasoned mercenaries, lay scattered around him. Eight men on the deck of the ship above hovered with guns ready, and three of the divers moved among the prisoners, taking weapons and checking wounds. The fourth, the smallest one, stood close to the captain, his MP5SD pointing at the man's face. Slowly, the Captain stood and raised his hands.

The man guarding him seemed preoccupied, his eyes moving quickly, hardly glancing at the captain. It was a ruse, and it worked. The captain aimed a kick at the hand holding the gun. He was stunned as the little man countered with a kick that sent him spinning to the deck in excruciating pain. His leg felt as if a pile driver had crushed it.

Kalil tried to gather his thoughts. This group had neutralized his boat in seconds! He knew the crew of Bring It Up Coral had almost entirely been military, but obviously, they were still training regularly. Only seasoned troops could respond that quickly and decisively! Knowing he'd underestimated them, he tried to think clearly.

So, the little man is experienced in martial arts! He's dangerous! I'll wait. The captain looked up at Mark Drumheiser with hate in his eyes, but Mark wasn't looking at him. His eyes were still moving around, seeing everything. Then suddenly, a pair of hazel eyes were boring into his own. The captain almost recoiled as he looked into those eyes. Their focus was so intense he could practically feel the stare as a palpable entity. Never before had he seen such eyes, and that confused him.

CHAPTER 29

"**I** thought you'd be better," C.G. said quietly. "Raise your hands slowly, Kalil!" he commanded.

Kalil realized that while he watched, someone had crept up from behind. He was never that careless, and he had a lookout. *What happened to him?* He waited for C.G. to move closer when Vince stepped up from the side, suddenly, there. A hand with a firm grip pulled his hands behind him and secured them before the man began to search. C.G. remained standing, his silenced pistol pointing at Kalil's chest. Vince was thorough, even finding the small pistol Kalil hid in his underwear. Frustrated, Kalil followed Vince onto the rigid raider and from that boat onto the *Bring It Up Coral* deck. Driver nodded to the two men and expertly positioned the rigid raider under the sling lowered by the crane, and the boat with its four passengers was lifted onto the deck. The entire team was there, sixteen men, all deadly, their bulky body armor evident under their coveralls. Kalil saw it now, realized what he had missed, and cursed himself.

"Abe and Sturdy, please bring your men on deck and transport the wounded to the hospital wing," Jim ordered. Kalil watched as six men, all armed with shotguns, appeared from below. The two largest, one a veritable giant, handed their guns to one of the team members, but the other four kept theirs. Kalil didn't know they had rehearsed this; he only saw the crew's professionalism.

"You are a military unit?" he asked.

"Ex-military," Jim said.

"You keep your crew sharp," Kalil said quietly.

"We're used to people trying to take what we salvage. The boat in the water without lights and you watching from the shore tipped us off. When your men fired at my ship, I took appropriate action," Jim stated flatly.

"So, you weren't expecting me?" Kalil asked, raising one eyebrow.

"Don't be stupid, you bloody wanker!" Lunch Box said as he flipped the safety on his weapon. He lowered it and looked at Kalil. "Too bloody right we expected you!" he said. "You're a proper Wally, you are!" Jim smiled at the Aussie's comments.

"You're predictable, Kalil. We've been watching you for some time now. You showed up when we recovered the treasures from the buried church. Driving a rented car under an assumed identity tipped us off. Then, your RAF goons gave us some laughs at the Vatican. Eventually, we put together your connection with the Committee of Five. Jacques Piaf is probably singing like a canary. You will, too," Jim added.

"You think you can torture me for information?" Kalil spat with disdain.

"That's not our gig, man," FM said. "We're a salvage outfit. We'll let the government boys get the information out of you."

"Mr. Miller, right you are!" Wade said. "Why don't you get a pair of shorts for our guest, strip him down and search him completely, and then give him a front-row seat to the salvage operation? He can watch us work while he waits for whoever will pick him up."

An hour later, Kalil was perched inside the crane tower. His hands were handcuffed to each side, and he was forced to spread his legs far apart to keep his footing. He wore nothing but the shorts they gave him and realized he was in for a very uncomfortable time. Every time the crane tower moved, he was jerked off his feet, holding on with his hands in desperation, swinging back and forth, banging his knees and sides of his legs on the unforgiving steel. When the sun was at its zenith, he was sure he was being cooked like a lobster.

He'd been on other ships and knew immediately that the crew of this one was different. For starters, there was no discernable rust on the crane. He could see where sections had been treated and repainted. The decks gleamed in the morning sun, and the windows were relatively clean. These men took pride in their work. Even now, some were repairing the damage from the battle.

Everyone worked, even the captain. There were no salutes and very few orders. At present, there were no signs of body armor or weapons. Kalil wondered where the guns were stored. He grunted and switched his feet to another position as cramps suddenly seized his side and lower back.

All day, he hung in the sun in his steel prison, watching teams of divers exchange places. Below the surface, he could see the bright flares of welders repairing the ship's hull. Looking around, he saw the two lookouts on the observation deck keeping their vigil. Every hour, two more would arrive to take their places.

As evening settled in, Wade climbed up, unlocked his handcuffs, and allowed Kalil to climb down. This was awkward because of his sore muscles, but he gritted his teeth, determined to show no weakness. He refused to bend even though he knew the men would know he hurt. Dorf and Mark were waiting to escort him to his cell. Watching them covertly, he decided not to try anything, knowing that these men would prevent any attempt to escape. It frustrated him, but he saw his chance.

Jim and Cecilia stood on the deck with Master Chief Warner discussing something as Kalil passed. Without warning, he struck out at Cecilia. Captain Shepherd went from still and concentrating to deadly motion so fast Kalil wasn't sure he saw it. He felt it, though. The captain's body deflected the kick while his arms blocked Kalil's hasty counterattack, and blows from seemingly nowhere seemed to rain upon him. He flew back and landed heavily, sliding across the metal deck with a grunt.

Just as quickly as he went down, he was up, his stance wary, and he was surprised to see that none of the men had tried to interfere. Jim stood calmly, watching, a slight grin on his face. His eyes, though, were what held Kalil's interest. They were not hard or fierce or filled with fire. Focus was the word that came to mind. Those eyes seemed to see everything, and for a moment, Kalil felt unsure, but only for a moment.

Even as Kalil noted this a circle of men surrounded him, with Jim alone in the center. Jim didn't move, and his stance looked relaxed. Kalil remembered how that changed. Captain Shepherd was younger than Kalil by about twenty years, and Kalil was no fool. He would have to attack quickly and with unexpected moves to overcome this man. All his training returned to him, and he sprinted forward suddenly.

As skilled and well-trained as he was, Kalil instantly realized he was overmatched. Not one of his blows landed, nor could he connect a kick. Captain Shepherd seemed to flow in and out of his vision, blocking kicks and punches with ease, his speed and balance frightening. A pile driver connected with his nose and eye, and Kalil landed on his back again, panting and almost seeing stars. He lay there for a moment, then pulled himself up and bowed.

"My compliments, Captain. You are a formidable opponent," he said through thick lips. He didn't remember being hit in the mouth, but exploring with his tongue found splits and blood and swelling.

"The next time you attack my wife, I'll kill you," Jim said quietly. Kalil blanched. Those words were spoken conversationally, almost easily, and he knew them for a fact. "Take him to his cell," Jim said.

Dorf and Mark stepped forward, motioning for him to walk between them. Limping, he allowed himself to be led to the only cell in the boat. It was not in a hold but in the galley, between the freezer and sub-zero refrigerator. Using Wade's design, the cell was secured by a two-inch thick bulletproof plastic door that slid down from the ceiling and two inches into the floor. Kalil noted that as he passed beneath it, he watched it slide home, cutting off any escape.

There were two small, narrow vents in the door and three in the back wall, four inches long and two inches high. Nothing covered the vents. A steel bunk-bed unit was welded to one wall, and a stainless steel toilet and sink occupied the other wall. The toilet was sealed, and the flush mechanism was automatic. The water in the sink was automated, too.

Kalil found a memory foam mattress and pillow, clean, crisp sheets, and a wool blanket on the beds. He stretched gratefully on the mattress and rested, letting his mind wander as work in the kitchen went on before him like a televised program through the transparent door.

The two strongmen were in charge of the kitchen, and from what he saw, they both knew their job well. Their crew worked around them, and he could see they loved what they were doing from their conversations and antics. Mostly, they ignored him, rarely looked his way, and were busy with their work. He discarded the idea of trying to lure one of them to help him escape. Grunting with displeasure, he stared at the ceiling.

His mind turned to Captain Shepherd. The man moved like lightning, countered every attack with ease, and Kalil realized that Jim could have killed him anytime he wanted. That shook him to his core. *One day, I will escape again, and I will find Chu. Perhaps Chu can kill him for me.* Chu was the only man who had ever bested Kalil in hand-to-hand combat . . . until now.

Kalil was a realist. He knew that American forces produced the best soldiers in the world. They were better trained, more motivated, and better supplied than any other military forces in the world. He had known that from the beginning. He resented it, and right now, he resented that more than anything else. But even that didn't guarantee that men lived. His mind turned with thoughts of how and when he could kill this new thorn in his side.

From the rear deck, Jim watched the boat full of wounded mercenaries limp away. Every one of them had been tended by Sean for their wounds and sent on their way with a stern warning. Jim knew they would not return. He despised men who sold their skills for hire to the highest bidder. They had loyalty only to money. This particular group had been motivated and savvy but unprepared for a military response.

Mark walked up and stood beside him for a moment without speaking. At last, he looked up at Jim, punched him lightly on the arm, and spoke.

"Don't brood over it, Shep," he said lightly. "They're worthless scum and always will be. We've seen their ilk before, haven't we?"

"You know, I was just thinking of Croy. He was a vicious sergeant, and the older he got, the worse he became. When he came up on charges, he knew he'd had it, so he hired himself out in the Congo. I heard he died there only two years later. AIDS took him. Poetic justice, that!" Jim replied.

"He was a good soldier once. Then, he lost sight of why we serve. Serving himself became his goal. Every one of those men is much the same," Mark observed.

"I'm glad we do what we do," Jim said, smiling down at his friend. "Better us than someone less skilled," he added with a nod.

"Oh, John wanted me to tell you Ira is on his way in a helicopter. They will land in about twenty minutes. Dorf and I will take the CH53 up so they can land on our pad," Mark added after a pause.

"Thanks, Mark. And good work today," Jim said, clapping him on the shoulder.

Sean approached them as they turned toward the bow. His face was relaxed and smiling.

"None of our boys were hurt, thank God, when they turned that .50 caliber on us. Dang thing wasn't very clean and hadn't been serviced in some time. Did you know that John and Wade confiscated it before turning that boat loose?" he reported.

"I saw," Jim replied. "How are we set for tomorrow's work?" he added as John and Wade joined them.

"We'll raise the ship tomorrow, probably before the Germans arrive," John said confidently. "Zeke says they'll arrive sometime tomorrow evening. We could be on our way by then!"

"Okay, let's get ready to receive Ira and his crowd," Jim said.

CHAPTER 30

Ira sat at a table in the dining room with Jim, John, and Wade. He was voluble in his apologies for Kalil's escape and their troubles. Jim listened with a slight smile on his face. He liked Ira. Ira loved his native country, Israel, in the same way Jim loved America. Both sacrificed much for their country without ever asking for anything in return.

"Just how did he escape?" Jim asked when Ira wound down.

"My orders were ignored!" Ira said with irritation. "Kalil was not placed in solitary confinement and watched at all times, nor was he placed in the highest security prison, as I instructed. After careful investigation and long hours of interviews, I discovered something I had only suspected. There was a traitor in our midst at the prison. Someone receiving payments to help when called upon, and I was able to discover all his indiscretions," Ira added.

"Was," Jim nodded. He knew what that meant. "How compromised were you?"

"I was not, nor were you. My country was. This displeased me, so I dealt with the matter with extreme prejudice," Ira replied. "The high-ranking official who appointed the warden of that facility has been dealt with as well," he added.

"Did he know who Kalil was?" Jim asked.

"No. That much I know for certain. He merely ignored my orders because of who I am. One of my own is now in charge of the prison system. Kalil will not escape again," Ira assured them. His eyes were lit with an inner fire as he said the last.

"Perhaps," Jim said. "He is a cagey one. Don't underestimate him. Chu trained him at some point."

"You killed Chu when you rescued me, didn't you?" Ira asked.

"Yes," Jim said with distaste.

"Let's have Kalil out here. I'd like to see his reaction to that," Ira suggested. "Sometimes a man's reaction to unwelcome news can tell us much."

Jim pressed his talk button. "FM, C.G., and Vince! Please escort Kalil to the dining room," he commanded.

Two minutes later, the three men entered the dining room. They looked at Jim as they passed, and FM spoke.

"You want him standing or crawling, boss?" he said.

"Just make sure he knows who is in charge, FM," Jim replied.

FM nodded, and the three continued through the galley to the brig. C.G. activated the door, and it slid silently into the ceiling. As FM predicted, Kalil came at them hard and fast. He quickly discovered that he was overmatched, and his resistance ended as quickly as it began.

FM handled the lesson, making it one Kalil would not soon forget. Kalil almost screamed in frustration as his blows were countered and blocked, and he was smashed to the floor, sliding back into the cell hard enough to hit the opposite wall! At least three of his ribs had been badly bruised, and his shoulder was out of the socket!

Vince jerked him to his feet, half dragged him into the dining room and dropped him roughly in a chair. He produced a pair of handcuffs and cuffed his hands behind him, passing the chain through the center bar of the chair. FM put leg irons on his ankles and then attached his legs to the support bar between the legs in the center of the chair using a pair of shackles. Kalil bore this, letting his head clear, licking blood from his lips. That they went to such extremes told him that these men knew more about him than he ever wanted anyone to know.

"You must consider me very dangerous," he commented, looking at his captors with contempt.

"No, just incredibly stupid," John replied, smiling at Kalil and shaking his head as if Kalil were a wayward pupil.

"Any one of my men could take you easily," Jim added easily. "They're all as good as I am, some better," he added, taking an unconcerned sip of his iced tea.

"I know who taught him, boss," FM said, following his instructions. "Guy named Chu, if I remember correctly. Am I right about that?"

"On the money, FM," Jim nodded.

"You killed Chu, didn't you?" Ira asked as if having a conversation. "If I remember, it was hand-to-hand combat. You were rescuing me at the time, and I remember it well. The fight lasted about three minutes, didn't it?"

"Yes," Jim answered simply, a note of sadness in his voice.

Kalil sat there stunned. *This man killed Chu? It can't be!* He looked at the men and realized that it was the truth. Then he was surprised by a look in Jim's eyes, a look he didn't expect. It was a look of profound sadness. This man would kill, but he didn't like it. That made him a member of a very select few really dangerous men worldwide. Kalil knew that such men existed and hated their existence with a passion that surprised even him. They represented the very thing he hated most: honor and morality. It made them weak and foolish, but he knew the opposite was true deep inside.

"I underestimated you," Kalil said quietly, his eyes full of hatred. "Next time, I will not."

Jim was as surprised as everyone else when he reached across the table and hauled Kalil and the chair right up into the air until their noses were almost touching. His eyes were as cold and empty as the grave. His huge hand was wrapped tightly around Kalil's neck, cutting off the flow of blood and air efficiently.

"There won't be a next time!" Jim snarled quietly. "If you escape again, I will personally hunt you down and kill you. As of this moment, you are a marked man."

Jim released him, and his chair thudded to the floor, almost tipping back, as Kalil gasped for air, his ears ringing, his vision clouded. That had been a close thing, and he knew with certainty that Jim Shepherd would do precisely what he promised. He sat there, his mind reeling, his spirit momentarily crushed. Fear, for the first time in many years, gripped his heart.

Who is this man? What kind of soldier was he? Why did he stop being a soldier? Kalil had no answers. Breathing hurt, and his head ached. Shaking it only made it worse. He heard a low moan break from his lips. Even that hurt.

"Captain," a new voice sounded. Kalil looked up through pain-filled eyes to see a junior officer standing at attention.

"What is it, LT?" Jim said evenly.

"An Israeli helicopter has asked permission to land," Finn said.

"Permission granted. We'll bring our prisoner up to meet them," Jim replied.

Kalil was released, jerked to his feet, and half dragged, half carried up the corridors to the rear deck. A helicopter hovered over the ship, *Bring It Up's* own CH53D Sea Stallion. A small four-man Bell 400 Turbo helicopter with Israeli markings sat on the deck with the rotor spinning. Kalil was dragged beneath the downwash of the blades and thrust into the hands of two Israeli soldiers. Ira Lehman climbed, grinning, into the rear passenger seat as Kalil was strapped in and then shackled to his seat. It felt good to see the man so disoriented. He vowed that Kalil would remain in prison this time.

"Thank you!" Ira yelled above the motors.

"You're welcome. If he escapes again, I get the privilege of hunting him down!" Jim yelled back.

Kalil's head snapped up at that and he stared down at Jim Shepherd. The green eyes boring into his own were as empty as a freshly dug grave, and Kalil shivered, sure he could smell fresh dirt. The doors were closed, and the soldiers lifted off with their prisoner.

Early the next afternoon, Jim watched as the cargo ship rose to the surface. A pumping crew leaped on board and began pumping out thousands of gallons of seawater, and slowly, the damaged vessel rose from the water as if the sea were reluctant to give up its victim. By evening, they were towing the ship toward Napoli.

Aboard *Bring It Up Coral,* the atmosphere was festive. Abe and Sturdy set a celebration feast before the famished crew. The dining room had been fairly quiet during the first twenty minutes of dinner. Now it rang with laughter, voices, plates and utensils, glasses clinking, all the sounds one acquaints with a festive feast.

Jim sat back in his chair, one arm around Cecilia, the other holding a tall glass of iced tea, listening to the banter around him. At the table beside his, a lively discussion was going on about sausage and sauerkraut. Sean held the floor at the moment.

"Yeah! I heard a story once from the outback about an Aussie, a Brit, and a German. The Brit and German were scientists studying the Australian saltwater crocodile. The Aussie was leading the expedition. He tried and tried to warn them to keep their distance, but one day, the Brit and German jumped into the river to take pictures of the crocodile in his habitat.

"The Croc immediately took the Brit down for a death roll, and he was never seen again. Three other crocs watched as the German swam to shore untouched. So the Aussie stepped up and asked why they hadn't eaten the German. The biggest one spoke up.

"I ate one of those Germans last week, and I've still got gas and diarrhea!"

Everyone laughed at the joke. Then the table exploded with laughter as Lee Roy lifted one leg and passed gas loudly. Cecilia, who had been listening and watching, waved a hand over her nose. Her cheeks were bright red. Being on a ship filled with men, she had often been treated with such ribald humor. Jim grinned at her and winked at the men at the next table.

Three days later, they towed the German cargo ship into port at Naples. Italian customs agents were present in large numbers and immediately began to inspect the ship's cargo. It was certainly not what the manifest claimed.

Bring It Up Coral still sat tied to the slip assigned when the German salvage outfit steamed into the harbor three days later. They demanded that the ship be released to them immediately. The Italian authorities refused. When the Captain protested too much, he and his crew were arrested and interrogated.

Jim heard all this from Villa Orvieto, where the crew spent a week of vacation. Rosa Calienté and the Siples had accomplished much in their absence, and the work on the ski lodge was progressing nicely. Gwyneth Shepherd and her staff returned to Live Oak after training Andrea's excellent staff. When the hotel was completed, most of them would train the staff that would work in that establishment.

Andrea spent his days going around and seeing what changes had been made, expressing his pleasure, and making the staff feel that their accomplishments were appreciated. Rosa, of course, glowed under his praise, and Jim smiled when he saw them walking hand in hand soon after Andrea returned.

Late in the week, Jim was in his office with Cecilia and Marvin, reviewing some paperwork, when the satellite phone beeped, indicating an incoming call. Finn lifted the phone and answered accordingly.

"*Bring It Up* Enterprises," he said properly.

"This is Sir Edward Marsh. May I speak to Captain Shepherd, please?" The precise voice on the other end surprised Marvin. Sir Edward Marsh, the great man himself, was on the phone. He quickly passed the phone to Jim.

"Sir Edward Marsh," he said.

Jim took the phone with one eyebrow raised. Sir Edward had never called that line before. "Yes sir, this is Captain Shepherd," Jim said.

"Is this line secure?" Sir Edward asked quickly.

"It is," Jim replied.

"Is anyone else listening in?" Sir Edward asked on top of Jim's reply.

"No sir," Jim replied, interested.

"Right, then. I'm an hour away. I'll tell you all about it when I arrive," Sir Edward replied. He sounded relieved, and Jim wondered what could be so important that a personal visit was required.

"LT, get the team together in the library in an hour. Sir Edward is coming. You should attend as well," Jim added.

Finn shot to his feet, saluted, and headed to his office. Jim sighed, hoping he would ask the men to come, not order them to be there. Some men accepted Finn, but he still rubbed them the wrong way, especially when it came to things like this. To his surprise and pleasure, Finn told the men that the captain had requested their presence at a meeting in the library. Marvin was learning.

An hour later, Jim met Sir Edward at the front drive. Sir Edward's face was haggard, his eyes puffy with heavy bags beneath, his hair uncharacteristically unkempt. His suit looked slept in, and perhaps it was. Jim grasped his forearm with one hand and shook his right hand with the other, welcoming him warmly.

Sir Edward smiled, his eyes suddenly lighting up, life slowly returning as his sagging body straightened. "God, I needed that!" he said, his lips finally parting to show teeth in a genuine smile. "I've had a horrible three days. I haven't slept in a bed, and I haven't had my feet on solid ground until today."

CHAPTER 31

Jim led Sir Edward up the steps without comment, three security personnel following closely. They were as tightly strung as Sir Edward, their eyes moving everywhere as if they expected attack, their hands moving almost unconsciously toward their weapons. Even inside the house, they didn't immediately relax. By the time they reached the library and watched the bookshelves open to reveal the secret room, then close behind them, they had relaxed only slightly.

It's bad! I hope we can help. Jim invited Sir Edward and his men to sit down at the table. There was room for everyone. The three men of the security detail watched the men rise as their Captain entered the room and waited to sit until he sat down. No one saluted, but there was the feeling of a collective salute in the air. Looking at each other, they sighed, almost fell into their chairs, and began to breathe deeply, working the kinks out of stiff muscles held too long in readiness.

"For those of you who have never met him in person, this is Sir Edward, Director of Operations, MI6. Rest assured, he could put a name to each of you and tell you more about yourself than you remember," Jim smiled lightly, taking his seat. He noted that the men waited until he was seated to follow suit.

"This is bad!" Sir Edward said, confirming Jim's fears. "It's another battlefront to which we have never been able to apply a military solution." He paused for a few moments to collect his thoughts. Then he opened his narrow briefcase, extracted a 64GB SanDisk flash drive, and handed it to Zeke.

Zeke fed it into his computer without comment, and every laptop on the table suddenly came to life. A dim picture appeared, showing foliage, rain, and drops of moisture on the lens. Then, a hand moved like a ghostly apparition and parted the branches. A storm-tossed sea appeared, and then, in the distance, a luxury yacht. It was at anchor, people sitting beneath the canopy watching the rain, occasionally lifting a drink to their lips.

As the men watched, dark figures suddenly appeared out of the water around the yacht. Jim recognized them as divers. No one on the boat seemed to notice them until one climbed onto the rear platform. A shot rang out, and the man who stood to look fell back with a faint cry, barely heard above the rain spattering on the leaves. Then, the figures clamored out of the water, all holding some weapon.

Women and children were forced to the port side, and the men were herded to the starboard side, where they were summarily shot, their bodies dumped in the ocean, disappearing beneath the surface. Eventually, they would come up again when the gasses in the body expanded. The women and children, now reduced to stark terror, were quickly bound, hand and foot. Each one had their feet lifted and attached to a rail post. Some of the smaller children were almost upside down, and their shrill screams could be heard now. A frightened child's scream of terror was penetrating. The men watched in horror as the pirates groped the women and children, laughing as they struggled.

A boat appeared, larger and much older than the yacht, a small container ship, stained and rusted from neglect. Most of the men on the yacht climbed aboard when it came alongside. Three remained in the yacht, and a few minutes later, the yacht lifted anchor and headed out to sea. The larger ship remained for some time, someone on the bow staring at the shore through binoculars. The camera did not move during this time, nor did the ghostly hand holding up the branches. Finally, the boat turned and left. Only then did the hand move, slowly letting the leaves fall back in place. Before the camera went dark, there was a brief view of the lower branches, leaf-covered ground, and the tip of the shoe.

"Do we know the registration of that yacht?" Jim asked in the silence that followed.

"We do," Sir Edward said with a catch in his voice. "A member of the British government chartered that yacht. Our Minister of International Finance and his family were on board. The Minister is the first to be shot."

"So they didn't know who he was!" FM said quickly.

"Correct, Mr. Miller!" Sir Edward said with a sigh. "Quite correct. It appears that this was a simple act of piracy. The women and children will be sold into slavery somewhere in South America or the Caribbean. We have no idea. What we do know is that this is the sixth such yacht stolen in the past three months. Each time, the same method is used."

"Where do the yachts end up?" John asked.

"The American Coastguard recovered one of them near Nassau, running drugs into Florida. The three men on the yacht claimed that their boss instructed them to deliver the drugs in the boat. They didn't know where it came from or how their boss got it. Then the French picked one up near New Guinea, also running drugs. The pilot told the same story. None of the others have been sighted."

"Bloody drug lords!" Chance said under his breath.

"Are acts of piracy up in the Caribbean?" Wade asked, almost on top of Chance's quiet comment.

"Very much so, I'm afraid," Sir Edward said.

"And do the pirates know they killed the Minister of International Finance from Great Britain?" Sean asked.

"No, they do not!" Sir Edward said with some heat. "At least, I hope not! I've spent the better part of the last three days hiring and teaching an actor to take his place temporarily until we can get this sorted out."

"You mean until we sort it out!" Zeke said, his chin thrust forward as it often was when he was determined.

"I can think of no one more qualified," Sir Edward said with a slight smile.

"I think our vacation just ended abruptly," Dr. Wozniac commented sadly.

"I'll need four more men," Jim said quietly, and every head turned.

"Who will you get?" Sir Edward asked, one eyebrow slightly raised.

"Zeke, do you remember a Marine sergeant we nicknamed 'Viper'?" Jim said.

"Oh, please! Not more Marines!" FM said, dropping his face into his hands in mock despair.

"Four more, actually," Jim replied with a grin.

"Oo-rah!" Wade boomed into the room. FM groaned.

"I talked with him two days ago. Admiral Runion suggested that he might need to be rescued from bureaucratic balderdash. Those were his exact words."

"Why four?" John asked slowly.

"That's all left of his unit," Jim said, his face suddenly grim. "Some congressman wants to make an example of them," he added. "His unit killed several hundred enemy insurgents. The congressman believes that kind of brutality has no place in our modern military and that evil America is prejudiced against the Muslims in that country.

"So, Viper resigns, and we rescue his sorry butt from boredom!" C.G. said with a grin. "Kind of like us!"

"Just who is this Viper?" Sir Edward asked.

"About the deadliest Marine you ever want to meet!" Jim said with feeling. "The three who made it out with him are on the same level of expertise and motivation as their sergeant. Actually, I believe they are sergeants themselves as well. I worked with Viper on a mission."

"Where do we pick them up?" FM asked, rubbing his hands.

"Key West," Jim replied. "They'll be briefed by Admiral Runion and then meet us there. Lieutenant Finn, get me four company credit cards with these names," Jim added. "Bill Dodge, Sam Colt, Roger Corrigan, and Sid Barrett will join the company. Also, make up the usual contract agreement and fax it to Admiral Runion." Jim sat back, satisfied.

"Jeeze, Jim!' Zeke said, his face slightly illuminated in blue from his computer screen. "The Marines are going to hate you! They all finished at the top at Fort Bragg's Delta training, one, two, three, and four. Barrett's the top marksman in the sniper class; Colt was born with a pistol in his hand; Dodge and Corrigan are the all-around soldiers the Marines want."

"Like I said, I worked a mission with them once," Jim grinned at Zeke. "Dodge made quite an impression. So did the other three."

"Could you possibly take on four more?" Sir Edward said quickly.

"Who?" Jim asked, curious.

"Sergeant Major Calvin Weston, Corporal Paul Donnelly, Corporal David Carr, and Sergeant Matthew Banks, from a special task force in the inner workings of the SAS," Sir Edward said, spelling each name. "They're young, motivated, and four of the best I've ever had. I spent the last three years training them for you specifically," Sir Edward added, a glint in his eye. Even those men hadn't known he'd been training them for that, but they did now. "Let's just say they have unusual qualifications,"

"Misfits like us, then," Jim said, nodding his head. He smiled. "Looks like we'll have to dig up another treasure ship somewhere in the Caribbean."

"We're takin' the Limeys?" Lee Roy said, as if shocked.

"Limeys, Mr. Brown?" Cecilia said with a raised eyebrow. "Do you have something against Limeys?"

Lee Roy looked at her and saw Jim cracking his knuckles and staring at him. He swallowed dramatically and nodded his head in the negative as everyone laughed.

"Can't be helped. We have to grease the wheels, you know, mate?" Chance said with a grin at Sir Edward. "Besides, I think I met this Weston bloke once. Does everyone call him 'Hobbs'?"

"Yes, they do!" Sir Edward said.

"Hobbs and his crew will hold up the British end mates," Chance said confidently.

"Good! Then that's settled!" Sir Edward sighed. "They'll meet you in Florida with the other four. Mr. Finn, I'll personally deliver the contracts you need to be signed," he added, looking at Marvin.

Finn nodded after making the appropriate notes in his book.

"You better have four more credit cards made up, LT," Jim ordered, nodding at Sir Edward. The two exchanged tired smiles.

"Thank you," Sir Edward said, meaning it. And so the team grew, and Jim knew he would have to have them working together quickly for the upcoming mission. Cecilia reached out and took his hand beneath the table and squeezed it gently. He smiled at her and then laughed out loud. He was young, doing what he loved best, surrounded by the best crew and friends a man could wish for. It would hurt to lose any of them, even the new men he didn't yet know. He resolved to have them riding the crest of that wave of perfection and keep them there. With pride, he accepted the resolve and welcomed this new challenge.

He saw the same resolve on every face in the room.